Deceitful Vows

Deceitful Vows

Trinity DeKane

www.urbanbooks.net

Urban Books, LLC
300 Farmingdale Road, N.Y.-Route 109
Farmingdale, NY 11735

ISBN 13: 978-1-64556-422-5
ISBN 10: 1-64556-422-3

First Trade Paperback Printing May 2023
Printed in the United States of America

10 9 8 7 6 5 4 3 2 1

This is a work of fiction. Any references or similarities to actual events, real people, living or dead, or to real locales are intended to give the novel a sense of reality. Any similarity in other names, characters, places, and incidents is entirely coincidental.

Distributed by Kensington Publishing Corp.
Submit Orders to:
Customer Service
400 Hahn Road
Westminster, MD 21157-4627
Phone: 1-800-733-3000
Fax: 1-800-659-2436

Deceitful Vows

by

Trinity DeKane

I see why women switch to pussy.

Hell, it's the same shit as fucking with a pussy-ass nigga.

A pussy is a pussy no matter who carrying it. Bitch-ass bum-ass ho.

Marriage didn't mean shit to him, and trust, I don't have any intention of sharing dick with na'n trick. She can have it, but not before I show my ass.

—Paula Smith Harris

Chapter 1

Sunday

Paula sat outside the house that she saw another bitch post on Facebook as being the spot where she and her boo, Michael Harris, were chilling. She prayed that it was a lie and that the bitch was just being salty. Paula refused to be friends with Michael on Facebook because she didn't want to see him flirting and chatting with other females. She had blocked his ass, and it didn't faze her because she knew where he was every night, but when her cousin sent her a screenshot of her man being tagged in a bae post, she jumped in her pink Crown Vic, grabbed her gun, and drove straight over to the house that was in the picture. It took her fifteen minutes to get there, and in those fifteen minutes she decided that shooting Michael's bitch ass would be too much. She wasn't going to continue to be that good ride or die chick for a nigga who didn't care where he stuck his dick. She worked and made good money, so it was nothing to live alone and make it. *But damn, is his head game fire, and that dick is fucking priceless!* she thought.

When she pulled up, she parked in the Lowe's parking lot across from the house and waited. Sure enough, not even ten minutes later, she saw Michael and a female she had seen several times with his sister walk out and sit down on the porch. He sat down on the porch, and the girl sat down next to him, and they appeared to be engrossed in conversation. A little boy who appeared to be around 5 ran out and started wrestling with Michael. Paula cringed inwardly, realizing that the boy had to be Michael's. He had been screaming that he wasn't ready for kids, yet he was playing daddy to another bitch's kid. Paula laughed aloud as she thought about the several times she had dropped his damn ass at this very house because he claimed she was his cousin. Paula never really clicked with his family and barely knew half of them, so she never doubted that the female was his relative.

"I got yo' bitch ass," Paula said aloud to herself. She didn't want to be seen, so she sat in the parking lot and waited for Michael to walk back into the house with his ho. When she finally pulled off, she called her cousin Tasha, who had sent her the screenshot.

"Bitch, I'ma fuck that nigga's world up. He is fucking with some bitch while I'm sitting at home like a good housewife. Fuck that nigga. Come over and help me pack his shit up."

"I'm on my way, cuz," Tasha replied.

Paula hung up and turned her music up with the bass booming from her speakers.

Paula was 26 years old and the vice president of one of the most prestigious day care centers in North Carolina's tristate area. Because of her "go get it" attitude and business ethics, she was one of the main reasons the company was so successful. She played no games. She made six figures a year between her bonuses and pay. She stood at five foot three and weighed 230 pounds. She was a big girl with class. She dressed appropriately for her size but always had a sexy flair to her style. She had brown skin and beautiful hair. She wore it natural, no chemicals at all. It was dreaded up and styled beautifully. She had nice, full lips and slanted light brown eyes. She had no children and had no desire for any kids until she had gained everything she desired in life. She knew that once she made the decision to have a child, she would be a full-time mother. It made sense to her to make all the money and life's mistakes before bringing a child into the world.

She grew up in the quiet suburbs with her mother. When she was a baby, her father had been killed in a car crash that took not only his life but four others. Paula didn't have any memories of him, but she had heard so many details about him, and what stuck most was that he was a great provider and loved her more than anything else in the world.

Because the accident was the fault of a tractor-trailer driver, Paula's mom received a settlement of $1.5 million, which, along with the $75,000 of his insurance money, left them well-off. Her mom put her in private school, and Paula's academic achievements soared.

Although Paula's dad was gone, Maria Smith kept Paula in touch with his family, which was how she and Tasha became close. Anytime Paula went out of town for vacations with her mom, she would always include Tasha, and vice versa. Tasha's family wasn't rich, but they were well-off enough that they lived in the suburbs also. When Tasha invited Paula to her school dance, Paula was excited because she had never been to a dance before. As soon as she hit the floor, her fate was sealed with Michael, and the rest was history. A year later, her mother fell ill and died, which left Paula the only option of living with her mother's mother, who moved into their home and managed the finances until Paula came of age.

Paula pulled up to an Exxon to get some gas before she ran out. She hadn't paid any attention to the gage earlier because she was heated, but her car beeped, alerting her that her car was close to E.

When she got out of her car, a young Mexican man was parked next to her. "*Mami*, you have a lovely car."

"Thank you," Paula replied, smiling. She loved getting props on her baby. She had a brown Tundra as well, but when she rode through the city to relax, the Vic was her choice.

"The driver is sexy as hell, too," he told her and winked.

"Thanks," Paula replied and walked into the store. She shook her head. It was too early in the day for foolishness, especially that day.

While Paula was standing in the checkout line, the door chimed, and she looked up to see the Mexican man walking over to her. He said, "Listen, I'm not trying to be rude or stalk you, but I wanted to give you this."

He handed her a flier that read:

> *Crown Vics all around, come show off your beauty and possibly win $15,000. If you think your Vic has what it takes, bring her out and let the CV Firm be the judge.*

"This is in South Carolina?" Paula asked.

"Yes, but I can guarantee that you will have a ball. There will be free food, plenty of contests, and an after-party. Shit, you might win the 'Rumpshaker' contest, also. Damn," he said, looking at Paula's ass.

Paula shook her head and brushed off the man's last comment, but after the day she was having, she was going to seriously give it some thought.

Paula told the guy she would think about it and walked off after paying for her gas. She filled her tank and drove home. "Now to get this nigga's shit out of my house."

***

"Get the fuck out of my house, you sorry-ass piece of shit. How fucking dare you come back here like everything is cool?" Paula yelled as she threw Michael's clothes out the door.

"Girl, what the fuck are you doing? You tripping for real. Put my muthafucking clothes back in the room."

"Fuck you and these li'l raggedy-ass clothes. Get the fuck out for real."

"What the hell are you tripping about? I ain't did shit."

"Where the fuck you been, Michael?" Paula asked.

"Man, you know I was at the bando trapping."

"Really? Really, nigga? Is that your final answer?" she asked, standing with her hands on her hips.

"Man, I'm telling you that I haven't been with no other bitch. That's on everything."

Paula grabbed her cell phone and showed him the picture of him and the woman he had just left. "Oh, yeah? Well, what the fuck is this?"

"Ma, where the hell did you get that from? You been spying on me?" he questioned angrily.

"You mad now? Get the fuck out of my shit. And to answer your question, yo' bitch shared this on her Facebook page, and someone sent it to me, asking me if we had broken up. So check that ho, not me. I can't believe that you would do this shit to me. Lying, telling me that's your cousin. Hell, even yo' dumb-ass sister was in on it, but fuck all y'all. Straight like that."

Paula started getting angrier and angrier. "And that li'l bastard of yours, yeah, I saw his ass, too. You can have all that. As a matter of fact, you can have your name back and this ring. I want out."

"You want what?" Michael asked as he stepped toward Paula.

Paula laughed and stepped closer to him. "What, ngga? You thought I was going to tremble or retreat? I will kill you, bitch, right where the fuck you stand. Like I said, I want out, meaning a d-i-v-o-r-c-e."

Michael stood stone-faced. "Paula, please don't do this. Please."

Paula shook her head as hot tears threatened to exit her eyes. She wiped angrily at them, refusing to let Michael see her pain. "Get out," she growled, staring him blankly in the eyes.

Michael shook his head. "I'm leaving, but I will be back."

Once Michael left, Paula sat down on her couch and allowed all her emotions to seep out. She cried, screamed, and cried some more. She threw objects against the wall and screamed some more until finally she was drained. She walked into her bedroom and lay across her bed, thinking about the first time she'd laid eyes on Michael.

Paula met Michael Harris at her cousin's school dance when she was 13 years old. She spotted him watching her when she was walking to the bathroom with Tasha. When they walked out of the restroom and started back to their table, Michael was waiting for her at the door.

"Hey, love. I'm Michael Harris, and you are?"

"I'm Paula, and this is my cousin Tasha."

"Yeah, I think we are in the same science lab," Michael replied, nodding his hello to Tasha.

Tasha barely spoke back, which caused Paula to give her that "don't be mean" look.

He walked them to the table and then asked Paula to dance. They danced to the Kids At Work song "Singing Hey Yea," and they were inseparable from that night on. Tasha didn't like the fact that her cousin was with him and voiced her concerns only once and never again thereafter. She decided that she would support her cousin's decision to date and then marry Michael and would be there to pick up the pieces when he broke her heart. In her mind it was inevitable.

Paula cringed as she remembered her cousin's warning and laughed, "I should've listened to Tasha."

She soon fell asleep and awoke the following morning ready to seize a new day. She had to find a divorce attorney and quick.

Chapter 2

After Paula called Chandra, her boss, and explained what had happened three days before, Chandra gladly gave Paula the day off. She was the kind of boss who held strong beliefs about love, marriage, and relationships. Paula loved working for her because she made her job enjoyable. Paula did have to promise to do some work from home that was time sensitive, but only after she spoke to an attorney. Chandra referred an attorney who had helped her out in her divorce, and she swore to Paula that she was one of the best. Paula thanked her, and after she got off the phone with Chandra, she took a shower, put on her best Armani suit, and drove to Tasha's house to see if she would ride with her to locate the perfect divorce attorney.

She was halfway there when her phone bleeped with a Facebook notification. She decided to wait to look at it until she pulled up at Tasha's. As she set the phone back down, she caught sight of the flier that the guy had given her at Exxon the day before.

"I might just have to check this shit out." She sighed.

When she finally pulled up in front of Tasha's house, she parked and got out. The sun was shining bright, and the warmth from it kissed Paula's skin. As she began walking to Tasha's door, she groaned, "Damn, I forgot my phone."

She walked back to her car, reached in through the window, and grabbed her cell. It was lit up, alerting her to another notification that had just come through.

"I almost forgot." She laughed.

There were two digital messages waiting for her in her Facebook Messenger from a contact she didn't know. She opened the attachments, and the smile on her face disappeared. The message Last Night followed each picture of her husband lying in what Paula assumed was Nicki's bed, asleep, with her lying under him with her arms thrown around his neck. Paula slumped back against her car, staring at her phone, tears clouding her vision. She began to shake and slowly slide to the ground. She felt so raw, like her insides were exposed to the nastiest disease.

A few seconds later she was being pulled up. "Girl, what's wrong with you?"

Paula held her phone out as she stood to regain her balance. The two ladies walked into Tasha's apartment, and Paula sat down at the bar.

"You know what's fucked up?" Tasha asked as she looked closely at the picture on Paula's phone.

Paula didn't respond as she sat on the couch with her left leg jumping uncontrollably fast.

"This nigga left you, his wife, in the state you were in and ran to his baby momma. Sorry-ass piece of shit," Tasha argued, not giving Paula the chance to respond.

"Tash, fuck that shit. I came over here to see if you would ride with me to check out a few divorce attorneys. The first firm I want to check out is the one Chandra suggested. She said that they helped her a lot," Paula stated.

"You know I'm down to ride. Let me go get myself together," Tasha replied.

Once Tasha walked to the back room, Paula got up and walked outside and got in her car to wait for her.

Paula was disgusted and felt that the life within her had been sucked out of her. A few minutes later, Tasha emerged, and they drove out in search of the perfect divorce attorney. They soon pulled into the parking lot of

Howard and Manchester Law Firm twenty minutes away from Tasha's residence.

They parked, and as Paula unclamped her seat belt and opened the car door, Tasha stopped her. "You sure you want to do this, Paula? You two have been through a lot."

Paula stared at Tasha, confused. "Tash, of all people I figured you would be okay with me doing this. You never liked Michael, and now you are questioning me about my decision? Listen, I'm not making any decision yet. I'm just really weighing my options."

"Okay, cuz, you know whatever you decide to do, I'm behind you. Come on, let's go talk to a man about a dog—your dog."

Tasha started laughing, and Paula shook her head. "Corny ass." Paula walked into the building with Tasha by her side.

The receptionist greeted them. "Welcome to Howard and Manchester Law Firm. How may I help you ladies?"

"Um yes, I was referred to you guys by Chandra Witherspoon. She said that this firm handled her divorce case," Paula said nervously.

"We do handle those, but do you have an appointment to speak with anyone?" the receptionist asked.

"Oh, no, I don't," Paula whispered, shaking her head and feeling kind of silly for not doing that first.

"Unfortunately, all of our attorneys are busy today, but I can set you up with an appointment with one of them for next Thursday," she informed Paula.

"Well, do you have any material I can look over?" Paula inquired. "After I read it, I will call you to set up an appointment."

"Yes, ma'am, we do have a packet here, and you call when you are ready, okay?" The receptionist handed Paula a light packet and gave Paula her personal card.

"Call me if you have any questions. You ladies have a fantastic day."

"Thank you, and you do the same," Paula replied.

The two ladies walked out and got back in the car. "Where to now?" Tasha asked.

"Shit, let's just ride." Paula laughed as she started her car and pulled off.

"I'm always down for that. Let's go get Angela and chase the wind."

Paula knew what Tasha was speaking of. Hell, she needed something between her legs, so why not make it a Ducati?

"Shit, let's get it," Paula agreed.

After Paula dropped Tasha off at home, she decided to call it a day. She drove home, and upon arriving there, she was unhappy and surprised to find Michael's car in her driveway.

"What the hell?" She sighed as she parked her car and turned it off. She sat there for a few minutes trying to calm her nerves because she knew if she laid eyes on Michael right then, there was no telling what would occur.

Finally, she got out of the car and walked into the house. An aroma greeted her. Michael was cooking. He must have heard her walk in, because he immediately advanced into the living room.

"How are you?" he asked.

"Michael, what are you doing here?" she asked, rolling her eyes.

"Like I told you earlier, we need to talk."

"Talk about what? I have really nothing to say to you," Paula said as she set her purse and folder down on the barstool and headed for the bathroom.

Michael began to follow her, but his eyes were drawn to the folder that she had set down. He walked over and picked it up and set it down quickly as if it were on fire.

"Paula, what the fuck?" he yelled.

"What are you talking about, Michael?" Paula asked as she walked out of the bathroom, drying her hands off.

"What's that?" he asked, pointing to the cream-colored folder with the Howard and Manchester Law Firm emblem imprinted on it.

"What do you think that is? I refuse to deal with a cheating, lying, sorry-ass man. I—" Paula began.

Slap.

Before Paula knew what had happened, Michael slapped her with a force that sent her flying backward onto the side table, and then falling hard to the floor.

Paula screamed out loudly from the shock and the sting of the blow.

"Baby, I'm sorry. Please forgive me," Michael cried as he rushed forward and knelt down to help her up.

Paula jerked away with her eyes glazed. "Get the fuck out of my house."

"Paula, this is my house too. I'm not going anywhere," Michael yelled back.

Paula stood up, holding on to the chair as she steadied herself. Once she was securely on her feet, she grabbed her cell phone.

"So you gonna call the cops on me now? It's not enough that you are trying to take everything I love from me, but you want me behind bars, too? I'm sorry, Paula. You know I've never hit you before. Dammit, I'm sorry."

Paula stared at Michael with a look that Michael had never seen before. "I'm taking everything you love? Nigga, if you loved me, we wouldn't be where we are right muthafucking now. You did this to us, and to make it even worse, you ran straight to the bitch who's in the middle of all this shit. Yeah, she sent pictures of you laid up in the bed with yo' son lying next to you."

Michael cringed as Paula showed him more damaging pictures of his wrongdoing, but technically he had done no wrong.

"Paula, yes, I went over there, but it was to confront her about why she put those pictures on Facebook. I haven't slept with her in years. You got to believe that."

Paula sneered, "And yet you keep getting photo-bombed at this bitch's house in her fucking bed. Nigga, you ain't shit. Get the fuck out."

Michael walked to the kitchen and a few seconds later walked back out. "It's not what you think, and I'm sorry that I put my hands on you, but this isn't over, Paula. Not by a long shot."

After Michael left, Paula fixed a chicken and shrimp salad and grabbed her peach tea out of the refrigerator. As she ate her dinner, she started reading over the material that she had gotten at the attorney's office. Thirty minutes later, Paula sighed and tossed the folder to the side and decided it was time to get ready for bed.

Paula took a shower and, afterward, put on her lace blue bra and panty set with a matching robe, fixed herself a cup of wine, and went to her office. She sighed as she flipped open her laptop and started working on the files that her assistant, Brea, had sent her.

She tried to keep her mind on what was in front of her, but she couldn't. She sighed and lay across the bed and closed her eyes, but she couldn't seem to shake the image of Michael lying in another bitch's bed. She didn't know what to do. She was angry and hurt, but she attempted to put on a mask around others. She could fool them, but she couldn't fool herself or her heart. The pain of knowing that her husband was a lying, cheating asshole had her regretting the very day she'd first laid eyes on him.

She tried to piece together why he cheated and when he had the chance to. He was home every night, which was why she ignored the talk about him and other women. She held him down from the time they got married, during his prison bid, and a few weeks after he came home from prison.

She applied herself in her work while he was incarcerated so that she could maintain and hold him down. She quickly climbed the corporate ladder and spent many late nights in the office. Was that why he cheated? Had she ignored him due to her work and he found pussy elsewhere? Shit, she figured any nigga would be happy to have a successful woman at home. Hell, she didn't trip when he spent his first two weeks home in the streets. She knew that after being locked up for almost two years, he wasn't going to want to be locked down in the house with her. But Paula had to admit that Michael was a bit distant when he was released. She just didn't know why. After he got the ripping and running out of his system, Michael had gotten a job as a forklift operator, which pleased Paula because he had made a decision to make money the right way versus the easy way. He never missed a day.

Paula groaned and turned frustrated at the thoughts that plagued her mind. Their sexual life was on point. There was never a dull moment. She went above and beyond to please him. She never told him no except when her period was on, and even then she found ways to accommodate him. She would give him oral sex or anal. But a few times she had turned him down because the cramps would be extra intense. Was that the reason? Did he cheat on her those nights because she wouldn't give him period coochie?

She sat up in her bed and whispered, "I need to get the fuck away from here for a while."

She grabbed her cell. "Cuz, you down for a trip?"

"You know I am," Tasha replied sleepily.

"I'ma slide through tomorrow, okay?"

"All right. Are you okay?" Tasha asked.

"Yeah. I just need to get away."

"I'm down. See you tomorrow," Tasha said and hung up.

The following day, Paula went to work and grabbed a few files to work on before she left for her trip. She didn't want to leave Chandra and the rest of the team with her work.

Paula left work early to go to the doctor and get herself checked out. She and Michael always made it a point to be checked out annually, but in light of all his dirt, she needed reassurance that she was clean.

Paula arrived at her appointment ten minutes early and sat in her car trying to make sense of everything. Michael had been living a whole other life, and she knew nothing about it. She felt stupid and used up. She decided to go on into the doctor's office and get the tests done and over with.

After a lot of probing, sticking, and digging, the doctor told Paula that she was disease free but that the gonor-rhea and AIDS tests were going to take longer to come back. He reassured her that he doubted she had anything at all and they would call her once the tests returned. She thanked the doctor and left.

She stopped at Sally's to get a plate. She was in the mood for soul food, but she didn't want to cook. When she finally arrived home, Michael was sitting on the porch. He had his hands clasped and his head bent.

"Is this nigga praying?" she mumbled. Paula grabbed her bag of food and got out of the car. "Michael, what are you doing here?"

"Paula, please, I need to talk to you. Can we do that?"

"I really don't have anything to say. I honestly don't," she replied.

Paula walked into her house and put her food down and walked back to the door and saw Michael in the same position she'd found him in when she first walked up. She groaned silently and walked back outside and sat down next to him. "Okay, Michael, talk."

"I know I can't change what I did or make that up to you, but I honestly love you and want to work on this. Please don't walk away from what we have created. I promise you—"

Before he could finish his statement, his cell phone began to ring. He looked at it and then at Paula. Paula knew from the guilty look on his face that it was another woman.

"Answer it," she said calmly.

"It's not important. It can wait," he replied.

"Answer your fucking phone, Michael," Paula said through clenched teeth.

"Paula, please don't do this."

"Don't do what? Michael, you are so full of shit. I had to go get tested today behind your nasty ass. I never thought in a million years that I'd have to do that shit. Then this bitch feeling so damn comfortable that she calls your phone when she wants? Un-mothafucking-believable." Paula stood up and stormed into the house with Michael close behind her.

"Paula, I love you. I don't want any other woman."

"Yeah, well, you could have fooled me. Just go check on your son and baby momma. I'm not in the mood for this bullshit. I'm tired, hungry, embarrassed, hurt, and I just want to be alone."

Michael shook his head. "I'm going to be staying with my mother. If you need me, that's where I will be, but we need to work this out one way or the other."

"Not right now we don't." Paula snickered sarcastically.

"I will be back," Michael said and walked out.

Paula sat down on her couch and leaned back, gazing at the photo of her and Michael on their wedding day. She leaned over and picked it up, swiped two fingers across the picture, smiling, then slung it against the fireplace, shattering the shards of glass everywhere. Paula walked over and stared at the glass and laughed, "Matches my heart."

Chapter 3

Road Trip

Early Saturday morning, Paula grabbed a bucket and her car cleaning supplies and placed them in the trunk of her Crown Vic. She was about to meet Tasha and Angela at the car wash so that she could get her car washed and they could shine up their motorcycles for their trip to South Carolina. Paula wanted her baby to shine. She wasn't too concerned about the contest because she knew her baby was sexy, with confirmation from anyone else. It was light pink with a tint that caused it to switch from pink to a pearl whitish color depending on how the sun shined on it. She'd had the paint custom-made to her liking. Paula's car sat on seventeen-inch white diamond, pink, and black rims, which were inside her black studded tires.

The inside held a pink and black leather interior with a clean black rug to complete it. The front grill of her car was chromed and shiny with her custom-made plate on the front that read, "Bougie & Ghetto Bitch," with green cat eyes underneath.

They were due to pull out for South Carolina in a few hours, and Paula was excited about it. She needed the vacation more than anything at that moment.

She pulled out of her driveway and rammed her motor, which hummed with perfection. Five minutes later, Paula pulled into the car wash, surprised to see that Tasha and Angela were both there. Paula admired Tasha, who was also a full-figured woman. She stood at five foot seven and was light-skinned with long, pretty, wavy black hair. Her boobs were huge, as well as her ass, but her stomach wasn't big at all. She wasn't a female you could toy with either. She would drag a ho quicker than lightning would strike a man standing in a mud puddle holding a wire hanger.

Angela was the lightweight of the three girls. She was five foot five, brown skinned, with a silky, curly afro. She weighed 157 pounds and was bowlegged. Angela was also into women. She had never had any desire to sleep with a man and only dated the hottest women in the tristate area.

As soon as Paula pulled up at the car wash and turned her car off, she hopped out. "Y'all beat me here. Damn, you on it today."

"Shit, look at you with those cute-ass jeans on. Damn, your ass popping in them." Angela laughed.

Paula turned slowly, showing off the jeans she had purchased the day before while she and Tasha had been out.

"All right, girl, you gon' make me cuff that ass," Angela joked, walking over to slap Paula on the butt.

"You know I like that shit. You better stop it." Paula laughed.

"My big baby." Angela laughed. She walked back over to her purple and black Ducati 929. It was one of the hottest bikes on their side of town. It had fluorescent lights that she had tailored to flash whenever she hit certain gears.

Tasha had a green and silver Ducati similar to Angela's. She had recently purchased it after wrecking her Harley two months earlier.

It took the girls an hour to get their vehicles cleaned and ready for their trip. Paula had her bags already packed and only had to stop by her house to drop off the bucket and pick up her bags. They were going to meet up at Angela's house because her uncle was going to let them use his trailer to put the motorcycles on and hook it up to Paula's car.

Two hours after leaving the car wash, the girls were on their way to South Carolina. Because of their last-minute decision to attend the CV event, they had to settle for a hotel farther away from the event, but they wouldn't complain because they found a nice hotel within a ten-mile radius from the Crown Vic gala.

As they traveled down toward Charlotte, the traffic was heavy, but it went unnoticed by the ladies. They were laughing, talking, and singing, enjoying the ride. As they crossed over into South Carolina, they were growing more anxious by the minute.

Finally, around three in the afternoon, they arrived at their hotel. They unlatched the bikes and the trailer and walked into the hotel to check in. Once they were in their rooms, they showered and got dressed. Paula wore her dreads up in a ponytail and a cute shirt that matched her diamond-studded Bougie & Ghetto plate, which also had the back out, and a pair of black jeans.

Tasha and Angela put on their biker jeans and leather Tims along with their gray T-shirts and short leather coats with diamonds on the back. They weren't part of any bike club, but they wore the matching jackets with Paula's logo, Bougie & Ghetto, branded on the back.

"Y'all ready to go?" Paula asked.

"Hell yeah. Been ready." Angela laughed.

They grabbed their helmets and keys and headed out the door.

"Man, I can't believe you two aren't going to ride with me," Paula whined jokingly.

"What did you think we brought our bikes for? Shit, I'm 'bout to show these South Carolina niggas what an ass really looks like on a Ducati. Ay." Tasha laughed as she danced down the hall of the hotel.

"That's a lot of ass she 'bout to show 'em, ain't it?" Angela laughed, watching Tasha sashay to the elevator.

"You damn right. They ain't ready." Paula laughed.

The ladies got on the elevator and rode it down to the bottom floor and left the hotel with a few eyes following them.

When Paula pulled up to the street where the Crown Vic contest was being held, she was in awe. There were so many people and cars lined up she felt like she was in heaven. The cars were just as sexy as hers, and the men were gorgeous. She glanced in her rearview and saw Tasha and Angela acting up on their bikes, and they were drawing major attention from the crowds. As the crowds cheered, Angela and Tasha went around her car with their bikes on one wheel. Paula laughed, "Show-offs."

When they pulled into the area where Paula had to register her car into the contest, Tasha and Angela were already checking out Paula's competition. They realized that as nice as Paula's Crown Vic was, several others outshined hers. They also knew that Paula didn't care if she won. She was just happy to be away from the drama in her life.

They waited for Paula to get into her position on the line, and they then parked their bikes in the same location.

"Girl, look at all these muthafuckas out here. I'm about to get me one of these dreads who will match my sexy and fuck the shit out of him. Y'all might have to save that nigga. I ain't had no dick in months."

"Shit, I ate some pussy a few nights ago, and dammit, I'm hungry again. Somebody's baby momma gonna ride this wave tonight. Unless Paula wants to be the one riding it." Angela laughed, licking her tongue out at her.

Paula knew that although Angela made her comments as if they were jokes, she was also serious. She didn't pay Angela much attention at all. She didn't care how desperate she was. She'd never fuck Angela, not because she had an issue with gay women, but because Angela was her friend. Hell, if she got horny enough, she'd fuck a bitch. Quick.

Paula lifted her hood and smiled as she admired her custom-built motor. She had put a lot of money into her car. She didn't have any kids, so she treated her car as if it were her baby. She loved her Crown Vic.

As they started mingling with some of the other people at the event, Paula was beginning to forget her problems.

Tripp

"Damn, look at that thick sista," Tripp murmured as he scanned the crowd, his eyes stopping to admire Paula's beauty.

"Oh, shit, she came," Ramon whispered, cheesing as if he had found his diamond in the rough.

Tripp glared at Ramon. "You know her?"

Ramon shook his head. "Not really. When I went up to North Carolina to check out Loraine, I ran into her at the gas station and gave her a flier and told her she should check it out. Baby bad as hell."

"Yeah, she sure is," Tripp agreed.

Ramon knew just by the sound of Tripp's voice that all bets were off where she was concerned.

When Tripp caught sight of Paula, he couldn't take his eyes off of her. There was something about her demeanor that intrigued him. She walked through the crowd as if she had already been crowned queen of VMC. He laughed and walked out to inspect the Crown Vics that were being judged.

But he was gonna make sure to invite her to their annual CV party that was going to take place later that night. She and her friends were going to be special guests of his.

"Girl, look at all these sexy-ass divas," Angela said, grabbing her crotch as if she had a dick.

Tasha, the only one in the group who seemed to notice everything, laughed, "Bitch, you act like yo' dick just got hard."

"I believe it did." Angela laughed.

"Muthafucka, you ain't got no dick. You got the same shit we got. Hell, yo' clit must've stood the fuck up, you long-clit bitch."

Paula, who was sipping on a Sprite, choked. "Man, you stupid, Tash."

"She just mad that my clit won't get hard for her, but ummmm, you already know what's goody, Paula," Angela laughed, winking at Paula.

"Angela, go on with that shit. Both of y'all got issues." Paula laughed.

"'Here comes the judge,'" Tasha sang, mimicking Flip Wilson.

Three of the sexiest men approached, one of whom Paula recognized instantly.

"I see you made it, sweetness. I'm glad you took my advice. Maybe you will follow through with the 'Rumpshaker' contest, too," Ramon joked only to get a threatening look from his companion.

"Man, don't disrespect her like that. Please excuse his sour mouth. I'm Tripp, and you are?"

"I'm Paula. Nice to meet you," she said as she extended her hand.

Tripp grabbed it and noticed her wedding ring. "Oh, I apologize. I didn't know that you were married, and here I am trying to . . . well, never mind that. You ladies take care," he said as he smiled at Paula.

"Oh, that's over. I don't know why she's still wearing that bullshit," Tasha spat out.

Paula groaned, "That's my loudmouthed cousin, Tasha. And that's my best friend, Angela."

Tripp smiled hard as he stepped closer to Paula. "So is that the truth? Because if so, I'd like to invite you and your friends to be VIP at our CV dance tonight."

Paula shrugged. "To be honest, I didn't come all the way down here to discuss that. But I would definitely be interested in being your guest tonight."

"Give me your full names, and here is the information for the dance tonight. All you need to do is give them your names, and they will let y'all in. Matter of fact . . ." he started and grabbed the paper back and took out his pen. "I'ma write my cell on the back so if you have any problems getting there or getting in, you can call me."

"Okay, that's a bet," Paula said, smiling at Tripp.

"Okay, well, let me get back to the business at hand, but y'all definitely enjoy yourselves out here, and I hope I see you all later," he said, looking more at Paula than anyone else.

"Well, I guess since I'm out with you, maybe I can tap that ass tonight," Ramon said, looking at Tasha.

Tripp frowned and popped him in the back of the head. "Bring your simple ass on."

Tasha frowned as well. "Ay, dude, come get my number. I'ma make you my weekend smash fest. And she comes with her own condoms. What's your size, bruh? I'm guessing medium or regular 'cause your walk tells it all."

Ramon started laughing and walked away with Tripp cussing him out about being disrespectful to women.

Tasha laughed, "Damn, what a chick gotta do to be taken serious around here? I'll fuck a li'l-dick nigga, too."

Paula started laughing hard. "Your ass is a lunatic."

Tasha shrugged and started twerking to the music that was streaming from Paula's radio.

The day seemed to fly by as the girls mingled and moved around, admiring all the cars that were there. After two hours, Paula and her girls left the Crown Vic event to get dressed for the gala. Just like Tasha figured, Paula didn't win the contest, but they all had met some very nice people. Paula had gotten several numbers from some of the men there, and Tasha prayed that she used at least one.

"Paula, which one of those sexy-ass guys are you going to mingle with tonight?" Tasha asked.

Paula shook her head. "None. I'm not here to focus on a man. Hell, I'm trying to escape troubles from one man now. I'm not going to leave one problem for another."

"Girl, it ain't creating problems. It's having fun and enjoying life. Hell, I can guarantee you Michael is."

Paula didn't respond as she grabbed her towel and headed for the shower.

"Girl, why you have to go there with her?" Angela questioned, hitting Tasha on her arm.

"Ouch. Well, shit, she needs to let loose, fuck it, and you know I'm not lying, Ang."

"Man, what the fuck ever." Angela fumed.

Tasha didn't say anything else. She pulled out her gray dress and pumps. She and Angela didn't speak again until it was time for them to leave, and even then, it was forced. Paula felt the tension but didn't say anything at all. She was there to relax, not play referee to two grown-ass women.

Chapter 4

When they arrived at the hotel where the gala was being held, they began to loosen up. As they approached the door, the doorman opened it for them and escorted them to the barroom. The ladies were impressed with the layout of the bar.

Angela leaned over and whispered, "Damn, it seems like everyone is coupled off. Shit, I'm about to tear up somebody's happy home. I need me a wifey." She quickly looked at Paula. "I'm sorry, boo. I didn't mean it like it sounded. I was joking."

Paula knew she wasn't joking, but she shrugged it off.

"You know I'm always saying shit without thinking," Angela said.

"Yeah, kinda like diarrhea at the mouth," Tasha replied sarcastically. "And you talk about me."

"Yeah, but, Tasha, you always have diarrhea at the mouth," Angela replied, rolling her eyes.

"All right, damn, you guys. That's enough of that crazy shit. Let's go have some fun," Paula said as she walked to the bar, leaving Angela and Tasha staring after her with their mouths agape.

Paula walked to the bar and ordered a lime margarita. When the bartender placed it in front of her, a deep voice chimed from behind her, "Ay, this drink is on me."

Paula grabbed her drink and half turned to find one of the most handsome Caucasian men she had ever seen. She smiled as she thanked him for buying her drink.

"What's your name, beautiful?"

"I'm Paula, and you are?" Paula replied, extending her hand to shake his.

"I'm Matthew Price," he replied.

"Nice to meet you, sir," Paula replied, smiling.

"Hey, how's it going over here?" another, slightly more familiar voice chimed in.

"Ay, what's up, Tripp?" Matthew asked.

"Shit, nothing at all. Miss Lady, how about you come with me to the VIP area?" Tripp said.

Matthew stepped backward and smiled. "Didn't know this was you, man. No disrespect."

"None taken. Enjoy your night, man," Tripp replied, taking Paula by the hand and leading her through the crowd to the roped-off VIP section.

Paula didn't put up a fuss because, if she had to be honest, she liked the way Tripp took control of the situation.

"You looking good, lady. So tell me about you," he said once they were seated.

"Well, as I told you earlier today, I'm Paula, I live in North Carolina, and I am the vice president of a prestigious day care center," she told him, cringing, thinking she sounded like she was on a dating show.

"Well, Paula from North Carolina, how did you enjoy the Crown Vic event today?"

"I loved it. I'm really glad I came down."

"I am as well." He smiled.

Paula sipped her drink, and she and Tripp talked for a while before he asked her to dance.

She again allowed him to lead her to their destination. As Frankie Beverly sounded out "Before I Let Go," Paula and Tripp performed a sensual swing dance that caught the eyes of several people in the bar. It was like they were made for each other. Their bodies flowed well together and connected as one.

After they danced, they returned to the VIP section and were approached by a tall Italian man. "What's up, boss man?"

"What's going on?" Tripp replied, reaching out to shake his hand.

"Shit, just wanted to come through and show my face. Um, we got that situation curbed, also," the man said, nodding his head.

"Cool. Listen, I'm trying to get to know this beautiful young lady right now, but we will talk at the office on Monday," Tripp said, smiling.

"Oh, no doubt. Didn't mean to interrupt at all. Y'all have a great night."

"Thank you," Paula replied.

"So, Miss Lady, tell me more about your job," Tripp said as he picked up his drink and took a sip.

Paula told Tripp about her work, and just as she was about to discuss her relationship status, Tasha and Angela walked over. Tasha said, "We have been looking for you, girl."

"Well, hell, I've been right here." Paula laughed.

Tripp slid over closer to Paula so that Angela and Tasha could join them. Before they knew it, Ramon and a few other people had joined them and were turned up to the max. Paula laughed and sat back against Tripp's arm, which was curled around her.

Tripp asked Paula if she could walk him to his truck before they left, and she agreed. He helped her up and again grabbed her hand, and they walked out of the bar to the parking lot. He walked over to his dark blue F-150 truck and opened her door. He helped her in and then walked to his side and got in.

He turned the interior light on and took his phone out. "Can I get your number?"

"Yes, you can."

Paula told him her number, and he looked at her. "You got your cell on you?"

"No, why?"

"Because I was going to call it to make sure you gave me your correct number. I know how you women do sometimes." He smiled.

"It's the right number, don't worry."

"Well, how long are you going to be in town?"

"Three more days."

"Oh, okay. Are you going to let me show you around?"

"Sure. I'd love that," Paula replied.

"That's what's up. I must say that you got some gorgeous lips and eyes. Make any man flip his wig," Tripp whispered.

"Thank you," she replied, lowering her head.

"You don't have to be shy, li'l lady."

Paula laughed, "I'm not shy. Well, not really."

He laughed and turned the music on. "You like jazz?"

"I love it. Sade is my favorite."

"Listen to this one," Tripp said as he flipped through the songs on the CD that was playing. He stopped as a deep male voice sang out.

Paula rocked her head to the beat and smiled as she recognized the second male voice on the song. "That's my man Kem."

"What you know about Kem?" Tripp asked her.

"Any song he puts out, I'm on it." She laughed. "Who is that singing with him?"

"What? You don't know Gregory Porter? Man, I thought you knew jazz," Tripp said, smiling.

Damn, that fucking smile got my coochie jumping, Paula thought.

The song continued to play, and Paula relaxed and closed her eyes so that she could enjoy the full vibe of the song. When she opened her eyes, Tripp was staring at her, smiling.

"What is it?" she asked nervously.

"Just admiring you. Is something wrong with that?"

Paula shook her head. *Damn, and he is saying all the right things.*

"Tell me, did you enjoy yourself tonight?"

"I most definitely did," she answered.

"What was your favorite part about tonight?"

Paula knew that he was fishing for a compliment, but she couldn't give it to him. She thought, *I can easily say you,* but instead she smiled and whispered, "Everything about today was memorable. I can't choose one specific thing."

Tripp smiled. "I'll take that."

Paula smiled, and Tripp reached for her hand and looked at her. "I pray for any loser who lets you go."

Paula turned her head and looked out the window. "I guess we'd better head back in."

"Did I say something wrong?" he asked.

"Nothing at all," Paula replied. "I just know my cousin and best friend. They will be searching for me with their war boots on if I don't."

"Let's get you back in there then."

Just as Paula had said, Tasha and Angela were scouring the bar for her, and when they saw her, Tasha advanced on her. "Next time you take yo' hot ass somewhere, tell us first. We been looking everywhere for you."

"Yes, mother." Paula laughed.

"That shit ain't funny. Had us looking everywhere for you," Angela chimed in.

"Okay, I will tell y'all next time," Paula whispered.

Tripp started laughing. "So y'all want to get a few more drinks?"

"I'd better not. I think my peoples are ready to go," Paula replied, seeing Tasha and Angela head for the door.

"I'm gonna be calling you tonight," he told her.

"I look forward to it." Paula smiled.

Tripp walked them to their car and waited until they pulled off before he sauntered back into the bar.

"Bitch, did you get you some dick?" Tasha asked.

"No, I didn't. You know me better than that, Tash," Paula replied, agitated.

"Mm-hmm. Let me smell," Angela laughed.

"Y'all two about to make me pull over and put y'all tails out of my car."

They laughed, and Paula turned her music up and drove to the hotel. Just like she figured, she had several missed calls from Michael and one missed call from a number she assumed was Tripp's.

"I'm gonna take a shower," she told Angela and Tasha.

"Mm-hmm, gonna wash that stank off your bootie," Angela joked.

"Man, y'all, please chill out with that," Paula groaned as she headed for the shower.

When she got out of the shower, she put her night-clothes on, sat at the desk in the room, and turned on her laptop to check her email for any messages from Chandra.

"Uh, nope. Put it away. You are on vacation, Paula," Angela told her.

"I know it. I'm just checking my email."

"I don't care what you are doing. We about to chop it up," Angela replied.

Before anyone could speak another word, Paula's cell phone rang. "We gon' have to chop it up after this phone call." Paula laughed, sticking her tongue out at Angela. "Hello?" she answered.

"So this is your number. Just wanted to make sure you made it back safe," Tripp said.

"Yeah, we made it. Thanks for checking on us."

"You know, I didn't get a chance to tell you my favorite part of the day."

"Yeah? And what was it?"

"As if you have to ask. It was meeting y'all."

"Oh, really?"

"Most definitely."

Paula smiled, and she and Tripp talked for an hour. When she hung up, Angela and Tasha were staring at her.

"Not tonight, y'all. I'm tired."

Paula hopped into her bed and pulled the covers over her head, leaving Tasha and Angela looking perplexed and mad.

The Next Morning

"Good morning, beautiful," a deep Southern voice drawled on the phone into Paula's ear.

"Good morning to you. Listen, I had a great time last night," Paula said as she turned to her left to check the time on the night table.

"I'm glad you did. I remembered you told me you're going to be in town for a few days, and I'm hoping you will let me convince you to allow me to show you ladies around. Kind of like your personal tour guide," Tripp told her.

"Well, how can I refuse your Southern hospitality, sir?" Paula laughed as she sat up in bed. "Let me get showered and dressed, and I will call you later."

"Say word," Tripp replied.

"Word." Paula laughed.

They hung up, and Paula jumped out of bed. "Ay, assholes. Wake up. Y'all wanna go on a tour of the city?"

"Hell yeah. I heard you over there whispering in the phone. I take it you like ol' boy?" Tasha questioned.

"Tasha, I don't know him like that, but I will say that I'm curious," Paula admitted.

Angela sighed and cursed. When she was sure that Paula and Tasha were looking, she looked under the cover and groaned, "Well, li'l kitty titty, looks like we might be out of the running for Paula's cooch."

Paula picked up an empty plastic bottle and threw it at Angela. "You so dang silly."

The girls laughed and ordered breakfast, ate it, then got showered and dressed. Paula called Tripp, who informed them that he would pick them up from the hotel in an hour.

Tasha grabbed her bag and pulled out her 9 mm.

"Tasha, what are you doing?" Paula asked.

"Bitch, we don't really know dude like that. Shit, I'ma blow somebody's head off if they try to do anything crazy."

Paula frowned. "Yeah, you got a point. Let me get my Taser."

The girls walked down to the lobby, and Tripp was waiting for them. "You look lovely."

"Thank you. You're looking suave yourself," Paula admitted.

"Well, let's go. Where would you ladies like to go first?" Tripp asked.

"This is your town, so take us where you want to, but keep in mind there are three of us to your one. Don't try nothing," Tasha replied.

Paula laughed and looked at Tasha, then shook her head. Tasha looked back with a funny look. "I ain't playing."

"Trust me, I wouldn't do anything to hurt y'all. Come on, I want y'all to see my studio," Tripp said as he walked to a burgundy Yukon. He walked over and opened the door for Paula and helped her in.

"Ohhhh, sookie sookie, a damn Southern gentleman. All right now," Tasha sang.

Paula laughed and Angela groaned. When everyone was inside the Yukon, Tripp pulled off. Thirty minutes later, they were pulling into the parking lot of a huge brick building.

"Damn, how much does it cost you to rent such a large building?" Tasha inquired. "I bet this shit is expensive as hell."

"Tash, you don't ask nobody anything like that. What the fuck is wrong with you?" Paula asked in utter shock. Paula had witnessed Tasha act out in a ghetto fashion, but never like she was in South Carolina.

Tripp laughed, "It's not a problem. I actually own this building. I had it built a few years ago."

"I can only imagine what kind of dent that must have put in your pocket. Come on, y'all, let's go in," Tasha said excitedly.

Paula shook her head at Tasha's behavior as they all walked inside the building. The attendant smiled as they approached. "Good morning, Mr. Moore."

"Good morning, Sherry. Have Kisha and Shock arrived here yet?" He picked up his mail and looked through it.

"Yes, sir, they are up at studio C, I think. Let me double-check. Umm, yes, sir, studio C it is."

"All right, thank you, Sherry. But listen, I need three passes for my companions here please."

"Okay, I got you, sir." She started typing on her computer, and Tripp, aka Tim Moore, escorted the ladies to the elevator and took them up to studio C.

When they arrived on the floor where the studio was located, Tasha began to speak yet again. "Damn, this shit fire."

Angela shook her head and laughed.

The studio was pretty much laid out. There were two porcelain lions that sat on either side of the doorway leading into the studio. The chandelier that hung from the ceiling was made of crystal and gold. As they walked farther into the studio area, there was a black leather couch sitting up against the wall with a few stools. The music equipment took up most of the space in the small studio. Behind the glass, on the mic, was one of the most famous lady rappers known.

"Oh, my God. Do y'all see who that is? Oh, my God. Please let me go say hello to her. I love her. I love her," Tasha squealed.

Paula groaned, and Tripp laughed, "Calm down, shawty. I will introduce you to her as soon as we finish this set."

The engineer walked up to Tripp and dapped him up, and then the producer walked over. The producer, who was introduced to them as Shock, kept eyeing Tasha and smiling. Tripp started laughing. "Ay, man, this is a new friend of mine, Paula, and these are her friends—"

"Tasha," she said, cutting Tripp off before he could introduce her.

"I'm Shock, and it's nice to meet you, beautiful."

"Mm-hmm. I'm Angela," she said after clearing her throat.

"Sorry, queen, I meant no disrespect," Shock said as he reached out to shake her hand.

"So how far have y'all gotten today?" Tripp asked as he waved at Kisha.

"We're just getting started actually," Shock replied as he winked at Tasha and headed back to the mixer. "Take it from the top, Kish," Shock said into his headset.

Kisha started rapping, and the girls were bopping to the beat. Paula could definitely relate to the song. It was as if Kisha were talking about her life.

"Let's try another rep. I'm not feeling that," Shock said into his headset.

"Okay, can we take it from the second hook though?" Kisha asked.

"From the top, baby girl," Shock replied.

"Serious? You weren't feeling none of that?" Kisha asked with her hands on her hips.

"Kish, you know I love yo' ass, but from the top."

"All right. You are a slave driver, man."

Everyone laughed, and the beat picked up again. This time when Kisha started rapping, Paula was feeling it and acting on it.

How could you hurt me, boy, after all I've been to you
If you didn't want me, baby, you should've moved on, but you
Wanted to play my love, play with my heart, play my feelings, boy, like I was a toy
Played with our future, fooled with our past. Now I'm packing up my bags, this is
Goodbye, don't call, don't write, just leave me alone
I'm so sick of hurting, so I'm moving on

Tripp stared at Paula in awe. Paula opened her eyes to find that everyone was staring at her, and Tasha was laughing. "My fucking bitch did that shit. Freestyled that shit. She got a voice on her, huh?"

"Damn, girl, you got some skills. Shit, you need to get on that hook," Shock told her.

"Oh, no. I couldn't do that." Paula laughed.

"Oh, yes. I will pay you to do the hook," Shock told her.

"Girl, go on and do it," Tasha said, nudging her.

"You think I should?" Paula asked.

"I do," Angela told her. "You sounded great."

"I don't want to interfere with Kisha's song though," Paula explained.

"Ay, Kish, listen to this chick sing and let me know if you think she should go on this track," Shock said.

"I'm on my way out," Kisha replied, removing her headset.

Tripp walked with Paula inside the booth and explained to her how to sing into the mic to get the best sound. He told her to freestyle what she had done earlier and to have fun with it.

Paula nodded and smiled, but she was terrified. She had never sung in front of anyone outside of Tasha and Angela.

Tripp walked back out with the others, where Tasha was all up on Kisha as if they had been longtime friends. Kisha didn't seem to mind though.

As the music began to play, Paula began to sing. She wasn't singing loud enough for it to be picked up, so they stopped the music, and Tripp went back in. This time he stayed with her.

When the music began again, he stood behind Paula. "Close your eyes and focus on the beat and what you want to sing. Block everyone out."

Paula did as he asked, and it was louder, but her voice was kind of shaky.

The music stopped, and Tripp turned Paula around to face him. "That was better, but you got to shake your nervousness. Look at me while you are singing. Sing to me as if your life depended on it."

Paula smiled, then turned back around as Tripp moved in front of the mic and smiled at her. "All eyes on me, beautiful. I know you like what you see." He smiled as he licked his lips.

Paula laughed and shook her head, letting them know she was ready. The beat started, and the sound that poured from her lips set Tripp's heart racing.

"Dammit, yessss. Put that on the track. You did that, ma," Kisha laughed as she walked back into the booth.

After another hour in the studio, Tripp asked the ladies if they were hungry. They all confirmed that they were, and he told them to pack it up so that they could go eat and then head back to his house to hang out. Shock and Kisha were also going to join them. Tripp took them to Passions, a five-star restaurant, which Paula didn't realize until they pulled up.

"Tripp, I'm not dressed to go into a place like that," she whined as they got out of the truck.

"You look fine to me," Tripp told her.

"I appreciate that, but really, I wouldn't feel comfortable going in there with this on."

"That's the bougie side of Paula." Angela laughed.

"Fuck you, Ang," Paula laughed.

"I got an idea," Shock interjected.

"What is it?" Tripp asked as the group of them stood around the truck.

"We can go back to my spot, and I will put a few things on the grill," Shock said.

"Let's get going. That sounds good to me," Tasha said, smiling at Shock.

"Tripp, take the girls to my crib, and I'ma go to the supermarket and grab a few things."

"Okay, bet. Y'all good with that?" Tripp asked Paula.

"Anything is better than me walking into a five-star restaurant looking like this." Paula laughed.

"Little lady, you want to ride with me and Kisha?" Shock asked Tasha.

"Definitely," Tasha replied, walking over to Shock.

Kisha laughed, "Hell naw, I'm not going to be no third wheel. I will ride with Tripp."

"Let's make a move then," Tripp told everyone.

Tasha and Shock drove off in one direction, and Tripp, Paula, Kisha, and Angela pulled off in another.

A few hours later, Paula found herself in the midst of some real ballers. When they arrived at Shock's house, Kisha had made a few calls and invited several people over. Paula had learned that Kisha and Shock were brother and sister and shared the house.

Angela had gotten drawn into a deep conversation with a few lesbians and was enjoying herself while Tripp and Paula were off on the balcony, talking.

Shock had put some steaks, ribs, and hamburgers on the grill, and Kisha made a pasta salad and baked beans. After the food was done, everyone spread out once more, but Shock and Tasha seemingly had disappeared. Angela walked over to where Paula was and whispered in her ear, "You know, your cousin's upstairs fucking."

"No, she isn't," Paula replied, staring at Angela with an uncertain expression.

"Girl, bye. She told me she was about to see what he was working with, and you know what she meant."

Paula shook her head, and Tripp stared at her in amusement. "Something wrong?"

Paula wanted to be angry, but the way Tripp was looking at her she couldn't be. "Ay, I'm nothing like my cousin, so don't get any ideas," she warned him.

"Naw, baby girl, I would never try you like that. I can tell you got some class about yourself," Tripp replied.

"As long as you know. Let's go back outside on the balcony. It feels good out there," Paula said, standing up.

"I'm right behind you." Tripp said as he placed his hand on the small of her back, allowing her to walk past him.

Paula loved the way the sky was riddled with different shades of red and orange. The sun was just setting, and the clouds that lingered in the sky were outlined in different patterns of colors. The air was fresh and warm.

They sat outside talking, and others started mingling in with the couple. Paula and Angela stood next to one another, arms linked together.

When Tasha reemerged, it wasn't hard to tell what she had been doing. Her hair was mashed, and her face was flushed, but the crazy thing was that when Shock walked out, he acted as if Tasha weren't even there.

Tasha walked over to them and smiled. "I need to go take a shower. Are y'all ready?"

Paula looked at Tasha as if she were crazy. "Hell no, I'm not ready to go. I'm just now beginning to enjoy myself. Call a cab."

"Are you for real?" Tasha groaned.

"I didn't tell you to go get laid. Now your ass feels nasty and wanna ruin my day. Nope, not gon' happen," Paula replied and walked off.

"You know that was foul," Angela told Tasha, "You didn't have to fuck that man."

"I came here to have fun too. What do you mean?" Tasha frowned.

"Yeah, but you can't get frustrated because we don't want to leave now that you got your rocks off, Tasha," Angela whispered harshly.

Tasha didn't say anything at first, but then she sighed, "Angela, why did I do this? This was supposed to be about Paula this weekend."

"Well, I don't think Paula is too concerned with any-thing concerning what your ho ass did." Angela laughed as she hugged Tasha. "You know what you can do?"

Tasha looked at Angela and laughed, "What can I do, crazy?"

"Tell that nigga to get you a rag and a bar of soap so you can wash your nasty ass, because apparently we ain't going nowhere."

Tasha doubled over in laughter, but when she stood up, she looked at Angela. "Fuck it."

Tasha walked over and rubbed Shock lightly across the arm and leaned over and whispered in his ear, "Can a girl get a wash rag to clean herself up with, dude?"

Shock looked at her and started laughing. "You most definitely can. I don't want you walking around here smelling all sweaty and shit."

After about an hour, more people started pulling up, and the girls were having a blast. Surprisingly, Shock started mingling with Tasha, hugging and all on her, standing behind her with his arms wrapped around her waist, and he even leaned in and kissed her on the neck.

Once the night was over and the girls were prepared to leave, Angela wasn't shocked at all when Tasha informed them that she would be staying the night.

Over the course of the next two days, Paula and Tripp spent a lot of time together. They rode around through the day and talked on the phone over the night. They ate breakfast together and then ate dinner. Paula had actually forgotten all about her troubles back in North Carolina. When the day came that they had to leave, she was flooded with a surge of anxiety.

Angela and Kisha had made a pact the night of the cookout that since they were the "leftovers," they would hang out together.

Shock had kept Tasha hostage for the remainder of their trip, and before he dropped her off at their hotel the morning that the girls were leaving, he promised her that he would stay in touch.

Chapter 5

Back to Reality

Paula was exhausted when she finally pulled up to her house. She had dropped Tasha and Angela off earlier and was happy to be home—that was, until she walked into her house to find it in shambles with a letter on the counter from Michael.

> *So this is what we doing now? You think you know every damn thing, but you don't know shit. Four muthafuckin' days I've come here to find you gone. You are still my wife, Paula, remember that.*

Paula cringed and yelled out angrily, "Oh, yeah, bitch? Well, we shall see about that."

The following morning, Paula called Howard and Manchester to set up a date to talk to an attorney. They told her that they were booked for the next month, but Paula didn't care. She had heard about their reputation and desired to have them represent her. She was given an appointment for one month later, and although she wanted an earlier date, she accepted it.

Chandra walked into Paula's office at lunchtime and smiled. "I see that vacation worked."

"Oh, my God, Chandra, it did. I felt at peace. That is, until I came home and found a note and a mess to clean up from Michael. You know, I think he was waiting somewhere. Watching and waiting for me to come home. I wasn't in the house ten minutes before he came banging on my door. It was awful. I swear that nigga is making it easier and easier to leave his ass. But . . ."

"But what?" Chandra asked.

"I slept with him," Paula answered as her eyes grew wide while she waited for Chandra's response.

"Paula, I can't tell you what to do, but how do you expect him to take you seriously?"

"Well, I put his ass out afterward, and I made him use a condom."

"Paula, either you want out or you don't, but you can't toy with that man's feelings like that. From the things that you have shared with me, he can become obsessed with you, which won't end well. Please be careful. You are so much smarter than that," Chandra said. "I'm going to go grab some lunch. You want something?"

"No, I've suddenly lost my appetite." Paula sighed.

"I didn't mean to be mean, Paula," Chandra whispered, walking toward Paula.

Paula waved her off. "It's not what you said at all. I understand, and I now realize that I made a stupid mistake last night."

"We all do at times, but you still got to eat. I'ma order Chinese. What do you want? It's on me."

"Beef lo mein, shrimp fried rice with an eggroll, and a large tea," Paula answered.

"For someone who wasn't hungry . . ."

Paula laughed, "When you said you were paying, I figured I should take advantage of that."

"Be right back then. You need anything else while I'm gone?"

"No, thank you," Paula answered.

After Chandra left, Paula sighed. Chandra was right about everything she had said. Michael had been texting her all day, confessing his love for her and begging to come back home. Tripp had also texted her a few times, which caused her to feel somewhat overwhelmed.

Once Paula was on her lunch break, she walked out to her truck and called Tasha. "Hey, girl, let's go out to dinner tonight."

"I can't tonight. I got a hot date, girl." Tasha laughed.

"With who?" Paula asked.

"Just this dude I met a few weeks ago," she answered.

"Where'd you meet him?" Paula asked.

"Girl, I really got to go right now, but I'm going to call you in a little while when I get home after work," Tasha said and hung up quickly.

Paula looked at her phone and laughed, "Turned away for dick."

She then called Angela to see if she wanted to have dinner, but Angela didn't answer. Paula sighed and got out of her truck and walked back into the office. A few moments later, Chandra walked in with her lunch.

"Girl, here you go," Chandra announced as she set Paula's plate down in front of her, and then she sat down across from her. "So tell me about your vacation."

Paula told Chandra all about her vacation and meeting Tim "Tripp" Moore. She shared with Chandra her feelings about talking to another guy outside of the one she was married to.

Chandra gave Paula the only advice she could think of. "Paula, your husband is out here doing his own thing, from what you have said, and you have needs and desires like the next woman. Go on and enjoy yourself. I know I would." Chandra picked up a huge bite of her beef and broccoli and stuffed it in her mouth.

Paula smiled and realized that she had a very good point. She was going to follow her own heart.

Later that evening after Paula left work, she stopped by the Food Lion grocery store and grabbed a premade chicken salad and a bottle of water. She had no desire to cook, nor did she want anything heavy on her stomach.

After she paid for her items, she left the store, got in her truck, and headed to the park that was a mile down the road. She sat in her truck and ate her salad and watched the couples who were walking together or just relaxing on the benches. A few had kids playing on the swing sets or merry-go-round.

She smiled as she saw one of the guys chasing a small child, who looked to be about 3, around the park. The little girl was laughing, and when he caught her, she hugged him. Paula sighed as she leaned her head back against the headrest. Closing her eyes, she said a silent prayer, asking God to ease her pain and give her some sign of which direction to go with Michael.

Twenty minutes later, Paula got out of her truck to throw her trash away, and she decided to walk the trails. She enjoyed it so much. She was relaxed, and when she left the park, she had decided that getting to know Tripp wasn't a bad idea.

She pulled up to her house, walked in, and headed straight for her bedroom. She hopped into bed and turned her television on and started to watch *Friends*. But again, Paula began to feel lost and distraught inside. She knew she had made a mistake by sleeping with Michael. He had been blowing her phone up all day. She scanned through the pictures on her phone that she knew she should have deleted but hadn't. They were the pictures that an anonymous person had sent her of Michael with his son—a son another woman bore him outside of their marriage.

Not only did it hurt her that he had stepped outside of their marriage and messed around on her and had a child, but when she was pregnant, he agreed that they weren't ready for a family and held her hand while she went through an abortion. Paula screamed as the pain ripped through her heart and stomach. She picked up her bedside lamp and slung it against the wall, causing it to shatter in a million pieces, much like her heart. Just as she was about to smash their picture that also sat on the bedside table, her cell rang. She smiled, seeing Tripp's number on the screen.

"Hey, lady."

"What's up, Tripp?" she asked, out of breath.

"You. But is everything okay?" he questioned.

"Yeah, I'm fine," she laughed.

"You sure are," he replied.

Paula blushed, knowing what he meant by the statement. "Did you work hard today?" she asked.

"I never work hard. I work smart." He laughed.

"I hear you. So, um, you've kind of been on my mind a little bit today," she admitted.

"Oh, really? Well, we've got something in common, except you've been on my mind a lot, queen," he replied.

"Tell me what you've been thinking about, and I'll tell you what was on my mind about you," Paula said as she lay back against her pillows.

"Just kept wondering how your day was going, beautiful. To be honest, since the day I met you, you've been on my mind heavy. I can't wait to see you again," he murmured.

"You can come to our city if you like. I'd love to show you around," she said.

"Word, just say when and I'm there," he told her.

"Shit, when are you free?" Paula asked.

"Well, how about three weeks from today? I should have all my affairs worked out by then," Tripp replied.

"Affairs, huh?" Paula asked jokingly.

"Not that kind. When I have my sights on a woman, I can't entertain anyone else. And I'm going to be honest right now. My sights are on you," he told her.

"Is that right?" Paula questioned.

"That's right. I know we just met, and it may seem crazy, but there's something about you that has piqued my interest, and I'd be a fool not to attempt to figure out what it is. I know you are going through something, and I don't mind waiting, but I don't want to wait if I have no chance. You understand what I'm saying?"

"Yes, I understand. I can't say what will happen, honestly, but I'ma keep it real. I don't know what I'm doing, Tripp. I don't want you to think I'm playing games with you. I like you, but my situation is crazy. I mean, you know I'm married, but right now we are separated."

Tripp was quiet for a minute, then he said, "Let me ask you a question. Do you feel in your heart that your marriage can be salvaged?"

Paula sighed and shook her head and readjusted the phone to her ear. "I don't think it can."

"Would you feel better if I fell back until you got the whole situation settled?"

"No," she answered a little too quickly for her own comfort. "I mean, I'm at peace when I talk to you. It's something I've grown to look forward to. But if you feel you need to fall back, I have to respect that."

"Paula, we are both grown adults, and I'm a patient man," he replied.

"Guess we are good then, sir," she laughed.

"Ay, you calling me sir now? I know I'm older than you are, but come on now, babe."

"I'm just being respectful, sir." She laughed hearing Tripp laughing as well.

"Oh, yeah. I got your sir, ma'am."

"Is that right?" she asked.

"Little lady, that's a conversation you aren't ready for."

Paula laughed, "I guess."

For the second time in the conversation, Tripp got silent. "Yeah, we aren't going to go there right now."

"I can respect that," she replied.

The two of them talked for an hour more, and when Paula finally pulled the covers up over her tired body, she fell asleep with a huge smile on her face. It had been a while since she felt so content.

The next day, Paula went to work and completed her day with no thoughts of her husband. Tripp had her mesmerized in a way, and she was feeling him in a way. At five o'clock, she punched out and headed home.

Paula walked into her house and kicked her heels off. She was tired and needed a massage badly. She took a quick, hot shower, and once she was finished, she dressed down in a pair of sweatpants and a T-shirt. She then made a peanut butter and jelly sandwich and had a cold glass of milk to accompany it. She sat back on her couch, folded her legs under her, and turned on the television to watch *Criminal Minds*. Soon the television was watching her as sleep claimed her.

At about 10:30, there was a loud banging on her door. "Open the door, Paula," a voice yelled.

Paula stirred, feeling like she must have been dreaming, but the loud banging sounded off a second time.

"What the hell?" Paula groaned angrily as she stomped to the door. "Who is it?" she yelled.

"It's your husband. Open the fucking door before I tear this bitch down," he ordered sloppily.

Paula frowned. "Is this nigga drunk?" Paula opened the door as Michael began beating on it louder and harder.

"Michael, what is it?"

Michael fell into Paula, trying to kiss her.

"Michael, move," she yelled, moving to the side.

Michael had to hold on to the wall to keep from falling. "Make love to me."

"Nigga, are you insane? You got the wrong fucking chick."

"No, I got the right chick. You are my wife, and you're going to make love to me tonight," he slurred as he crisscrossed his way farther into the house. He made it as far as the couch before falling on to it and clocking out.

Paula stood staring at him with her hands on her hips, when suddenly a devilish grin grew on her face and a wicked thought crossed her mind.

She grabbed her cell phone and called Tasha and then Angela. "Hey, come over here now," she told them.

Angela was ready, but Tasha was reluctant. "Bitch, do you know what time it is?"

"What we are about to do will be worth a few hours of lost sleep. Just come on." Paula laughed.

Paula looked at Michael and walked over to him. "You want to fuck, huh? Okay, all right, I got you, nigga."

Paula proceeded to take his shirt and shoes off and waited for Tasha and Angela to arrive to take the rest of his clothes off. When they arrived, Paula had them assist her with his pants. They had to pause for a second as Michael began to stir a bit. Once he was still again and snoring, they finished their task.

Tasha was the first to take notice of Michael's blue boxers, which were thin. Her eyes grew wide, and she laughed, "Damn, cuz, I see why your ass was stuck on his ass. Bruh got a piece on him."

"Tasha, keep your eyes off his dick. That ain't what you over here for. Come on, help me get him in the car," Paula said.

"Girl, hell naw. You better pull that damn truck up to the edge of the porch," Angela laughed.

Paula explained to the girls her idea, and just as she thought, they were all for it.

"Wait, Tash, go get me some duct tape." Paula laughed.

Tasha went to the kitchen. She looked in the closet, took out the gray roll of tape, and handed it to Paula. "Turn him over."

Michael was so drunk and out of it that he didn't realize what was going on. They taped his hands together and then his feet. Paula left the house, got into her truck, and pulled it around to the front of the porch. The three ladies proceeded to put him on the bed of the truck.

Angela sat in the back with Michael to ensure that he didn't wake up in the mist of riding and hurt himself. Tasha followed close behind them in Michael's car. When they turned onto the street where Michael's baby mother lived, they turned the lights off, slowly pulled up to Nikki's house, and killed the motor.

Paula looked at Angela. "Okay, let's go."

By the time they got off the truck, Tasha was walking up.

"Tasha, you and Paula grab his feet, and I'll get his hands," Angela whispered.

They struggled to get Michael off the truck because he had seemingly started to wake up.

Paula laughed, "Man, let's hurry up and get this fool off this truck."

After they laid Michael at the bottom of the steps, Paula ran up to ring the doorbell. "Tasha, get my cell phone so we can get this live. They like Facebook? I'm going to give them Facebook."

Tasha took Paula's phone and aimed the camera at her. She waited for Paula to ring the doorbell, then went live on Facebook. The title of the video was, When wifey drops husband off to his side chick.

Nikki opened her door. When she saw the three ladies standing in her yard with Michael lying at the bottom of the steps, she flipped. "Yoooo, y'all can't leave him here like that."

"He's your mothafucking problem now. You wanted him, and you got him. You all on social media with my husband laid up smiling and shit, well, you got the whole damn nigga. Good night."

Tasha laughed, "I got it." She stopped the live video, then tagged Michael and Nikki in it.

They laughed at Nikki's behavior when she realized that she just might have a baby daddy all to herself.

The following day, Michael called Paula, begging her to ask Tasha to delete the video, which had gone viral. Paula had taken a little flack for the video as well, but she didn't care. Maybe Michael would get the picture. He was no longer wanted.

Chapter 6

Paula decided to go stay with Angela for a few days. Michael knew where Tasha stayed, and she wanted to avoid him at all costs. Angela had recently moved, and Paula knew she could hide out there for as long as she needed to. Sleeping with Michael had been the worst move she could have made. But she was horny that night and knew that Michael would fuck her the way she needed to be fucked. That was the one thing he was good at doing.

For the first few days, Paula was at peace. She went to work and back to Angela's. She and Tripp were on the phone each night, chatting as if they had known each other forever.

He had even sent her flowers to her job. Tripp seemed to be a very sensual, kindhearted, and funny man, but there was something about him that Paula felt was off. She had even voiced her opinion about it to Angela, who quickly jumped to Tripp's defense.

"Paula, girl, if you don't stop that shit . . . I can understand if you aren't ready to move on, but don't try to find fault with a good man. Tripp got all the qualities you can want in a dude. Just take your time and get to know him."

Paula nodded her head in agreement, but her heart felt what it felt. Something just wasn't right.

Friday morning, Paula went to work feeling renewed and refreshed. After spending the previous evening video chatting with Tripp, Paula's mind was put at ease. Her bad feelings were put to rest as Tripp revealed to Paula his bad relationship experience. He told her that when he loved, he loved hard, so when his last girlfriend hurt him, he had to take time to get over the pain. He assured her that he understood if she was reluctant about starting a new relationship when she was technically still in one. But he prayed that she would allow him to be her friend and comforter.

Paula smiled and giggled aloud as she remembered how Tripp had recited the Shai song "Comforter" in her ear.

She sat at her desk, humming and typing up a "request for service" form for one of their clients.

"Looks like someone is feeling good today." Chandra laughed as she peeped into Paula's office.

"Most definitely." Paula laughed.

"Well, Miss Giggles, meeting in twenty minutes, okay?" Chandra laughed as she closed the door.

Paula went through her day with no thoughts of her husband. That was, until she clocked out and found Michael standing at her car.

"Michael, what are you doing here?"

"What the hell do you think I'm doing here? You pull a disappearing act on me two weeks ago, come home and fuck me like nothing ever happened between us, put me out again, but not before embarrassing me on Facebook by leaving me naked on Nikki's porch, and then you disappear on me yet again. What the hell did you think I was going to do?" he yelled, causing people to look in their direction.

"Michael, please leave. I work here. You can't come here and disrupt my workplace," Paula whispered harshly while unlocking her car door.

Michael pulled Paula back away from her car and snatched her keys from her hand. "Dammit, I'm getting real sick of this bullshit. You gonna listen to me, and I mean it."

"Michael, let go of me," Paula growled as she attempted to jerk free of his grasp.

"I'm not letting go of shit. You are gonna talk to me, dammit. I'm hurting. Can't you see that?" he cried.

Paula had grown angry and began assaulting Michael with her words. "You sorry-ass piece of shit. How dare you come here telling me that you are hurting? Bitch nigga, all the things I've been to you, done for you, and you fucking go off and fuck another bitch and have a kid."

"I wasn't the only one fucking around, so stop acting like you are innocent," Michael fumed.

Paula stared at Michael. "What the hell did you just say to me? Huh? Nigga, you got a whole damn kid. But you didn't want one with me, so you went with me to kill our child. And as far as you saying I cheated, you got the wrong bitch on that."

Before Michael could respond, a policeman pulled up, and Chandra was walking over. "You okay, Paula?"

"Yeah, I'm fine. I just need to get away from him," Paula replied as Michael released her arm.

"Ma'am," the police officer said as he got out of the car, "is there a problem here?"

"Oh, my God," Michael groaned.

"Officer, I am Chandra Walker. I am the owner of this business establishment, and I would like for you to inform this man that he is no longer allowed on this property and that if he comes back here, he will be arrested for trespassing."

The police turned and asked Michael for his ID and wrote his information down in his notepad. "Sir, I have been asked to inform you that you are no longer allowed on this property. If you violate this order, you will go to jail. Do you understand what I have just said to you?"

"Yeah," Michael replied and walked away.

Before he got into his car, he looked at Paula. "I really can't believe that you are doing this after all we have been through."

"You okay, Paula?" Chandra asked as she rubbed her arm.

"I'm just tired of the constant drama behind his mistake. I don't know what to do." Paula shook her head and then lifted it upward to keep the tears from falling. She refused to waste any more tears over Michael.

"Paula, you know you are my girl, but whatever you do, please don't allow Michael back on this property. This is a place of business, and we can't have that kind of activity around here."

"I understand," Paula replied, feeling somewhat embarrassed that Chandra felt the need to tell her that.

Chandra smiled at her and walked with Paula to her truck. When they got to the truck, Paula turned toward her and said, "Chandra, I really am truly sorry about today. None of this is professional at all."

"I've been where you are, so no worries. It's going to get better. Go on and get some rest, boo," Chandra said as she turned and headed for her own car.

Paula got into her truck and drove to Angela's house, but she didn't immediately get out. She sat in her truck, trying to figure out what she could do to get Michael off her ass.

She decided to call his mother. It had been a minute since they talked, and she felt it was time to reach out. She knew that his mother didn't care for her that much, but she at least respected her. She didn't know what all Michael had told her, but she couldn't have Michael disrupting her workspace like he had just done.

She dialed Sandra Harris's number, and as soon as she picked up, Paula began to speak in a rushed manner.

"Hello, Sandra, this is Paula, and I was wondering if we could talk for a few minutes."

"Hello. What do you want to talk about, Paula?" she asked in a nonchalant tone.

"Well, I'm not sure what all Michael has told you, but I'm quite sure you know of his infidelities and son. I just found out about it, and I asked him to leave. He informed me that he was staying with you."

Before Paula could finish, Sandra stopped her. "Get to the point of this call."

"Well, your son is showing up to my job, and he almost went to jail today. You need to talk to your son and tell him to stay away from me. Please."

"Ma, hang up the phone. Paula ain't talking about shit," Paula heard coming from the background.

"Tammy, shut your mouth. You don't have nothing to do with this. Seems to me if y'all tended to your own business, none of this would be going on." Sandra growled, "Paula, I will talk to him when he gets home. Goodbye."

Paula got out of the car and walked into the house. Angela had cooked dinner and picked up a movie that they had been waiting to see.

"Girl, I got the last copy of *Fifty Shades Freed*. Don't be trying to come on to me while we watching this movie either." Angela laughed.

Paula started laughing and then began crying.

"Hey, sis, no, don't do that. What's wrong?" Angela asked.

Paula didn't say a word, but Angela held her best friend until she fell asleep.

Chapter 7

Paula hadn't been home in a couple of weeks, but she decided to return to her house since Tripp was visiting for the weekend. Staying with Angela was great, but Paula needed to kick it with Tripp on her own. She knew that if they hung out at Angela's, she and Tasha wouldn't give her and Tripp a break. She had Angela drop her off because she didn't want Michael to cruise through and see her car in the driveway. She had glanced out her window a few times and witnessed him riding by. She texted Tripp and told him to leave his car at the hotel and catch a cab over to also keep the lurkers from seeing him and reporting to her soon-to-be ex-husband.

She wasn't worried about Michael walking in because she had recently had the locks changed.

Tripp was due any minute, and Paula had her house smelling like Southern BBQ. She had heard Tripp speak about how well his mother cooked, and she was going to show him that, even though she was a businesswoman, she could still throw down in the kitchen. She had neck bones smothered with onions and gravy, cabbage simmering, and her special mac and cheese baking. She was going to put her cornbread on last. She knew that she shouldn't have another man in the home she had built with Michael, but she didn't give a fuck at that point.

Tripp had gotten a hotel room to stay in, but he was going to stop by and eat dinner with her before they hit the streets of B-Town. She was excited to be going out with Tripp, not because of him, but because she was ready to show the whole town that she didn't have a problem getting another man.

Paula's cell phone began to ring just as she was taking her mac and cheese out of the oven and putting her corn-bread in. "Hello," she answered after wiping her hands on her apron.

"Girl, what you doing?" Tasha asked.

"Cooking. You know Tripp is in town, and he will be here in just a bit. I'm about to take a shower right quick. Y'all still gonna meet us at Trinity's Lounge tonight, right?"

"You know we are. What time?"

"Let's say ten-ish," Paula replied. "But look, I've got to go."

"All right. Don't do anything I wouldn't do." Tasha laughed, "Hell, or do."

Paula shook her head, laughing, "Bye, stupid."

Paula hung up with Tasha and walked to her room. She found the perfect pair of dress pants and a cute sleeveless blouse.

She turned her music on and hummed to the song "Slowly" by Syleena Johnson. She danced her way into the bathroom and turned the water on. She then checked her locks in the mirror before wrapping them up. She jumped into the shower and washed up thoroughly before getting out.

As soon as she opened the bathroom door, she was greeted by smoke. "Oh, shit. My cornbread." She grabbed her robe and raced to the kitchen.

She slung the oven door open and pulled her black-ened cornbread out. "Fuck."

Just then her doorbell chimed. "Oh, no," she whined.

Tripp had arrived. She walked to the door and opened it with a smile. "Well, hello."

Tripp frowned jokingly. "Seems like you may be having a few issues in here, lady. Are we going to have to go out for dinner tonight?"

"You funny as hell. No, we aren't. Come on in. I just had a small mishap with the cornbread."

Tripp walked in and sat down on the gray plush couch in Paula's living room. He admired the decor in her home and the cleanliness. He looked at the fireplace and paid close attention to the picture of Paula and who he assumed was her husband. Paula followed his gaze and knew that Tripp had to have questions about her situation, and she decided that she was going to clear the air but after she got dressed.

"I will be right back. Let me get dressed real fast."

"Take your time, cuteness."

When Paula returned, she walked to the kitchen with Tripp behind her. "So what's this charcoal treat?" he laughed, pointing to the burnt cornbread.

"Tripp, if you don't sit your butt down . . . I got this."

"You sure?"

Paula turned and gave him an evil look.

"Okay, okay. I'ma sit down, Miss Top Chef." Tripp laughed as Paula threw her potholder at him.

"I'm sure you have a few questions about my li'l situation, so let me tell you a li'l bit," Paula began as Tripp sat down on the barstool behind the island in her kitchen. "I met Michael when I was younger, teenaged years, and we fell in love and got married right after high school. He at some point cheated on me and created a whole family, and I just recently discovered it. He claims he wants me and this marriage, but I don't. I'm filing for divorce and never looking back."

Tripp frowned. "I don't understand why a man would cheat on his wife, especially a woman of your character. I mean, I only know of what you have told me, but in getting to know you over the past few weeks, you seem like the kind of woman any man would love to have. But let me ask you this, are you sure a divorce is what you want?"

"Why would you ask me that? Honestly, I'm not sure what I want, but feeling like I am and the hurt that I've felt not only because of his cheating, but the kid, is an issue that I doubt I can get over. Listen, let's just enjoy this meal and one another's company."

"I'm with you on that, but listen, beautiful, I'm not trying to invest my heart and time into this," he said as he pointed at the both of them, "and then I get hurt, you feel me? I'm not so nice when I feel violated."

Paula stared at him for a second and could see how serious he was about that statement, but then she quickly replied, "I wouldn't play with you like that, Tripp. I know what it feels like to be hurt."

"So what's all on the stove, love?" he asked, refusing to say what he really wanted to say.

"Well, you just have to wait and see." She laughed.

She began fixing their plates and handed Tripp one. She took the other one and led him to her kitchen table.

"I have beer, tea, wine, and water. What's your pleasure, sir?" she asked, smiling.

"Whatever you recommend, ma'am," he replied, admiring her smile.

"I'm going to have tea," she told him.

"I guess I am too."

Paula walked over to her fridge, poured their drinks, and took them back over to the table.

"You might have some skills here. This looks and smells delicious," Tripp admitted.

"Taste it," she said.

"Not until you sit down," he replied.

Paula smiled and sat down. "Now eat," she ordered.

"Blessing first, ma'am," he laughed.

"Ugh, I feel so bad. Go ahead. You are the guest."

"Heavenly Father, we come to you as humble servants who will bend to your will. We come to you today to give thanks for this meal we are about to either enjoy or regret eating, dear Father. Bless those who aren't as fortunate as we are, dear God, and lastly bless the beautiful hands that prepared this meal. Amen."

"A praying thug? Who would've thought?" Paula joked.

After Tripp said the blessing, the two ate their dinner in silence.

"Babe, you did that. You put your whole damn leg and foot in it," Tripp complimented her.

"Thank you. Let me clean this up, and then we can chill out before Tasha gets here," Paula said as she stood up, clearing the dishes off the table.

"Can I help?"

"Sure," Paula replied, smiling.

They cleaned up the kitchen while talking and learning more about one another. They then walked to the living room and talked more about their failed relationships. Tripp told Paula that he could relate somewhat to how she felt. He told her that he had been in a relationship for almost ten years, and just when he was about to propose to her, she left him. He learned later on that she had been cheating on him with his best friend, and it caused him to lose it.

She was the first woman he had ever loved enough to propose to. He told Paula that he made a vow to himself that he would never allow another woman to hurt him like she did. Paula told him that she understood and vowed the same thing. They chopped it up until Tasha arrived to pick them up.

Chapter 8

Paula and Tripp got out of his truck and walked into Trinity's After 7 Lounge. Tasha and Angela met them when they got out and walked with them toward the club. Tasha had picked Paula and Tripp up and had driven them to get his truck, and they drove to Angela's to pick her up.

Paula had on a pair of tight denim capris with slashes all over showing her pretty golden thighs. Her shirt was money green with a butterfly slash in the back, exposing her back and the green lace bra she wore. She had on a pair of green heels with a gold chain locked around her ankles. When they walked in, she knew that all eyes were going to be on her and her entourage.

They all looked sexy, and Tripp was looking handsome in his dress slacks and Polo shirt. His muscles were protruding through the shirt. His height of six foot three and 225-pound body were looking good to Paula. Tripp had light skin with a short cut. His lips were pink and luscious looking. His teeth were straight and pearly white with a thin mustache outlining them. What really caught a lot of ladies' eyes were his dimples. Paula really liked him, and she forced herself to ignore the negative feelings that she was having about him. She basically put it in her head that the negative feelings were because she was married and had never thought of any man outside of her husband in that kind of way.

When the group walked in, Paula and Tripp grabbed a table while Tasha and Angela walked around the club.

"So what do you think about our little town so far?" Paula asked Tripp as she flagged over a waitress.

"It's okay so far. I hate that I've got to leave tomorrow."

"Oh, you aren't staying 'til Sunday?" Paula questioned, watching the waitress walk over.

"What can I get you two to drink?" the woman asked.

"I want a Tom Collins," Tripp answered.

"And I'll take a Blue Motorcycle please," Paula chimed in.

"Separate tickets?" the waitress asked, smiling at Tripp.

"No, all together," Tripp replied, looking at the waitress with distaste.

"Okay, gotcha. Be right back with your drinks," she replied as she ducked her head.

"You wanna dance?" Tripp asked as Jaheim's "Every-time I Think About Her" began to play.

"Sure," Paula replied, allowing Tripp to pull her up and lead her to the dance floor.

The two stepped and danced close together. Tasha and Angela walked toward the table and caught sight of the couple on the floor.

"They look good together, don't they?" Tasha said, nudging Angela.

"I'd look better with her," Angela replied and walked to the table where Tripp and Paula had been sitting.

Tasha frowned as she watched Angela. Was Angela serious?

After a few seconds, Tasha walked to the table and sat next to Angela, who was talking to a chick at the next table. Tasha had to admit that Angela had true swag. She worked at her uncle's car shop, where business was booming daily. Angela was one of the top mechanics in the North Carolina area and made a great living doing what she loved. Angela was light brown skinned and had a close fade with the sides highlighted a blond color. Her abs were toned, and her bowlegs were very shapely. When Angela ventured out, she dressed with a thuggish style that most women were attracted to. Hell, and some men.

Tasha laughed as she listened to Angela explain to the woman that her tongue worked more magic than any dick could and she could prove it. When Angela licked it out and wiggled it at the woman, Tasha spat out her drink and hollered, "Girl, yo' ass ain't got no kinda fucking chill."

Angela looked at Tasha and winked, and moments later the woman was pulling Angela to the dance floor. Tasha joined them on the floor and danced until her knees buckled.

Four songs later they were all back at the table, laughing and talking, when suddenly Angela's eyes fixed on the entrance of the club. "Oh, my God, Paula, look who the fuck just walked in."

Paula looked at the door and froze. Standing at the door glancing around the club was Michael. As soon as he locked eyes with her, he began walking in her direction. Paula's heart began to beat hard and fast. Her breath was short, and she began to perspire a bit. She breathed a sigh of relief when Michael sat down at the table facing them instead of coming over to where they were seated.

"Friend of yours?" Tripp asked, breaking Paula's trance.

"Fuck, more like a relative. That's my husband. I don't know how the hell he knew I was here," Paula whispered.

No one at the table uttered a word. Tripp motioned for the waitress to come over, and he ordered a round of drinks for everyone at the table.

When the waitress came back to the table and Tripp paid the tab, he leaned over and whispered in Paula's ear, "You wanna dance with me the next song?"

Paula smiled. "Definitely."

Tripp grabbed Paula's hand and kissed it, then sucked on her finger. Paula's eyes grew wide at the gesture, but she groaned when she saw Michael glaring at them. Michael stood and started walking in their direction. It was obvious that he was drunk and looking for trouble.

"Paula, I need to talk to you. Now," he slurred once he reached them.

"Michael, don't do this here," Tasha pleaded.

"Bitch, mind your business. That's what's wrong now, too many of y'all in our shit. I don't know who the fuck you are, bruh, but this is my wife you're sucking on, playa," Michael growled.

Paula shook her head. "Michael, you are what's wrong in our marriage. You and that greedy little dick of yours. You couldn't keep it in your pants, and it cost you our marriage. Don't you dare sit here and act like anyone else is to blame."

Tripp didn't say a word, but he kept his eyes on Michael and Paula.

Michael laughed, "Paula, I'ma ask you one more damn time to come and talk to me. Please."

Paula again declined. "Michael, you are drunk, and I really have nothing to say to you. As you can see, I'm busy at the moment."

Michael's face changed immediately. His eyes grew dark and threatening, and before anyone knew it, he snatched Paula's hand from Tripp's and yanked her up from the table. Tripp snapped and stood up before Tasha and Angela could move.

Pow.

Tripp punched Michael clean in the face, knocking him down between the tables. "You tripping, playa," he said, referring to Michael as Michael had addressed him. "You don't put your hands on a female. Especially this one right here. You got life all the way fucked up. I will break your fucking neck. I suggest you find something safe to do, because you about to get fucked up, playa."

Michael tried to stand up but couldn't.

Paula looked at Tripp with tears in her eyes, which angered Tripp even more. He wanted to take Michael's head off.

"I'm ready to go. This shit is crazy," Paula whispered shakily.

"I know you aren't shocked. Y'all poked that angry bear. What did y'all think was going to happen?" Angela asked, looking at Michael with pity.

"Angela, what the fuck? You know what? Never mind. Are y'all coming or no?" Paula said, looking downward.

Angela walked over to Paula and hugged her. "I didn't mean it like that, sis. You know I'm on your side, but when Michael walked in, we all knew that it wasn't going to be pretty."

"Paula, y'all go on. I'm just beginning to enjoy myself," Tasha replied.

"You sure?" Tripp asked.

"Yeah, you two go ahead," Angela confirmed.

Paula and Tripp walked away, but it broke Paula's heart to hear Michael calling her name like he was. She never looked back though. Once they were in the truck, Tripp looked at her. "Are you okay?"

"Not really, but I will be. I just can't believe that happened. I'm sorry that you had to get involved in such a mess. But I thank you for helping me back there. I didn't want your first time visiting me to be full of drama."

"Paula, it's not your fault. I hope I'm not speaking outta turn, but the dude seems to really love you and appears to be heartbroken."

"Humph. I doubt it," she replied sadly.

Tripp didn't respond to her remark. He figured he'd let it go, so instead he asked her, "Where to?"

"Your hotel room," she replied, looking him in the face.

"If you want me to stay until Sunday, I will. I can handle my business Monday." He pulled out of the parking lot of the club.

"No, it's okay. I think I need to chill by myself for a while anyway," Paula replied.

"Understood, queen."

Tripp turned the music up just a bit, and Paula laid her head against the headrest and closed her eyes, trying to again make sense of her life.

Twenty minutes later they arrived at the Marriot Inn. Tripp parked and got out of the truck, walked over, and opened Paula's door and helped her out. He held her hand as they entered the hotel.

Paula walked into the hotel room, exhausted from her experience at Trinity's Lounge. She didn't know how Michael knew where she was, and then he walked in drunk as hell. She was surprised at how calmly Tripp handled the situation. He had definitely earned a few brownie points.

"I'm gonna take a quick shower. Can I use one of these towels?" she asked.

"You know you can. You want me to join you?"

Paula laughed, "I think I got this."

Tripp smiled. "I will behave. I've been dealing with you now for a month, and I haven't stepped out of line yet."

"I know, bae, but just give me a few more minutes of privacy. I won't be long, I promise." She stood up on her tiptoes and kissed his lips.

"All right. Hurry up so I can get in the shower," he said.

She walked into the bathroom and stared at her reflection and mumbled, "What are you so nervous about? You aren't a virgin."

"Did you say something, babe?" Tripp yelled out.

"Oh, no. I'm just singing," she lied.

Paula got in the shower, and as promised, she was in and out quickly. She put her Caress soap back in the box and stepped out of the shower. Afterward, she brushed her teeth and put her robe on and walked out of the bathroom. When she stepped into the bedroom, Tripp lay on the bed with his shirt off and pants undone. His dark chest looked like a ripple of chocolate, and the muscle tone of his stomach was spectacular. He rose when he heard her take in her breath.

He smiled and stood up. "My turn, huh?"

She dropped her gaze and shyly walked past him, grabbed her lotion and deodorant, and sat on the bed. As she put her lotion on, Tripp began to completely undress in front of her. She squeezed a small amount of lotion in her hand, but before she could rub it in, Tripp was taking off his drawers. She couldn't believe how magnificently his body was sculpted, from his arms and chest to his abs, thighs, and dick, which was the showstopper. It wasn't even hard, and it was huge. She dropped the bottle of lotion on the floor, which made Tripp look at her.

"See something you like?"

"A lot," she answered, and as if she were in a trance, she shook her head, looked away from Tripp, and finished putting her lotion on.

While Tripp was in the shower, Paula's phone began vibrating. She looked at it but didn't open it, seeing Michael's name pop up. She shook her head and turned her phone off. Finally, she lay under the covers. She began to relax a bit until a few minutes passed and she heard the shower turn off. Her heart quickened, and she quickly turned on her side, feigning sleep.

When Tripp entered the room, he slid into bed next to Paula and pulled her back against his body. Paula melted and couldn't resist rubbing her buttocks against Tripp's pulsating dick. She bit her bottom lip, trying not to moan aloud. Hell, he had barely touched her and she was on fire. The soapy fragrance emanated from his body, which drove her insane with desire. She turned, facing him, and buried her head in his chest and wrapped her arms around his neck.

"Girl, don't start nothing you can't finish," he whispered into her hair.

Tripp loved the way Paula smelled, and he wanted her so badly, but he didn't want to rush her into anything she wasn't ready for.

Paula was lost in wanting Tripp, and all common sense was gone. She smiled, sat up, and turned Tripp onto his back. She got on top of him and kissed him deeply on the lips. Their tongues played hide-and-seek for a few minutes before she began trailing light kisses down his torso.

"Damn, Paula, you making a nigga feel something he shouldn't."

Paula looked up at him and shook her head. "Just fuck me, Tripp. I need this so damn bad."

Tripp groaned and flipped Paula onto her back and started kissing her stomach and sucking her nipples, paying close attention to Paula's reaction as he did so. Her body jerked from the pleasure of his lips on her skin, and the soft moans that escaped her lips made his dick jump with wanting.

He slid her down to the middle of the bed and positioned himself between her legs and began massaging Paula's clit gently, slowly at first and increasing speed as time went by. He then slid two fingers inside her, twisting them softly from left to right as Paula's hips mimicked his actions. He bent down and kissed her neck and removed his fingers and licked them after he had

Paula suck them. He grabbed her legs and put them on his shoulders and slid quick and hard inside Paula, causing her to cry out.

"Shhh, I got you, baby," he whispered.

Paula had never had a man the size of Tripp inside her, and it was somewhat painful, especially with him being so rough.

"Baby, be easy, damn," she groaned.

"I'm sorry, baby," Tripp said as he slowed his hips to a speed that Paula liked.

They made love, and although Paula came, she wasn't satisfied. Tripp had all that dick and couldn't fuck. She had just figured out what wasn't right about Tripp.

Damn, he's the perfect man in every way except where it counts the most, she thought as they both drifted off to sleep.

The next morning after Tripp left, Paula sat back, thinking that it was her karma for sleeping with Tripp before she had even filed for divorce.

Paula pulled her Tundra out of the parking lot of the hotel. She needed to take a day just for herself and ride alone. As she passed through Burlington, she spotted Michael's car at TJ's barbershop.

She quickly crossed into the turning lane and swooped into the parking lot. She immediately spotted Michael sitting in the chair facing the window. Beside him was his son. She felt her fingers begin to tingle and her face tightening. She laughed in spite of wanting to cry. Without really thinking, she got out of her car and grabbed her iron from the trunk and walked over to Michael's car. She stood at his car with her eyes glued on Michael's face, mentally willing him to look up. As if feeling her presence, he glanced up, and Paula smiled at him evilly, blew him a kiss, and with angry tears burning their way down her cheeks, she smashed his back windows out.

Michael jumped up and raced out of the barbershop with his son right behind him. "Paula, wait. Paula."

"Daddy, who was that lady, and why was she hitting your car?" the little boy asked.

Paula shook her head and quickly walked to her car. She noticed that one guy was standing outside videotaping her.

Michael raced over to Paula's car, trying to stop her from closing the door, but he was a few seconds too late. "Paula, please let me talk to you," Michael begged as he hit her window.

"Get your little bastard son and get back in that barbershop and leave me the fuck alone from this point on, Michael. I hate you for making me feel like this."

Paula pulled off, leaving a trail of smoke behind her. For the first time since finding out that her husband was living a double life, Paula broke down.

Paula drove to the nearest Best Western, and once she arrived and parked in the parking lot, she sat in her truck for a few minutes. She wiped her tearstained face and searched her console for a tissue. She found a few napkins and blew her nose. After taking a few moments to regain her composure, she exited her truck. Her legs trembled as she began to walk. She stopped short and placed her hand on the hood of her truck.

"That mothafucking bastard," she growled.

She shook her head and moaned as she rubbed her hand across her stomach, trying to control the sickening feeling that engulfed her. She finally steadied herself enough and continued into the hotel. She walked up to the attendant and asked if they had any available rooms. After the attendant confirmed that they did, Paula paid for a room for a week. She needed to vent, cry, and figure out where her life was going if she divorced Michael.

When she received her key card, she walked to her room, and once inside, she slid to the floor and wept. She wept for all the wasted time that she had invested in a marriage that didn't weigh in the same for her husband. She wept for the pain she felt knowing that the only man she ever loved didn't love her enough to stay true. She wept for the child she aborted because she and her husband mutually agreed it wasn't the time for a child. She wept from seeing her husband be the best father to a child he had with another bitch, and lastly, she wept because of the anger she felt toward her husband. She felt that she could literally kill him.

Chapter 9

Two Days Later

Paula got off work and decided that it was time to talk to Michael. She pulled out of the parking lot and grabbed her cell phone. "Hello, Michael, how are you doing?"

"I'm good. I'm glad you called. Are you okay?"

"I'm not, but I think we need to talk," Paula replied.

"I agree. Are you at home?"

"I'm actually staying at the Best Western over here off of Huffman Road for a while," she answered.

"Why?" he asked.

"Needed to think without the usual interruptions."

"Okay, well, do you want me to come over now?"

"No, give me about two hours. I'm just getting off work, and I have a few stops to make," she told him.

"Just call me when you are ready for me," he replied.

"I will."

"Paula, I love you," he whispered.

"Yeah, okay." She sighed and hung up.

Paula hung up and drove to Lucky Bamboo to get them some food. She wanted everything to be perfect. After she got the food, she went to the Dollar Tree and grabbed some candles and other things that she needed, and then she went to the liquor store to grab a bottle of peach Cîroc and some juice. Everything else she needed was already at the hotel.

Two hours later she had everything set and ready for her night with Michael. She sat on the bed and impatiently waited for him to arrive. Her phone had been ringing off the hook for three days. Tripp had been calling nonstop and texting her phone, pleading with her to talk to him. She felt bad for ignoring him, but for her the attraction just wasn't there.

Knock. Knock.

Paula stood up and checked herself once more in the full-length mirror on the wall. "Here goes," she sighed. She turned and looked back at the room, and satisfied with how it looked, she walked to the door to let her "husband" in.

"Damn, all this for me?" he asked as he entered the room, admiring what Paula had put together.

"Are you hungry?" she asked as she led him to the small, round wood table that she had set up gorgeously. There were flowers, wineglasses, and plates and utensils that she bought all from the Dollar Tree.

"Yes, but what's going on? You trying to poison me?" He sat down, and she began fixing him a plate.

Paula laughed, "Really, Michael? You don't trust me now?" Paula took Michael's fork and lifted a good amount of his pepper steak and rice and ate it. "Satisfied?"

Paula then poured their drinks and looked at him and laughed, "Which glass would you like?"

Michael looked at his wife and shook his head sadly. "Whichever one you'd like me to have."

Paula swallowed hard as she witnessed the pain in her husband's eyes, but then, as if she were snapping out of a trance, she cleared her throat hard and handed him his glass. She snatched her hand away as Michael's fingers lightly rubbed hers.

"How was work?" she asked as she took her seat across from his.

Michael put his fork down and stared at Paula for a moment. "I'm sorry, Paula. I swear to God that I never meant to hurt you like this. If you'd just listen to me and let me explain—"

Paula cut him off before he could finish. "Michael, please, let's not ruin dinner by talking about this right now. We can talk about whatever you like later on."

Michael dropped his eyes from hers and felt his heart start pounding hard. How was he going to get his wife to forgive him?

Paula excused herself and walked into the bathroom. When she reemerged, she had on a white lace gown with a pair of crotchless panties. Michael looked shocked as his eyes almost bulged completely out of their sockets.

"Are you just going to stand there gawking, or are you going to come and join me on the bed?"

"Paula, last time we did this, you walked away like it meant nothing. I'm not doing that again," Michael replied, sitting at the table and refusing to move.

Paula walked over to him and leaned down and kissed him deeply, then moved his chair back a bit so that she could sit on his lap. She lifted her lips off his and grabbed his hand, led it to the wetness between her legs, and then resumed kissing him.

Michael moved his fingers lightly across her clit as if he were afraid it was going to bite him, but hearing her whimper against his lips was his release. He picked her up and carried her to the bed and undressed, never removing his eyes from hers. When he was completely naked, he lay next to her and once again began massaging her moist area, but this time he was giving it his most thorough massage. Paula lifted her hips as his finger slipped inside her. She moaned and grabbed her breasts and began pulling gently on her nipples. Not missing a beat, Michael moved her hand with his free hand and began sucking on her breasts. As he sucked and fingered her, Paula moaned louder and louder and rocked her hips faster and faster, and as she increased speed, so did he.

Michael gently turned Paula on her side and used his legs to open hers, but just as he attempted to slide his rock-hard dick inside of her, she stopped him. "Michael, wait."

Michael froze as he realized that his wife was handing him a condom.

"Are you serious?" Michael asked, but she didn't have to answer, and he couldn't honestly blame her for handing him the condom.

He took the condom and slid it on. He was surprised that his dick didn't go soft as his heart broke knowing his wife didn't trust him. He raised Paula's leg and slid inside her. He felt her pussy muscles contract as she took all of him in. He slowly moved his full length in and out of her. She grabbed his arm and clasped it as he began moving in and out hard. He slammed inside her, repeatedly ignoring her cries.

Paula tried to move away a bit, but Michael slid down and clamped her leg down with his free leg and continued his sexual assault on her. When he finally freed her legs, it was momentary. He turned her on her back and moved in between her legs and once again found her wetness with his man tool.

He began to roll his hips, grinding deep and slowly inside of Paula. Paula felt like she was in another world lost in a wave of confusion and pleasure. Michael grabbed her dreads and pulled them as he nuzzled his lips against her throat. Paula wrapped her legs around his waist and fucked her husband with a burning fire that only he could smother.

"Let me on top," she whispered.

Michael moved and lay on his back, and Paula climbed on top and sat upright with his dick inside of her, but she didn't move right away. She stared at him for a few seconds but then began rocking slowly and passionately. Michael held her hips as she moved rhythmically. He had to bite down on his lips to keep the cries from escaping. Paula closed her eyes and leaned forward, placing each one of her hands on either side of his head and kissing him. Michael's eyes sprang open as he felt powerless tears hitting his face. Michael didn't know why, but it angered him and hurt him at the same time that she was crying. He began to slam her down hard on his dick and watched as Paula squirmed. He felt her hands gripping the pillow his head was on, and he slammed her even harder until he felt her lift up.

"Paula, what the—" He stopped moving, and his hands fell from her waist.

Paula sat on him, still moving her body with a .38 pointed at his face. "Don't stop, Michael. Get your last nut."

Paula began to move a bit faster with a steady and controlled hand holding the gun. Paula cried as she came once again, and even though the situation had turned cold, Michael came with her. Afterward, Paula stood up, still holding the gun. "Get up, Michael."

Michael moved slowly and laughed, "Do you think I give a fuck about dying? I'm already dead without you."

Paula realized that even though she wanted Michael dead, she couldn't kill him. "Why did you do this to me?" Paula yelled. "I would've never treated you with such disrespect. You broke my heart, and every time I see you with your child, it shatters all over again."

At that point her whole body was shaking, and she dropped the gun and began to cry. Michael walked over to console her, but Paula began to plead with him in a voice that he had never heard before. "Please leave. I have never wanted to kill someone before in my life. You've hurt me in a way that I never imagined you would. If you love me, Michael, please go."

Michael stood up, feeling defeated. With his shoulders slumped, he silently picked up his clothes. After he was fully dressed, he walked to the door and paused with his hand on the door handle. He didn't look at Paula but spoke clearly for her to hear him, "Paula, you should have killed me. I'm leaving, but I want you to know that I'm not going to let you go that easy. Yeah, I fucked up, but hell, you fucked up too. Next time, Paula, pull the mothafucking trigger."

Michael walked out of the hotel room, leaving Paula to tend to her aching heart and confusion at his statement that she had also fucked up. He couldn't have been talking about the club situation with Tripp because Tripp didn't come into the picture until after Michael's infidelity.

Chapter 10

One Week Later, Tuesday

Paula hadn't seen or talked to Angela or Tasha since the incident at the club with Michael, but Tuesday after she got off work, she drove to Angela's to get her belongings. She made sure that she went during the hours that Angela worked. She wasn't ready to see either of them. She didn't know how Michael knew where she was that night, and she knew it had to be one of them. They had been blowing her phone up, and Tripp had as well. Surprisingly, the one person who hadn't attempted to call her was Michael, and she didn't know what to feel about that. Maybe he was giving up on winning her back. She was confused. As hard as she tried to get him to leave her alone, she had to ask herself if that was what she really wanted to do.

Her routine was the same day after day. She would go to work and then back to the hotel and think about her husband. She needed to get to the truth in her own feelings. He was her husband, but just when she figured she would try counseling with him to see if they could salvage their marriage, she was hit with more Facebook drama.

On Wednesday she was browsing Facebook, and Tammy, Michael's sister, had posted a recent picture of Michael and Nikki playing with their son. Paula could've jumped through her phone and into that picture and beaten the shit out of Nikki and Michael if only wishes could be granted. The picture tagline read, My brother and his baby mother doing their grownup-ish. Family time with my ONLY nephew.

Paula started cursing, "Dumb-ass bitch. I can put a stop to all that shit if I want to."

Before Paula realized what she was doing, she picked up her phone and scrolled through her contacts. When she found the name she wanted, she pushed the send button.

"Hello?"

"Hey, it's me. Are you busy?" she asked.

"Hell no. I've been waiting to hear from you for over a week now. What's good? Are you all right?" Tripp asked.

"I'm still going through it, but that's not why I called. Do you have any plans for the weekend?"

"If you're trying to come down, any plans I may have can be changed to another time," Tripp told her.

"Are you sure? I don't want to stop what you got going on."

"Paula, just come on," he commanded.

"Okay, well, I will see you Friday evening," she said softly.

"Sounds good to me."

The two of them talked for almost an hour, and once they were off the phone, it took Paula two more hours to fall asleep.

Friday

Paula woke up and packed up her clothes. She was going to head straight to South Carolina once she got off work. She was going to see if she could get off of work early so she wouldn't have to ride in the late-evening traffic. Tripp had texted her to let her know that he had enjoyed their conversation the previous night. She smiled, and although the feeling was mutual, the excitement of seeing him just wasn't present. She just needed to get away from the problems of her life.

She checked out of the hotel before she left for work. When she arrived at work, she completed the billing and new consumer admissions by midday. She clocked out and hopped in her truck, praying that the little getaway she was about to take would help clear her mind.

When she got to her truck, she called Tripp.

"Hey, babe, what's up? Where you at?" he asked as soon as he picked up his phone.

"I'm just now leaving work. I'm going to be on the highway in a few."

"Okay, sounds good. I can't wait to see you," he said softly.

"Same here," she replied, rolling her eyes up. She hated feeling like she was using him, but Tripp felt like a safe haven to her. "See you soon," she said before hanging up.

After four hours of driving in heavy traffic, Paula arrived at her destination. Tripp was waiting for her on the porch of his house with a bouquet of roses.

She smiled as she walked up on the porch. "These for me?"

"You better know it. Who else would they be for?" He laughed as she took them from him.

Tripp leaned in to kiss her, but she turned her head so that his lips would land on her cheek.

"I feel so icky. Can I take a shower right quick?" she asked.

"Sure, let me show you where the bathroom is and get you a towel and rag. Then I'll get your bags and bring them in. Are you hungry?"

"Not really. I'm just tired."

"I understand. I will order something later if you feel like you're hungry. I'm not too hungry myself," he told her.

Tripp showed Paula where the restroom was and gave her a rag and towel and showed her where the soap was. Paula got into the shower and closed her eyes and allowed the water to run down her face and down her back. She let out a long breath of relief.

When she got out, Tripp had her bags on the bed and was walking out of the closet with his robe on. Paula cringed, knowing that Tripp was expecting sex. Paula walked in and sat down on the bed and started putting on her deodorant and other smell goods when Tripp walked over and took Paula in his arms. But to his surprise, she was stiff and unresponsive to his advances. Tripp pulled back and stared at her crossly.

"What am I not doing right? Tell me and let me please you how you desire to be pleased. I'm a man before I'm anything else, and I guarantee you I can put it on you right. I really like you, and I will do whatever I have to do to keep you."

Paula didn't want to hurt his feelings, but she couldn't lie to him either.

"Tripp, it's like we click in every department except for sexually. You aren't attentive to my needs. You hurt me the last time, and I was very much disappointed."

"Damn, really? Why didn't you say anything to me?" he asked as he sat down on the bed.

"I didn't want to hurt your feelings. I mean, you are the perfect guy, but we just aren't compatible in bed," Paula told him gently.

"Paula, give me a chance to fix this. I am not a selfish lover. I can make you cum so fucking hard you won't ever question my sex. I mean that for real. I don't know if you realize this, but I am falling for you, and I can't lose you. Matter of fact, that ass ain't going nowhere," he growled, lifting her up in his arms.

Tripp carried Paula in the bedroom and made love to her until her whole body was trembling from orgasms. She couldn't see straight when he was finished. Not even Michael had ever made her cum so many times. Her legs were shaking, and she felt so much better. She lay in Tripp's arms and fell asleep immediately.

She was awakened the next morning with round two, which to Paula was even better. In the end, she wrapped her legs tightly around Tripp's back and held him in place, urging him to stay put. She was sadly mistaken by her earlier assumption that he couldn't fuck. That mothafucker was a beast. She had just gained a different level of respect for him.

Paula sighed as she thought, *it's time to put that call in. They need to serve those papers.*

Paula left South Carolina feeling refreshed and more alive than she felt in a long time. Tripp had mesmerized her with his passion. All she had to do was tell him what she wanted, and he delivered. Tripp even went down on her and ate her cooch like it was a juicy peach. He licked it and sucked it and then twirled his tongue inside her woman's cave. Her legs began to tingle just thinking about their sexual encounter. Paula could honestly say that he had given her pleasure. But before she left, he had received a phone call, and for the first time since she'd known him, he took it into the next room. Paula couldn't help but wonder if he was talking to another woman. She honestly couldn't get mad if he was, but he was the one who had said he wasn't going to entertain another woman while they were dealing with one another.

The Next Day

Paula went to work around 9:50. She received a text from Tasha: Cousin, please call me ASAP. It's an emergency.

Paula hadn't talked to Tasha or Angela since the night they were at the club and Michael showed up, but she was over her anger. It really didn't matter who had called him. Paula walked quickly to her office door, shut it, and then dialed Tasha's number.

"What's up?"

"Man, Paula, I've really fucked up this time," Tasha cried.

"Fucked up how?" Paula asked.

"Paula, what the hell am I gonna do?" Tasha asked in a shaky voice.

"First off, you need to calm down. What's wrong?"

"Bitch, I'm pregnant."

"You're what?" Paula asked, hoping she had heard her wrong.

"I said I am pregnant," Tasha growled slowly. "I can't have this baby. Can you meet me at the clinic after you get off?"

"Tasha, no. Don't do that," Paula whispered, instantly realizing what clinic Tasha was referring to.

"I can't have this baby. I'm not ready, and the father isn't either. This could ruin my life."

Paula cringed as the memories of her pregnancy sprung to her mind. "Okay, I will meet you there at about five fifteen. Is that okay?" Paula asked.

"Yes, thanks, cuz. Please don't tell nobody," Tasha begged.

"You know I won't, but are you sure this is what you want to do?" Paula asked.

"I don't have a choice," Tasha told her.

"All right. See you later." Paula hung up with a heavy heart. Tasha would never forgive herself after that day. She knew that because she had yet to forgive herself for what she had done years ago.

Paula finished out her day and left her office and headed to meet Tasha.

The procedure took about two hours, and when they left, they vowed to never mention it again. Paula drove Tasha home and told her that she would be back once she went home and got some clothes. Tasha didn't say a word. She just dropped her head and walked straight to her room and lay down in her bed.

Paula shook her head when she walked out, knowing exactly how Tasha was feeling. For the next few days Tasha was distant, but she eventually bounced back to her crazy, outspoken self.

Chapter 11

"Ay, man, we still on for tonight?" Michael asked his coworker and longtime friend Miguel as they punched out at the time clock.

"Shit, I don't have anything else to do. What time we meeting up?" Miguel asked.

"How about eleven? Hell, shit don't start jumping until that time anyway," Michael replied, walking out of the building.

Miguel stopped abruptly at the top of the concrete steps and nodded his head. "Looks like you got company."

Michael looked over to where he was parked, and standing next to his car was a tall white man with a sheriff's uniform on. "Fuck."

He walked down, and as he approached the car, the man walked forward. "Michael Harris?"

"Yes, that's me."

"You have been served."

The man walked away, and Michael leaned back on his car.

He removed his hat and wiped at his sweaty forehead. His hands shook as he read the paperwork: "Petition for Dissolution of Marriage."

Miguel walked over once the sheriff pulled off. "Everything okay, man?"

Michael looked up. "Hell naw. She wants a divorce. What the fuck happened to 'for better or worse?'"

"Damn, I don't know what to say. Bruh, dead ass, you need to talk to her," Miguel told him.

"How? Every time I'm around her, shit goes left. Not to mention she got this nigga around her now."

"Fuck dat, nigga. She is your wife, and if you don't have any plans to fight for her, then don't stress about that damn paper in your hand," Miguel told him as he gripped Michael's shoulder.

Michael sighed and shook his head. "Man, these have been the worst few months of my life. Then to top it off, I got a baby momma who stays trying me with my son. Shit. I'ma talk to you later, nigga."

Michael dapped Miguel up and got in his Chrysler 300 and pulled off.

Miguel stood in the middle of the parking lot and shook his head as he watched his best friend pull off, then jumped in his car and drove off in the opposite direction.

Everybody on my dick about the drama between Paula and me, but there are always two sides to a story, trust. I know I don't owe not one muthafucking soul an explanation, but I refuse to be the bad guy. Men always get the short end of the stick, but fuck that. I'm coming at ya! I got my flaws, but bae ain't innocent! She says I'm her regret, but I still love her, and I'ma fight for mine! I'm not the only one to blame, one hundred!

Man, how did I get myself into this shit? I love my wife and didn't mean for things to end like they did, but I'ma do everything in my power to win Paula back! If she thinks that nigga gonna take her from me, she got another think coming! Fuck she thought? But damn, I got a whole other problem—my baby mama! Damn, a brother really did fuck up!

—Michael Harris

***

Michael walked in and was greeted by his mother. "How was your day, son?"

Michael sighed and plopped down on the sofa. "Well, my day was okay until I walked out and the sheriff was there to serve me with papers. Paula wants to dissolve our marriage." Michael picked up one of the small pillows and threw it over his face. "Mom, what am I going to do if Paula divorces me? I love her so much, and I know I messed up, but I can't see myself living without her."

Sandra walked out from the doorway of the kitchen with her pink and white ruffled apron on and approached Michael, wiping her hands on her apron as she sat down. "You will be okay either way. I know you love Paula, but sometimes love runs its course. People come into our lives for a reason, a season, or a lifetime. If it's meant to be, you will work things out no matter how bad things appear or may become. Talk to God about it."

"Thanks, Momma," Michael whispered with the pillow still over his face.

Sandra walked away, humming a hymn from The Canton Spirituals. She knew her son was hurting, but he had messed up, and she couldn't blame Paula if she never forgave Michael. But whatever happened, she vowed that she would be by Michael's side.

Michael lay back on the couch and started thinking back to the day that his problems first began.

He had walked into their house, and she started bitching from the gate about a Facebook picture she had seen of him chilling with another chick. He first tried denying it, but when she flashed the picture in his face, he didn't know what to say. As soon as she threw his ass out, he headed straight for Nicki's house. Once he hit the threshold of her living room, he blanked. "What the fuck was your problem posting that shit on Facebook, bitch?"

"I didn't do shit," Nikki yelled.

"Well, if you didn't do it, who the fuck did?" Michael raged.

At the same time, they both looked at Tammy, Michael's sister, who was fidgeting with the remote and refusing to look at either one of them.

"Tammy, you did this shit?" Michael asked angrily.

"Michael, she isn't right for you. Your place is here with your son," Tammy finally spoke up.

"That's not your damn call. You are my sister, not my momma, and even she can't tell me what the hell to do or who I should be with or love," Michael roared.

Just as he was about to go in even more on both women, his son walked in. "Daddy, why are you yelling?"

Michael froze, not wanting to cause his son any discomfort. He put on a fake smile and turned. "Hey, baby boy, yo' momma and Auntie Tammy just played a stupid game with Daddy, and I'm just telling them to stop it."

"They were bad, Daddy, whaten they?" Tavon asked.

"Yes, they were. Come on, let's go and get you ready for bed, okay?" Michael said as he grabbed Tavon's hand and led him to his room.

"You staying the night, Daddy?"

"Not tonight, but I'll tell you what, I will stay until you go to sleep. Deal?"

"Deal." Tavon laughed.

After reading Tavon a story and putting his pajamas on, Michael lay across the bed and fell asleep himself. Waking up at 4:00 a.m., he kissed his son and left.

Michael jumped up, sat up, and slid his shoes on. He had to see what the hell Paula was trying to do to him. He didn't want the divorce, and she knew it. Why was she trying him like she was? He had to go find out.

"Ma, I'll be back in a few," Michael yelled as he walked to his room to get his keys.

"Son, I hope you aren't going over there to Paula's. You gotta give her space," his mother told him as she walked into the front room.

"She is my wife, and I got to talk to her," Michael replied, walking past his mother and ignoring her pleas.

"But, Michael—" she started but was abruptly shut down as Michael walked out the door and to his car.

"Dear Lord, help that son of mine and keep his black stupid ass out of jail," his mother whispered, shaking her head as Michael hurriedly pulled out of her driveway.

On his way to Paula's, his cell phone began to sound off. "Yeah, what is it, Nikki?"

"Damn, you don't have to answer the phone like that when I call. I didn't sleep with yo' ass last night. Anyway, I need you to watch your son for a little while."

"Watch him when?"

"Now."

"Listen, I'm on my way to talk to my wife, so whatever you have planned is just going to have to wait, or you can find someone else to watch li'l man," he retorted and hung up.

Seconds later his phone sounded off again. Michael shook his head and continued to his destination. As he pulled up, Paula was attempting to pull out. He swooped in quickly behind her, blocking her exit.

Michael hopped out of his car and approached Paula on the driver's side. "I need to talk to you."

Paula rolled her window down. "What is it?"

"What the fuck are you thinking about? You sent me divorce papers and didn't have the damn courtesy to warn me," Michael growled.

"Like your ass didn't know they were coming. Nigga, get your car out of the way before I push that bitch out of my path," Paula warned Michael as she pressed on the gas.

"I'm done playing with you. You will get a divorce over my dead body," Michael boomed.

"Oh, really? We will see about that," Paula growled.

"Paula, I mean, why are you so angry with me? This has got to be deeper than my cheating," Michael said.

"Michael, please just move," Paula cried.

"It's that nigga of yours, ain't it? He all up in your head, huh?"

"Michael," Paula started.

"Naw, he can't have you. If you don't give us a chance to work this out, then I have no other choice but to make your life hell."

Paula's face grew blank, and her eyes held a cold glare. She turned her car off, got out, stood directly in front of Michael, and said, "How dare you stand there like I'm to blame for this breakdown in our marriage? You did this to us. Michael, let me ask you a damn question. For five years," she started, waving five fingers in his face, "you kept your child a secret. You lied to me repeatedly. Why didn't you tell me about him, huh?"

"Because I knew you wouldn't be able to accept knowing that I fathered a child outside of our marriage, nor would you be able to accept him. I fucked up, but I only lied because I didn't want to lose you," Michael explained.

Paula's face relaxed, but her eyebrows drew close together, and her stare deepened with disappointment. "Michael, do you realize that you took any opportunity from me to forgive you for your mistake? You held me hostage in a sham marriage. You don't know what would have happened had you told me about your son, but instead I had to find out through Facebook. But I guess the thought that I could possibly forgive you never crossed your mind," Paula sighed. "Michael, please just leave."

Michael reached for Paula and tried to pull her into him. He wrapped his arms around her waist. "Paula, please don't do this."

"I can't do this with you right now. Let me go," Paula growled as she pushed at Michael's chest.

Michael dropped his arms away in defeat and headed back to his car. Paula got back into her car and waited for Michael to pull off.

Michael got back in his car and sat there for a second, thinking about what Paula had said. He acknowledged that she was right about a lot that she had said to him, but he had his own questions. "Why after five years did Nikki and Tammy decide to reveal my secrets all of a sudden?"

Chapter 12

Michael woke up early Saturday morning to the annoy-ing voice of his sister. Michael lay in bed, staring at the ceiling. "I hope she isn't here trying to stir up shit with me, because I'm not in the mood."

After a few minutes, there was a light knock at his bedroom door. "Michael, are you up?" his mother asked.

"Yeah," he replied.

"Breakfast is almost ready if you want to eat," she told him.

"All right, I'll be out in a few."

After Michael got up and washed his face and brushed his teeth, he headed down the hall toward the kitchen.

"What's up, bro?" Tammy greeted him as he walked into the kitchen.

"Yeah, what's good?" he replied, barely looking at her as he headed to the counter to pour himself a cup of coffee.

As he headed back to the table, he stopped short and kissed his mother on the cheek. He approached the table and sat at the far-left side, as far away from Tammy as he could.

"Rough night, huh?" she asked, staring at him over the rim of her glass of orange juice.

"Not really," he replied coldly.

Mrs. Harris couldn't help but notice the distance between her kids, but she decided she wasn't going to interfere with whatever they had going on. "Breakfast is ready if y'all want to fix your plates."

Michael waited for Tammy to fix her plate, and once she was seated, he went to fix his. Once he was seated at the table yet again, he began eating, and Tammy started laughing. "You know, I never imagined the day would come that we wouldn't be close. We have always been able to talk to one another, Michael. I want to know why you are so cold to me."

"You know damn well why I'm acting like I am to you, Tammy. Don't sit here trying to act like you are oblivious to what my issue is with you 'cause mom is sitting here," Michael said as he looked up.

"All right, what is going on? I was going to stay out of it, but now you two are really tripping. There is nothing that should come between a brother and sister," their mother fussed.

"That's what I'm trying to tell him, Mom. I don't want to lose my brother at all, which is why I'm here trying to talk to him."

"I have nothing to say to you. Listen, Mom, I got a few runs to make, but I will be back later," Michael said as he stood up and cleared his dishes from the table.

"Michael, don't leave like this," his mother pleaded.

"I can't sit here like everything is okay."

Sandra gave him a half smile with a sadness in her eyes that broke his heart. "I won't pressure you, son."

"Thanks, Mom," he whispered.

Without glancing at Tammy, he walked out of the kitchen.

Michael decided against his better judgment to refrain from telling his mother about Tammy's part in his and Paula's marriage woes, but he also wasn't going to sit there and listen to Tammy preach about his marriage and parenting issues, especially since she had no clue what it meant to be married or be a parent and deal with a bitter bitch whose only joy in life was making him miserable. All he ever did was keep it real with Nikki from the point of penetration to contraception to a baby being born. He didn't want Nikki and wasn't going to be with her no matter what happened between him and Paula.

Michael again brushed his teeth, walked into his room, got dressed, and slammed out of his mother's house without saying another word to either woman. He called Miguel. "Ay, what's up? What's on the agenda for today?"

"Same shit we were planning on doing yesterday. We are going to chill, drink, and have a good time," Miguel laughed.

"Well, damn, I'm out and about now. Are you home, dude?" Michael asked.

"Yeah, we out here playing horseshoes in the back."

"Oh, shit, hell yeah. I'm on my way. Y'all niggas ready to lose some real money?" Michael laughed as he hung up the phone.

Michael stopped by the ABC liquor store and purchased a bottle of Cîroc and a bottle of gin. He needed to get white-boy wasted and Mexican faded to get the issues that he was going through off his mind.

Michael woke up feeling worse than he did the day before. Not only was he more confused about his situation, but his head was banging as a result of a massive hangover.

"Oh, my God. What the fuck did I do last night?" he groaned.

"Your ass got drunk as hell, nigga. You drank all that hard white gin and Cîroc," Miguel replied.

Michael jumped when Miguel spoke, not realizing that he was still on his couch and was surrounded by his boys.

"We need an intervention, man. You're going downhill fast. You can't let your baby momma's behavior or your wife's decisions cause you to lose focus on yourself, bro. This ain't you," Sean chimed in.

"Yeah, you're a better man than this," Miguel agreed.

Michael sat up with his head bowed. "Y'all don't know what I'm going through. My wife was my everything. Do y'all know she is seeing some other dude now? And we aren't even divorced yet."

Miguel looked at Michael and frowned. "Why are you concerned about what she is doing? Don't you have a side chick too?"

"Hell no. What are you talking about?" Michael questioned.

"I'm talking about that chick you were on the phone with last night. You told shorty you wanted to see her, but you passed out on the couch before you could even hang up the phone," Sean answered before Miguel could respond.

"I did what?" Michael groaned. He grabbed his cell phone and scrolled down. "Nooooo," he yelled once he saw the name of the person he had called. He slapped his forehead and leaned back against the cushions of the couch. "Man, what am I going to do?"

"I know what you're not going to do. You're not going to continue to sit here feeling sorry for yourself. Get the fuck up and get yourself together. We are going out, nigga," Miguel told him.

"Man, I don't feel like doing anything today. My head is killing me," Michael complained.

Miguel and Sean started laughing. "Boy, get yo' ass up, and let's go take all your frustrations out on the basketball court. Tory, Amp, and Jay challenged us last night to a game, and we can't go without a third. Hell, you put a hundred dollars on the game, nigga."

"I did what?" Michael shouted.

Sean and Miguel laughed as they walked into the kitchen to eat.

"Come on, nigga, fuel that body up."

Monday Afternoon

Michael got off work and headed straight to Nikki's house. He had to find out why she chose to let their secret out of the bag after five years. When he pulled up in her driveway, his son immediately ran out. "Hey, Daddy."

"Hey, little man." Michael smiled as he picked his son up and carried him into the house. He loved his son and treated him with as much love as he could shower upon him. He was a small-framed child with dark skin and light brown eyes, and he was very smart and mature for a child of his age.

"Where's your mother at?" Michael asked.

"She is in her room lying down. She isn't feeling good, Daddy," he answered.

"She isn't? What's wrong with her?"

"She's been kind of mean. I think it's her mommy's time," he whispered.

Michael started laughing. "Her mommy's time, huh? Well, go tell her I'm here and that I would like to talk to her, please."

"Okay, but um, after you talk can we go get something to eat? I'm hungry."

"You haven't eaten today?" Michael asked sharply.

"Not since this morning," he admitted.

"What the . . ." Michael began, but quickly halted his words as his son stared up at him. "Go outside and sit on the porch, okay?" Michael said softly.

"Okay," Tavon said.

Once Tavon was outside sitting on the porch, Michael walked back to Nikki's room. "Nikki, I need to talk to you now," he roared as he walked to her bedroom door. Michael was immediately met with a disgusting view. There were dirty clothes everywhere, but what really got his stomach churning was the foul odor and the used condoms that were visible on her nightstand. There was a Mountain Dew bottle next to her bed that he was sure she had used to spit cum into. At least, that was what it look like to him.

"Man, bitch, how the fuck you got this shit lying around for my son to see? You are a trifling-ass woman."

Nikki turned quickly, struggling to get away from in between her covers. Her hair was tousled, and her eyes were wide. "What are you doing here, Michael?"

"I came to talk to you about a few things, but instead I'm greeted by my son telling me he is hungry and hasn't eaten anything since this morning. Then I walk in here, and you laid up back here with this room looking like a nasty-ass trap house where hoes entertain their johns. I'm going to take my son to my mother's, and I will bring him back when you call me and tell me that this house is fit for him to be here, you stupid-ass woman."

Michael stormed out of the room with Nikki running behind him, tripping over the debris that cluttered her floor. "Michael, wait. Please don't take my son. You have no right."

"No right?" Michael growled. "I just may have lost the only woman who ever meant anything to me because you and my sister thought that it was time that you air out my secrets, but you coming at me saying I have no rights. Bitch, if I lose my wife, I'm gonna take every damn dime I have to take all my rights and get custody of my son. Hell, now that you have told my wife about him, even if we work things out, I'ma take my son."

Nikki ran behind him. "Michael, you promise you're gonna bring him back?"

Michael turned and looked at her. "Nikki, leave me the fuck alone before I fuck you up."

Michael walked out of the house and put on the biggest smile he could for Tavon. "Hey, you wanna go see Grandma and see what goodies she got cooked up?"

"Yes," Tavon screamed with excitement. "Bye, Mommy."

Nikki waved back, looking like a troubled wench.

Chapter 13

Michael was tired and lonely. He missed Paula with his entire being, but he decided to fall back for a little bit to tend to his son. It had been two days since he had taken his son from Nikki, and she had yet to contact him. He was so glad that his mother was there to help him. His life was in total shambles, but he refused to corrupt his son with his foolishness. He didn't know what to do about anything concerning his life, but the one thing he was certain of was that he wasn't going to let his son suffer because of it.

As soon as he pulled up to his mother's house, he smiled. His son was sitting on the porch with his mother, and they were splitting peas together.

"Hey, Daddy, you see this? It's a pea," Tavon told him excitedly.

"Yes, I see. Hey, Mom, how you doing today?"

Michael walked into the house, leaving his mother and son on the front porch to finish picking the peas. He walked in his room and grabbed his towel and bath rag and went and took a hot shower. He then dried himself off, put on his nightclothes, walked into his bedroom, and lay across the bed. He looked long and hard at the picture of him and Paula that was on his nightstand.

Suddenly his son walked in and ran and jumped on the bed. "Daddy, who was that lady? I remember her." He lay next to Michael on the bed.

"That's my wife," Michael replied quietly. He didn't want to lie to his son.

"Oh. Daddy?" Tavon asked, looking up from the picture.

"Yes, Tavon?" Michael replied.

"Is Mommy your wife too?"

"No, just this lady, and her name is Paula. It's too much for you to understand right now, but as long as you know I love you, the rest of this is irrelevant. Do you understand what I'm saying?" Michael asked.

"Not really, and I love you, Daddy. Daddy?" Tavon continued.

"Yes?" Michael replied, smiling.

"She is very pretty."

"Son, she is gorgeous. I mean, perfection." Michael laughed and grabbed Tavon and started wrestling with him.

Michael went to work the next day, and on his lunch break, he decided to text Paula. He initially felt that giving her space was best, but he needed to reach out to her. He decided that a text would be better than calling. He sent his text, praying that she would respond.

Him: Good afternoon, Paula.

After about three minutes, his phone beeped.

Her: Afternoon to you as well, Michael.

He smiled and quickly texted back.

Him: I pray that your day has been a blessed one.

Her: Yes, it has, and how about yours?

Him: It's been okay. I just wanted to check on you. I'm not gon' hold you up.

He didn't want to overdo it since she'd replied. Just that little bit of conversation made him smile. It took everything in him to refrain from texting, "I love you."

Her: Thank you, Michael.

Him: No doubt, queen.

Michael went back to work and finished out his day smiling. When he got off work, he was humming and ready to get to his son.

"Nothing is going to ruin my day," he sang aloud.

Michael drove home with nothing but Paula and his son on his mind. He stopped by the grocery store to pick up a few of his son's favorite snacks. When Michael finally arrived home, his mother had a guest. One of her church members was there.

Michael walked in and spoke to them, then asked if there was any word from Nikki. His mother shook her head and smiled sadly.

"Tavon, come on and let's go get us some pizza," Michael said.

"Yay. I like pizza," Tavon shouted as he ran and grabbed Michael's hand.

"Mom, do you want something?"

"No, me and Beulah are going to choir practice, and I'll just grab a sandwich or something while I'm out," she told him.

"Okay, enjoy yourself," Michael said and headed out the door. He locked Tavon in his car seat, got in, and turned his radio on. "You ready, guy?"

"Yes. Daddy?"

"Yep," Michael answered.

"Does Mommy still love me?" he asked sadly.

Michael was stunned by the question, and he honestly didn't have the answer. The way Nikki had been acting as of late, he truly didn't know if she did, but he wasn't going to crush his son's heart. "Tavon, you know she loves you. Maybe her phone is messed up, so she couldn't call. You know Mommy drops stuff."

Tavon wasn't having it. "But she could drive her car."

"Yes, well, maybe she didn't have enough gas to drive her car."

"Oh," Tavon replied, looking out the window.

Michael looked at his son through his rearview mirror and noticed that he had dropped his head and looked very unhappy. Michael sighed, "I will go check on Mommy tomorrow when I get off work, okay?"

"Okay," he exclaimed, sounding a bit happier.

They went and sat down in Pizza Hut and ate their pizza, then afterward went to the park and then back home. Tavon had fallen asleep by the time they pulled up to Michael's mother's house. Michael got out of the car and unlocked Tavon's car seat and picked him up and carried him into the house. When he walked in, he laid Tavon down on the couch, but Tavon immediately sat up.

"Well, since you're up, let's get you a quick bath," Michael said.

Michael ran Tavon's bath and heard his phone beep. "Who the fuck is that?"

He called Tavon in and helped him undress, then washed him up. "Okay, son, let's get ready for bed."

"But I'm not sleepy yet," he replied, yawning.

Michael laughed, "Well, pretend you are."

After Michael laid Tavon in bed and read him his favorite children's book, he went and got his nightclothes and took a shower. He was tired and was ready to lie down. As soon as he got finished with his shower, he walked back into his room and checked his phone and saw that he had a text message waiting. He opened it up and shook his head as he read what it said.

Tammy: Michael, we need to talk. I know you are upset with me, but I'm your sister dammit.

Michael: I have nothing to say to you. You should've remembered that I was your damn brother before you started playing games with my marriage.

Michael turned his phone off and lay across the bed. He couldn't sleep as the last few months started replaying in his mind. He thought back to the day that he had gone to his and Paula's home and she wasn't there. He had sat there waiting for her damn near all night. He was going to lay everything on the table and had decided that he wasn't going to leave until they talked and worked shit out, but she never showed up. He left but returned the following day only to get a repeat of the previous day. Michael was angry and smashed up a few things and wrote Paula a short letter letting her know that he had been there.

The next time he heard from Paula was when she texted him asking him to meet her at Trinity's Lounge only to be greeted by her in another nigga's face. Hell, he had been drinking prior to arriving at the lounge and was basically done for. He shouldn't have even gone out, but seeing Paula's text, he couldn't, he wouldn't, miss out on the chance to talk to her. He didn't remember how he made it home, but when he woke up, he remembered feeling violated to the max. He finally felt how Paula must have felt seeing him on Facebook with Nikki.

At some point, lost in his thoughts, Michael drifted off to sleep. When he woke up the next morning, he had pushed his own problems to the back burner of his mind so he could focus on his son's. He was going to go see what the fuck was going on with Nikki and why she hadn't attempted to check on Tavon. He couldn't fathom what was so important that she couldn't pick up her phone to call.

Michael got up the next morning at six and got dressed. He tiptoed into the room where Tavon was sleeping and kissed him on the forehead and left. He stopped at Biscuitville and got some breakfast.

As he pulled up to the window of the drive-through, the young lady who took his money smiled at him. "About to make that money, huh?"

"Yeah, that's a must for me," he laughed.

"You must have a family to take care of?" she asked, fishing to see if Michael was taken.

"Thirteen years and counting," Michael said, showing her his wedding band, which he never took off.

"Lucky lady," she replied, handing Michael his food. "Have a nice day."

"You too," Michael replied before pulling off in the direction of his job. When he reached his destination, he sat in his car and ate his breakfast.

"Come on, man, you sitting in here feeding your face, and you are going to be late," Miguel said as he walked up to Michael's car.

"A brother hungry as hell. I'm coming." Michael laughed, stuffing the last bite of his sausage and egg biscuit in his mouth. Michael got out of his car and locked his car doors, and then he and Miguel headed inside the building.

"Man, I talked to Paula yesterday," Michael said, cheesing big time.

"Word? What y'all talk about?" Miguel asked.

"Well, technically we didn't actually speak, but we texted. I was happy she didn't ignore my ass," Michael told him.

"Well, was it a good conversation? I mean, textization?" Miguel asked, trying not to laugh.

Michael laughed at Miguel's lame joke. "It was pleasant but short. I didn't want to overdo it. But I'll tell you what, if I ever get the chance to show her, I'm going to be the best damn husband to her, and that's on God."

"I hope it goes how you want it to, because I'm tired of seeing you moping around like you been doing," Miguel told him.

"I haven't been that bad," Michael replied.

"Damn lie. Shit, you were about to drown in depression, but you look chipper these days and sober," Miguel told him.

"Hell, I had no choice. Tavon has been with me for a few days now," Michael explained, "but that's a good thing. I'm thinking about going for custody."

"For real? How would that sit with Paula?" Miguel questioned.

"That's the part I'm not sure about, but I'm hoping that one day she would at least meet him and spend time with him. I'm a father first. I love my wife though, and I honestly want them both in my life," Michael admitted.

"Well, I'm sure everything will work out, but damn, if you and wifey work shit out, that's going to be the end of our club nights. No more strippers, no more chasing, no more anything . . . well, not for you," Miguel chided.

"I won't have any need for those hoes then. Shit, I don't have no need for them now. I just be riding along," Michael laughed.

"Man, go do some work." Miguel laughed as they clocked in.

Michael went through his day working extra hard and through his lunch break because he informed his boss that he needed to get off an hour early to handle some personal business. His boss agreed only if he worked through his lunch break.

At three o'clock, Michael clocked out and headed to his car. Once he was in his car, he checked his phone, and after calling his mother to check on Tavon, he headed to Nikki's house.

He turned the radio up as "Hush" by Jaheim flowed from his speakers. Fifteen minutes later, Michael was pulling up to Nikki's house only to find that she wasn't home.

"Fuck," he groaned and slammed his fist down on the steering wheel. He was livid. "What the hell am I going to tell Tavon now?" Michael spun out of Nikki's driveway and headed home. When he arrived, he was taken aback at the sight that fell upon his eyes.

Chapter 14

Michael pulled up in the grassy area of his mother's yard. His heart was beating hard as if it were trying to leap out of his chest. He watched as his wife and his son sat on the porch, talking. She was smiling at him, holding his hands, and he was smiling hard at her.

Michael finally got the nerve to get out of the car, and he walked nervously to the porch. "Hey, it's nice to see you," he said.

"Well, you had some mail at the house, and I wanted to bring it to you. I honestly wasn't expecting you to be here," she replied, still looking and smiling at Tavon.

"My daddy said you were gorgeous," Tavon told her.

"Is that right?" Paula asked, laughing.

"Yeah, 'cause he said you were his wife, but my mommy wasn't," Tavon told her.

"Tavon, go in the house," Michael cried.

"He is okay," Paula laughed. "Actually, Tavon asked me to stay for dinner, and I told him I might," she said, eyeing Michael while Tavon played with her fingers.

"Please do," Michael said, trying not to sound too happy.

"So where is the mommy?" Paula asked.

"Mommy is MIA," Michael replied, hoping that Paula wouldn't get in her feelings about Nikki.

"Oh, man, that's wild," Paula replied. "So how about we take little man here to the park?"

"Are you serious?" Michael asked.

Paula sighed. "As much as I want to be angry right now, I can't," she replied, looking at Tavon. "But I don't want you to get the wrong idea about this, Michael."

"Oh, no, I won't. I'm just happy that we can actually talk without arguing," he replied. "Let me go take a quick shower and I'll be ready."

"Okay, I will sit right here with Tavon. He can tell me more about his favorite food list," she said.

"You be good, Tavon," Michael warned.

Paula looked up, and her eyes met with Michael's brown eyes, and she couldn't look away. *Damn, he is sexy as fuck,* she thought.

Tavon patted Paula on the leg and said excitedly, "Look at me."

Paula jumped and turned to watch Tavon, who turned half flips in the yard. She laughed and clapped.

Michael walked into the house and spoke to his mother, then quickly grabbed his clothes and rushed to the bathroom, pausing to check if Paula was still there. He smiled as he watched her playing with Tavon. Was that it? Was Tavon the blessing that was going to bring Paula back to him?

Michael walked into the bathroom and jumped in the shower, whistling a tune that he hadn't whistled since his breakup with Paula. After he got out of the shower, he got dressed and cleaned up his mess in the bathroom. When he walked out, he went to inform his mother that they were about to leave.

His mother eyed him oddly and whispered, "Are you sure Nikki will be okay with you and Paula taking him out?"

Michael frowned, wondering why she would ask him such a question. "Paula is my wife, and Nikki can't tell me whether I can have her around my child. I don't dictate who she has around him. Ma, come on. Don't kill my positive vibe with this nonsense."

Sharon smiled. "Son, I'm not trying to kill your vibe, but you know how messy that baby momma of yours is."

"Yeah, well, I'm not concentrating on her or anything else at this moment. I will see you in a little while. Can I get you something while I'm out?"

"No, I'm okay. You just go on and enjoy your family," Sharon told him as she folded up the last of the laundry she had washed.

"Okay, love ya, Ma." Michael walked out the door. "You guys ready?"

"Yeah," Tavon yelled, running to the car.

Once they were all safe and secured in the car, they pulled off. Michael drove his car, and he drove with ease. He was praying that his day would end on a positive note.

When they arrived at the park, they got out of the car, and they all played around as if they were all 5. Paula and Tavon got on the merry-go-round, and Michael turned it. Tavon held on tightly to Paula as they spun around. Paula seemed to enjoy Tavon's presence more than Michael could've imagined she would. Tavon immediately latched on to Paula. If he got on a swing, he urged Paula to get on one right next to him, and Michael alternated between pushing each one of them. Paula smiled and laughed so much that she had to take a break, which didn't last very long.

Tavon rushed over to the bench where Paula was sitting and grabbed her hand. "Come on, Miss Paula, watch me run. I can run fast."

"Oh, yeah?" she laughed. "Well, let me see."

Tavon started running, and Paula clapped her hands and cheered him on. After playing around for a little while longer, they left and headed to Wendy's, where they ate, and then headed back to Michael's mother's house. Paula hugged Tavon and promised him that she would come back the next day so they could hang out again.

The next day, when Michael got to work, he was all smiles. He wasn't going to waste time getting his work done. He was ready to see Paula and spend time with her and his son. It felt like they were bridging a connection to becoming a family.

Michael felt wonderful. Miguel noticed the change in Michael and had to ask him where the change came from.

"Ay, bruh, you all smiles today, looking goofy as fuck. What gives?"

"Well, if you must know, I have a family date with my son and my wife," Michael laughed.

"What?" Miguel asked, staring at Michael in shock.

"Yeah, you heard me. We went out yesterday, and at Paula's suggestion, we are going back out again today," Michael announced proudly.

"How did that happen?" Miguel asked.

"Hell, I got off work yesterday, and when I pulled up, Paula was sitting on the porch playing with Tavon. He asked her to stay for dinner, but instead we went out. We went to the park, hung out, and then grabbed burgers from Wendy's. Man, I felt alive, and if you had seen the way Paula was with Tavon, man . . ."

"So what are you guys going to do today?" Miguel questioned.

"Well, we were thinking about taking Tavon to the city park then to Mayberry Ice Cream Shop for hot dogs," Michael said.

"Oh, okay, that sounds like fun. Tavon will enjoy that," Miguel replied.

"Yeah, man. I'm not gonna think too much about anything, but I am happy," Michael told his friend.

When Michael walked off, he couldn't help but smile. He had just said that he wasn't going to put too much thought into hanging out with Paula, but he had to be honest with himself if no one else. He was going to use his current situation with Paula to turn things around for them.

He knew that Nikki was aware by that time that Paula had been there visiting him and Tavon, but he didn't care. If she even attempted to intervene, he was going to make her sorry. She had played a major role in the destruction of his marriage, and he'd never looked at her the same. She was and always would be his baby momma, but that was it. Tammy, on the other hand, he'd have to deal with differently because she was his sister. He laughed, imagining the looks that the two of them must've had when they learned that Paula was back. Michael finished his day so that he could go on home.

He clocked out and talked to Miguel for a few minutes, then jumped in his car and heard his phone beeping. He pulled it out of his pocket and saw a text message waiting for him from Paula informing him that she would meet him at the city park, which was a local kids' zone where children went to play games, ride on fun rides, and eat kid-desired food.

He called his mother to see if Tavon was dressed and ready to go, and once she confirmed that he was, Michael hung up and headed down the highway. At one point he checked his rearview mirror and could have sworn that he saw Nikki's car behind him, but when he checked it a second time it was gone. He didn't know if he was paranoid imagining it or if she was indeed behind him, but he'd make sure she would feel his wrath if she was playing with him. He didn't know what kind of hold his sister had on Nikki, but Nikki needed to realize that between him and Tammy, she would rather have her as an enemy than him.

Michael finally arrived home and sat in his car for a few minutes waiting to see if Nikki was going to pull in. After two minutes and nothing, he got out and walked into the house. He walked in and hugged Tavon then his mom.

"I'm about to take a shower, and then we are out of here, my boy," he said to Tavon.

"Okay," Tavon said as he leaned back and finished watching *Scooby-Doo*.

An hour later, Michael texted Paula and told her they were on their way.

When he and Tavon pulled up to the city park and got out, Paula was waiting for them as she promised. Michael helped Tavon out of his seat belt, and as soon as he was free, zoom. He flew to the rides that were going and yelled for Paula to follow him.

"Tavon, get back here," Michael ordered.

Paula laughed at how excited Tavon appeared.

Tavon stopped on command, but he was jumping up and down. "Look, Daddy. The train is going."

"I see," Michael replied.

"Can we ride? Pleasssee?" Tavon begged.

"Yes, we can. Gotta get some tickets first," Michael told him. "I'll be right back. I'ma go get some tickets. Do you want something to drink?" he asked Paula.

"Yes, get me a Sprite. Tavon, what do you want?" Paula asked as she took his hand.

"I want a drink too, Daddy," Tavon cried.

"Okay, I'll be right back," Michael told them.

Paula and Tavon sat on the bench and waited for Michael to return. When he did, she stood up and took her drink. Instinct made Michael place his hand on her lower side as they walked, but after he realized what he had done, he removed it. Paula looked at him and smiled.

"Okay, little man, what shall we do first?" Paula asked.

"I want to get on the train." He laughed.

"Okay, well, let's go get on the train."

Michael kind of stayed behind, causing Paula to look back at him. "Come on, Daddy. You are coming too."

The way she said "Daddy" made Michael's heartrate accelerate. He smiled and walked quickly to join his wife and his son. They rode the train three times, and then got on the carousel. Tavon was having a blast. They then walked the park, and when they got to the bridge overlooking the rocky creek, Michael leaned over and took a penny out of his pocket. "You want to make a wish?" he asked Paula.

She gazed in his eyes and smiled, then nodded. "You have to blow it first," Michael told her.

Paula blew the penny and closed her eyes. When she opened them, Michael tossed the penny in.

"What did you wish?" he asked.

"I can't tell you. If I do, it won't come true."

"Superstition." Michael laughed. "Come on, tell me or give me a hint."

Paula laughed, "Nope. Not gonna do it." She walked away, twisting her hips and trying to tempt Michael. At least, that was what he thought.

Michael jogged to catch up with Paula and Tavon, and they walked through the park for a few minutes more before Tavon was screaming for food. They ended up going to Mayberry, a local ice cream shop that also sold food. Tavon ate a hot dog and then a cup of cookies-and-cream ice cream. Paula and Michael ate the same, except Paula ate sherbet instead of ice cream. When they finished eating and walked back to the car, Michael saw a deep scratch on the side of his car. He wanted to flip out but decided against it. He had a feeling that Nikki was responsible, and he would deal with her on his own time, not while he was with Paula.

Michael asked Paula if she would follow him to his mother's house so that they could talk, and when she agreed, he got in his car and waited for her to get in hers and pulled off, ensuring she was behind him.

When they got to their destination, Michael got out of the car and lifted his sleeping son from his car seat and carried him in the house, then put him to bed. He walked back outside, and he and Paula stood beside her truck. "I know we've been through a lot, and I know I'm mostly to blame. I noticed that your phone was blowing up there for a moment. I assume it was a man friend."

Paula shrugged. "Yes, it was. To be honest, he is a good guy."

Michael's jaw began to twitch as jealousy sat in. "The nigga who was at the lounge that night?"

"Yes," Paula replied.

"So is it serious between you two?" he asked, looking at her hard.

"He is just a friend. I'm not trying to build anything with anyone right now. I think I reacted how I did with him because I was hurting and wanted my taste of revenge," Paula confessed.

"You know, you could've had all the revenge you needed had you shot me that night," Michael whispered.

"I don't think I will ever forgive myself for that night. I wasn't in my right frame of mind." Paula sighed.

"I understand that. I wanted to strangle you and that nigga the night at the club and probably would have if I hadn't been drunk. Are you still seeing him?" Michael asked.

"Honestly, I haven't seen him in a while, but we do talk on the phone."

Michael shook his head. "But I'm wrong."

"I think it's time for me to go. I don't want to argue," Paula replied, walking backward a bit.

Michael quickly switched it up. "I don't want to argue either. Please stay a little bit longer. Listen, can I take you out to dinner Friday night? Just you and me? Please."

Paula didn't immediately answer, but truth be told, she missed her husband. "Yes, we can do that."

"Okay, I will work out all the details," he said.

"Okay, great. I really have to go. I got work in the morning."

"Me too. May I have a hug?" Michael inquired.

Paula instantly went in for the hug, and after two minutes, they separated, and Michael waited for her to get in her truck and drive off. He was hurt, angry, and happy at once. It was a feeling he had never experienced before.

"That nigga got to go," he sneered to himself.

Chapter 15

Paula looked beautiful. Her dreads were placed up in a perfect bun, and her hips were swaying as she walked from left to right, inviting Michael's eyes to watch them. The beige dress that she wore showed her huge, busty cleavage, which Michael longed to bury his face in.

He cleared his throat, as it was hard for him to speak. "You look good, Paula. I mean, that dress looks perfect on you."

"Well, thank you. You always knew what to say to make a girl feel good," Paula replied.

"Paula, it's not to make you feel good. It's the truth."

"Are you ready to go get some dinner? Where is Tavon? I'd like to say hello to him."

"Oh, I didn't mean to be so rude. Come on in, Paula. Come on in," Michael said, suddenly realizing he had held her hostage on the front porch, admiring her beauty.

Unbeknownst to Michael, while he was checking Paula out, she was checking him out as well. Her ass kept gazing at his juicy lips when he spoke, and the dimple in his left cheek sent her heart racing. She couldn't help but notice the muscular tone underneath his button-down Polo shirt. *And, Lord,* she thought, *the way he walks away with his bowlegs makes my insides tingle.*

As she walked into the house, Sharon greeted her. "Hello, Paula, how are you doing?"

"I'm good, Mrs. Harris, and you?"

"Well, I'm making it. You know, Tavon has taken a real liking to you. All he talks about lately is his daddy's wife."

Paula gave her a half smile and looked at Michael, then back at Sharon. "Well, you know, I like him too. He is a very sweet and smart young man. I'm glad to have the opportunity to spend time with him."

"Paula," Tavon yelled from the hallway. He took off running and hugged her.

Paula sat down on the couch and talked to him for a few minutes until Michael spoke up. "Paula, we have to go if we don't want to be late for dinner."

"I'm coming. I will see you later, Tavon." She smiled, giving him a hug.

"Okay. Bye, Daddy. Bye, Paula," Tavon said as the couple walked out the door.

"Whose car are we taking?" Paula asked as they walked out.

"It doesn't matter to me," Michael replied. He was just happy to be having some positive one-on-one time with Paula, and that time it was going to be on his terms. No guns and no mess.

"Here," Paula said as she handed him her keys. "You drive."

Michael hesitated a little bit, and Paula laughed as she realized that Michael didn't trust her after that last stunt she had pulled on him at the hotel with the gun. "I'm on my bougie status tonight, so you are safe. You need to pat me down?"

Michael laughed, "I wasn't worried."

Paula smiled and gave him a knowing glance.

"All right, maybe just a little bit," Michael admitted.

He walked around and opened the door for Paula to get in, and once she was safely in, he returned to the driver's side and got in the truck.

"Where are we going?" she asked.

"Just strap on your seat belt and relax. I got you," Michael replied as he started her truck and pulled out of the driveway.

They barely spoke on the drive, but they constantly exchanged smiles and glances. When they pulled up to their destination, Paula was instantly impressed. "Oh, my God, Michael. You know I love this place."

"That's why we are here tonight. This is your night."

Michael got out of the truck and walked around to help Paula out. "You know, I got the prettiest chick on my arm, and I feel whole again."

Paula laughed, "I'm not doing so bad myself. I've got a very handsome man by my side."

"Oh, shit, was that a compliment?" Michael joked.

"Just a smidge." Paula laughed.

Michael and Paula headed into Gregory's, a five-star restaurant with a jazz club inside. When they walked in, the hostess ushered them up. "Name and reservation time?"

"Oh, man, a reservation?" Michael murmured.

Paula looked away in embarrassment.

"Harris. Michael and Paula Harris," he said, nudging Paula.

"Boy, don't play with me like that." She laughed.

"Wait one minute," the hostess replied as she motioned for a server to come over.

"Right this way," the server replied after looking at the reservation chart and taking two menus.

They were seated near the middle of the restaurant. The server took their drink orders and left them with their menus. Once she set their wine and water on the table, she inquired if they were ready to order.

"I will have the pasta and lamb ragu with a light white sauce," Michael told her.

"And I will have the island duck with mulberry mustard," Paula told her.

"Okay, I will be back in a few with your meals," the server said and walked away.

"I can't believe we are sitting here," Paula bubbled as she beamed with excitement.

"I wasn't going to half step on this night," he confessed.

"I'm impressed," she admitted.

Michael bowed his head. "I'm glad. I want to thank you for taking the time out to get to know Tavon. It means a lot to me and him."

"Well, when I went to your mother's, I wasn't expecting to see him, but when Sandra introduced me to him and he came over and shook my hand, I became curious. He grew on me instantly."

"God works in mysterious ways. Again, thank you."

"You're welcome."

They sat for a few minutes, and Charlie Wilson's "Chills" was playing. Michael wanted so badly to reach out and take Paula's hand, but he wasn't going to push his luck, at least not so early in the night. He stared at Paula, and she stared back. Unspoken words that screamed from the two of them were expressed. Michael quickly turned his attention to couples around him, and he hoped that the vibes he was reading from Paula weren't mistaken.

He looked back. "Paula, I know I've said this once, but damn, you look beautiful. There is no other woman in here tonight who could hold a candle to your beauty."

"You trying to make me blush?" Paula replied, smiling.

"It's the truth." He finally found the nerve to take her hand in his. When he realized she wasn't pulling back, he smiled and gave it a light squeeze, then let it go. He took a sip of his wine and glanced around the room.

The dance floor was filled with couples, and Michael prayed that Paula wouldn't turn him down when he asked her to dance. "You want to dance?" He held his breath waiting for her response.

"Sure." She allowed Michael to take her hand and lead her to the dance floor. Michael pulled her close as "Don't Come Easy" by Raheem DeVaughn played.

Neither spoke at first, but then Paula leaned back and stared up at Michael. "This feels good. I'm glad we did this."

"I am too. I hope this won't be the last time you allow me to do this. I want to show you that I am worthy of you. I want to gain your trust again," he whispered.

"It's not gonna be easy, but we can take it one day at a time and see what happens," she replied gently.

Michael smiled and pulled her closer. He wasn't going to push it. Hell, he was just happy she was finally cooperating. *At least she didn't say it wasn't possible.*

After they finished their dance, they went back to their table, and five minutes later, their food arrived.

"This looks delicious," she drawled.

"Yes, it does," he agreed. Michael took his first bite and smiled. "We got a winner."

"Let me taste," Paula replied as she aimed her fork for Michael's plate.

Michael laughed, "No way. Eat your own food."

He moved his plate out of her fork's path, and she laughed. "Oh, you're going to let me taste it."

"You think?" he challenged her.

Paula slid her chair closer to Michael's and gave him her best enticing smile, batting her eyelashes at him. "Please?"

"You don't play fair," he whispered.

She lifted a small amount of his food to her lips, and his eyes followed her fork's path, lingering on her lips. Paula closed her eyes. "Mmmm, yes, it is good." She opened her eyes and saw the look of longing on Michael's face and continued, "Here, taste mine." She lifted a small amount of her food and fed Michael.

Not wanting to cause either of them any discomfort, Michael frowned. "It's not as good as mine."

Paula laughed and shoved him. "Liar."

They ate their dinner and danced a bit more before deciding to leave the restaurant. They headed back to Michael's mother's house, and upon arriving there, they sat in the car and talked for another hour. When he got out of Paula's truck, he walked around to help her out and walked her to the driver's side.

"I really appreciate tonight, Michael. Thank you."

"I thank you for coming out with me, Paula."

Paula leaned in and kissed him. He wrapped his arms around her waist and pulled her in closer. Michael watched her pull off. He couldn't walk into the house with his dick hard, so he walked up to the porch and sat down for a few. When he was straight, he went inside.

"How was it?" his mother asked, who appeared to be up waiting for him.

"It was very nice."

"Well, I'm going to bed. I just wanted to make sure you made it in," Sharon replied as she got up off the couch and went to bed.

Michael walked into the room where Tavon was and kissed him on the forehead and went to bed. When he finally went to sleep, he had the biggest Kool-Aid smile on his face.

Saturday Afternoon

Michael asked his mother if she could watch Tavon so he could hang out with Sean and Miguel. She agreed to watch him, and he headed out. He was in a wonderful mood after the night he and Paula had spent together.

He pulled up to the park, and his friends were there waiting for him.

"What's up?" he said as he walked up. "Y'all ready to get y'all asses whooped?"

"Man, you ain't about to whoop shit. Let's do this." Sean laughed as he bounced the ball.

They played the first game, and Sean won.

"Ha. I told y'all ass I wasn't here to play," he yelled as he danced around the court.

"Nigga, whatever. Shit, game two," Miguel said.

"Let's do this," Sean replied.

"Hell, I need a second to catch my breath." Michael laughed.

"Oh, shit, don't tell me your ass is out of shape." Sean laughed, bouncing the ball in Michael's direction.

"Hell naw. Tavon been keeping me busy. But you know I'm enjoying my time with him," Michael told them.

"Yeah, that's not the only person keeping you busy lately. How is that going anyway?' Miguel asked.

"Man, I took my wife out on a date last night, and I swear I haven't felt as connected with her as I did last night in a long damn time," Michael admitted as he took a swig of the water he had.

"Well, that's what's up. I'm glad you two are back talking again," Sean chimed in.

"I know. Well, y'all ready for this second round?" Michael asked as he stood up and faked left, then snatched the ball from Sean.

"Oh, word, Let's do this then." Sean laughed.

After a second win for Sean, Miguel again prompted another game.

"Damn sore loser, huh?" Sean laughed.

Michael sat back down on the bench, sweating and breathing hard. He looked down and checked his phone. He had three missed calls from Paula. "Oh, shit, what the fuck is going on now?" he groaned. He picked up his phone and pushed the call button. "Yeah, what's up, Paula?"

Miguel and Sean watched as Michael's smile turned into a frown instantly.

"What? I haven't seen that bitch since I went to her house and took Tavon. That's on my life," Michael yelled angrily. He paused for a minute, allowing Paula to talk, which couldn't be heard by the other men. "You know what? Fuck it. I'm tired of all this bullshit. I'm going to handle this shit right motherfucking now. If you want to keep listening to the bullshit, that's on you. I've fucking had it. I've done everything that I know of to get you to talk to me, to work this out, but damn it, enough is enough." Michael then smashed his cell phone down against the cement pavement.

"I'm going to kill that bitch," Michael growled furiously as he stomped hard and fast to his car.

Miguel looked at Sean and shook his head, knowing exactly where Michael was heading. "We can't let him go over there."

Sean looked at Miguel with his eyebrows raised. "And how are we going to stop him from going?"

"Bro, I ain't never seen him this mad. Come on. If we can't stop him, then we're riding," Miguel said and then turned and walked to Michael's car.

Sean sighed and followed suit, muttering to himself, "Man, I hope this is not about to land us in jail."

Michael drove like a bat out of hell out of the parking lot. "Ay, bruh, slow down or you're not going to make it over to Nikki's house," Miguel warned.

"Man, I'm tired of that bitch. I'm going to kill her," Michael told them.

"Nah. We're not going to let you catch no charge. Just say what you need to say and bounce," Sean said from the back seat.

"Man, what did Paula say?" Miguel asked, staring at Michael.

"Nikki messaged her on Facebook and told her that I was still chilling with her. Man, on God, I don't want or deal with that ho, and I know somehow Tammy is behind this bullshit as well. I'm sick of both of them. She said she told her that she didn't want her around Tavon either. She said that's why she should have kept her distance. Man, I swear to God, these hoes are going to feel me." Michael's knuckles were turning white as he gripped the steering wheel tightly.

No one spoke another word as they rode to Nikki's house. When they pulled up, there were two other cars there besides Nikki's and Tammy's. Michael popped open his glove compartment and pulled out his .45.

"Man, what the fuck you about to do with that? I'm not going to jail for no bullshit," Sean cried.

"I don't know who is in there, and I will put a hole in a nigga's head or a bitch if they think I'm going to be touched."

"Man, Michael, come on now," Sean cried, trying to reason with Michael.

Michael hopped out of the car and headed straight toward the house.

Sean looked at Miguel. "This is your fault, man. We could have stayed at the basketball court."

"Man, shut up and come on," Miguel said as he hurriedly ran to the house, watching Michael snatch the front screen door almost off the hinges.

"Bitch, why the fuck you keep playing with my life?" Michael fumed as he walked up on Nikki, who was sitting on a barstool.

She and everyone else saw the gun, and her eyes went wide. "Michael, I didn't."

"Shut the fuck up with that lie you about to tell. You have no goddamn right telling my wife that you don't want her around my son," he cried, kicking a coffee table over and causing the three men who were visiting to move quickly out of his way. "Now I'm going to tell you and you," he said, pointing at Tammy, "to stay the hell out my life. On everything I love, you will regret it if you don't. Let me ask the both of you a question: who made y'all the decision makers of my life? Huh?"

"Michael, she ain't—" Tammy started.

"Bitch, don't you dare say she isn't right for me. I know who I want, and it's not her dumb ass," Michael shouted, pointing at Nikki.

"Michael, please listen. I'm your sister, and I've seen what she is about. She thinks she's all that, and no one should have to hide the fact that they have a child, no matter how he came about. I did this so that my nephew could have a chance at a real family," Tammy explained.

Michael started laughing. "First off, I don't have a sister anymore. You are dead to me. Secondly, Paula is all that and then some. Third, I hid the fact that I had Tavon not because of how Paula would have reacted, but because I was ashamed of what I did that brought him here. I love my son, but I was married. And you know what? After all that you two have done to try to destroy my marriage, Tavon still doesn't have the real family you desired him to have. Oh, and since you want to bring up hiding things, which one of these niggas is here for you?"

"Michael, listen," Tammy started with a pleading glare.

"Nah, I'm done listening. Whoever's fucking you, I hope that he straps up real good with your herpes-carrying ass, and those are facts."

Miguel and Sean were in the background, snickering at the fact that Michael had just exposed Tammy.

"Michael," Tammy yelled.

"Fuck you, bitch, and fuck you too, Nikki." Michael stormed out, leaving an air of heated, feuding voices.

As Michael, Miguel, and Sean got back in the car, Sean started laughing. "Damn, bruh."

Michael threw him a silencing glare as he put his gun back in the glove compartment.

No one said another word until they arrived back at the park where their cars were.

"Man, you good?" Miguel asked.

"Hell no," he answered, "but I will be. It's like when things start working in my favor, shit starts backfiring. Maybe it's my karma. But why am I the only one karma is catching?"

"Paula still doesn't know you know about her and dude?" Miguel asked.

"Naw, and right now I'm not sure I want her to know that I know. I'm just tired, Miguel," Michael sighed. "I'll talk to y'all later, bro."

"All right. If you need to talk, I'm available," Miguel told him.

"I know, and thanks," Michael said.

"You know it, bro."

After Miguel and Sean got out, Michael drove to his mom's house. It was time that she heard what her daughter had been up to. Maybe she could talk some sense into her.

Michael rode around for a while before he headed home. He didn't want his mother or Tavon to be affected by his stormy mood. He drove to the local bar and sat in his car, seething. He wanted to go in and take a drink badly, but after sitting in his car for almost forty-five minutes, he decided against it. Just as he was about to pull off, he heard a light tapping on his window.

"Well, hello again, handsome."

Michael looked up and saw the young lady who worked at Biscuitville staring and smiling down at him. He rolled his window down and smiled. "What's up?"

"Shit, just chilling with my homegirls. You coming in?" she asked, looking at him as if he were a snack.

"Not at the moment. I got some things to take care of, but I might come back," he told her.

"I'm going to be there for a minute, so if you do, maybe we can chill," she replied, leaving no question to her advances.

"That's what's up," Michael said, then rolled up his window.

When he arrived home, he was ready to bear all to his mom, but when he walked in, he was greeted with anger.

"What the hell is wrong with you?" his mother raged. "Going over to that girl's house with a gun that you are not supposed to have, number one, then telling your sister's business, and then saying she was no longer your sister. I didn't raise you like that."

Michael couldn't believe his ears. How was he the bad guy? "No disrespect, Mom, but how can you speak on something when you don't know the facts? See, everybody wants to paint me as the bad guy. I'm always unheard and misunderstood."

"Enlighten me then, son. Explain to me and help me understand why you felt the need to belittle your sister like you did. Y'all are family, and she is your sister. I didn't raise y'all to act like y'all are acting," Sandra cried.

"Did your child tell you that she and Nikki are the reason I'm facing a divorce? They are the ones who told my wife about my son. Then they started harassing her and telling her that she needed to stay away from Tavon just when she was starting to accept him and was on her way to forgiving me." Michael began pacing, and for a few minutes, his vision was blurry.

"All I know is that it's your fault that you are facing a divorce. Had you not cheated on Paula in the first place, you wouldn't be in this predicament. Honesty and loyalty are the vows that you took, and you have to live by those vows, not your sister and not Nikki. You can't blame nobody but yourself."

"What, really, Ma? So you must feel the same way Tammy feels, huh? Paula isn't right for me?" Michael asked with tears building in his eyes.

"I never said that, Michael. It's up to you to fix your marriage, but as long as you are here, you will treat Tammy as you have before—like your sister, dammit," Sharon fussed.

"You right. I will be out of here in an hour. Where is Tavon?"

Sharon glanced at Michael for a minute then sighed, "Nikki got him."

"Nikki? Oh, my God, really? I took him because her house was unsafe for him, and you sent him back?" Michael groaned.

"She is his mother, and I couldn't keep her from taking him. Tavon was just as thrilled to see her and leave with her, but I don't want you to leave. I just want you and Tammy to get through this," Sharon explained.

"If I don't get Paula back, I can be six feet under and she still won't be forgiven. I'll be out as soon as I get my things." Michael turned and walked to his room, packed up the majority of his things, and started carrying them out to his car. As he grabbed the last of them, he walked into the living room where his mother was seated, looking bewildered and lost.

"I love you, Momma," he whispered and left her house.

When Michael got into his car and pulled off, his initial thought was to go get his son and snatch him from Nikki's home again, but he decided against it. He didn't want to get hemmed up over at Nikki's house and the situation to be seen as anything more than what it was, so instead he drove back to the bar to get a drink.

When Michael pulled up and parked, he shut his phone off, as it had been ringing nonstop since he left his mother's house. He was going to call her back, but he just wasn't in the mood to apologize to her for storming out like he did. He knew he had been disrespectful, and it broke his heart, but he wasn't going to let anyone tell him that Tammy was righteous while she meddled in his life. He had already owned up to his wrongdoings that led to the breakdown of his marriage, but who the fuck were Tammy and Nikki to decide his wife wasn't right for him? Nikki was just some ho he'd fucked the first night he met her while visiting Tammy when he had gotten out of prison. He had even used a condom, which broke while he was fucking her.

When Michael walked into the bar, he searched the room to see if he could find a vacant spot in the back. He wasn't in the mood to be bothered by anyone other than the waitress who would take his drink order. Having no such luck, he sat on the far end of the bar and turned his phone back on and texted Paula.

Baby, please believe me when I tell you that I am sorry for all the pain I've caused. We chilled the whole week, and it's not fair that you are allowing those bitches to pull us apart when we were coming back together. Please call me.

He set his phone faceup and ordered a beer and a shot of gin. As he sipped his beer, he kept checking his phone. After about ten minutes he texted her again.

Please call me. We need to talk.

Finally his phone beeped.

Paula: I have nothing more to say.

Michael: But I'm telling you that I haven't been dealing with her like that. I will file for custody or visitation of Tavon, and we won't have to deal with the messiness. I love you.

Paula: I just can't. All I keep thinking about is your deception.

Michael: Damn, baby, I made a mistake. One fucking mistake.

Paula: Yeah, but that one mistake brought forth a handsome, innocent young man whom I would always have to see if I take you back, and I'm not sure that it would be fair to me.

Michael looked at the message and started to get angry. He was tired of apologizing for his mistake when she hadn't even confessed to her own indiscretions.

Michael: Cool. I can't force you to believe me or trust me, but damn it, at least admit to your bullshit.

Paula: What bullshit? I haven't done anything to apologize for.

Michael: Really? You sticking to that lie?

Paula: Lie? Tell me what I did.

Michael shook his head and started laughing, then texted: Forget it. You win.

Paula: No, tell me, because you keep saying I did something. Speak now or forever hold your peace, no pun intended.

Michael turned his phone off without responding and ordered another shot of gin.

"I see you came back," a soft voice said from behind him.

Michael turned and saw the young lady from earlier. "Yeah," he replied.

"Damn, don't look so gloomy. What's wrong? You must have problems at home."

"You could say that," he replied.

"I can help relieve your mind a bit," she told him.

"Oh, really? How do you propose to do that?" Michael asked.

"Shit, let's get out of here and I will show you," she purred.

Michael ordered another shot of gin, and the bartender eyed him harshly. "Are you sure you need another one?"

"I asked for it, didn't I?" Michael responded nonchalantly.

"Bro, this is the last shot," the bartender informed him.

"Just pour it," Michael replied, slamming his money down on the bar.

The bartender slid Michael his drink and watched as he downed it. He then stood up after he finished his drink and started digging in his pocket to get his keys out. He grabbed his cell phone off the bar top and looked at the young lady. "Let's do this."

Michael and the girl walked out to his car, and as soon as he unlocked the doors and they were inside, the girl was all over him. She had her lips all over his neck and her hands digging in his braids. As aroused as the girl was, Michael wasn't feeling it. He closed his eyes, but Paula's face was there.

Wait a minute, he thought. *I'm about to make the same mistake I made when I met Nikki.*

"Hey, yo, stop," he whispered gently to the girl.

She ignored him and slid her hands downward and grabbed his dick. "Don't worry. I won't tell your wife."

Michael pushed her, instantly angered by her statement. "Bitch, I don't know your name and you don't know mine, so don't think I'm one bit concerned about you telling my wife."

"I thought you wanted this," she said, trying to grab Michael's crotch once more.

"And I thought I told you to stop. Get the fuck out of my car."

"Fuck you, nigga. You must be gay," she slung at him.

Michael's face turned up, and he had a look of contempt in his eyes. "Naw, I'm just not that thirsty for a thot-ass bitch who's just looking to get dicked down. My shit A1, but you won't find out. Now like I said before, get the fuck out of my car." Michael leaned over and opened the passenger's side door.

"Loser," she snapped as she stepped out of the car and slammed his door.

Michael laughed, "Boy, what a motherfuckin' day."

As he pulled off, he dialed Miguel's number, and when Miguel answered, he asked him if he could lay his head there for a few nights. Miguel said yes with no hesitation.

Michael lay back on Miguel's couch, and as hard as he tried, he couldn't fall asleep. He kept thinking back to the day he had caught three years in a federal prison for selling and distributing drugs. He only did it because he knew that they needed to make ends meet. Paula had made boss moves and was bringing in the majority of the income, and he felt like less than a man.

He wanted to be the provider of their family and made the wrong decision on how to make that happen. He only had to do a year and a half, but while he was in there, he had received numerous letters from his sister and other individuals about Paula's indiscretions. He had received one picture in particular that broke his heart, and that was Paula all cuddled up with some nigga he had never seen before.

Michael sighed as he buried his head into the cushion of the couch and finally dozed off. It seemed like since he and Paula had separated, sleep was the hardest thing for him to get.

Chapter 16

Michael decided it was time for him to look out for himself. He called out from work, and his first task was to find an apartment. He put in several applications and then called around to check out a few divorce attorneys. He could already tell that Paula wasn't trying to talk to him, and although he felt like giving up, he wouldn't.

Sean had told him that he was a fool to continue to chase a woman who no longer wanted him, but the week that he had spent with Paula proved to him that she still loved him. They both had their faults, but he prayed they could get past it. He called Lee & Associates and then made an appointment with Mr. Aaron Lee for that day. Michael stressed that he needed help immediately and that his employer wouldn't allow him any more time off.

After his appointment was set, he decided to pay his mother a visit. He couldn't go another day leaving things like they were. He drove straight to his mother's and pulled into the driveway and parked. He sat in his car for a moment, then got out. He walked up on the porch and knocked on the door. When she came to the door, he noticed that her eyes were puffy and dark. He didn't like the idea that it was because of him that she looked like she did.

"Hey, Ma, can I come in?" he asked, unsure of her attitude.

"Son, you know you don't have to ask to come into my home," she replied sadly.

Michael walked in and sat down.

"Are you hungry?" she asked.

"No, ma'am. I already ate," he told her.

"Are you okay?" She rubbed his arm.

"Not really. I have so much on my mind and heart, but the one thing I hope I can fix right now is me and you. I never meant to disrespect you. I love you, and you have been nothing but supportive through this whole ordeal. I will never disrespect you again, but I'm asking you to let me and Tammy deal with our situation ourselves and respect whatever happens."

"Son, I love you too, but I can't sit by and let the two most important parts of me separate. You are all I have. I can promise you this, I will let you two work this out, but if y'all don't soon come to some understanding, I will intervene," she vowed.

Michael smiled. "I expect nothing less from you."

"I want you to know that Tammy should've never intervened in your life like she did, and I gave her a piece of my mind also. Paula is good for you, Michael. I know it and Tammy knows it. She is just being Tammy as usual, messy and all. I hope you two can work this out," Sharon said.

"We will see. Tammy has a lot of things to work out within herself," Michael said.

"I wasn't speaking about your situation with Tammy. I'm talking about you and Paula," she corrected him.

Michael smiled. "I'ma fight until there is no fight left in me."

"I expect nothing less," she replied, sitting next to him and grabbing his hand. "It takes a real man to own up to his mistakes and attempt to make amends for them. Do what you feel you must with regard to Paula, and I will support you."

"Thank you, Ma. I have to go now, but I will be back tomorrow," Michael told her.

"Do you got somewhere to stay tonight?"

"Yeah. Miguel is letting me stay at his crib for a few days. I applied for an apartment, so hopefully they will call me soon," Michael answered.

"You know you can come back home. I'on trust that boy."

"Ma. He good people." Michael laughed.

"Yeah, so you say."

Michael stood up and bent down and hugged his mom and kissed her on the cheek. "See you later."

"Be careful out there, and get rid of that damn gun," she told him.

"Momma. You cursing?" he replied in shock.

"Forget all that. You heard what I said."

"I already have." He laughed.

"Boy, I'm not playing with you."

"All right, I will. I promise."

"Okay, now," she said, hugging him again. "Please talk to Tammy."

Michael rolled his eyes upward. "I will, but right now I'm on my way to see a man about possibly saving my marriage."

"Good luck." Sharon smiled, nodding her approval.

Michael walked out, feeling like a great weight was lifted off of him. He hopped in his car and put in his Jeezy CD and turned his music up as "Pretty Diamonds" started playing. He drove over to Church Street and pulled into the parking lot of Lee & Associates and got out, grabbing his wallet and the papers he had been served with. As he walked into the building, he looked around and pushed his alarm on his car.

"May I help you, sir?" a young receptionist asked as Michael approached her desk.

"Yes, ma'am, my name is Michael Harris, and I have an appointment to see Mr. Lee."

"Oh, yes, we have you down for two o'clock. Please have a seat, and I will let Mr. Lee know that you are here," the receptionist replied, smiling while looking Michael up and down.

Michael sat down and grabbed an *Ebony* magazine. His hands were sweaty, and his mind was on everything except the woman who was sitting at her desk checking him out.

After a minute or so, the receptionist called Michael's name, but he was so caught up in his thoughts as he pretended to read the magazine that he didn't hear her.

"Mr. Harris," she repeated.

Michael jumped. "Yes."

"Mr. Lee is ready to see you."

"Thank you," he stammered.

"You're welcome, sir," she purred.

The receptionist stood up and escorted Michael to Mr. Lee's office. When he walked in, she smiled. "Mr. Lee, this is Mr. Harris. He has a two o'clock appointment with you."

"Yes, come on in," Aaron Lee replied as he stood up to greet Michael. The two men shook hands, and the receptionist took her leave. "Have a seat please, Mr. Harris."

Michael sat down, taking in the attorney's appearance. He was a short, stocky older black man. He wore thin gold-framed glasses, which sat on his rounded nose. His head was slightly balding, and the hair that he did have was salt-and-pepper. His goatee matched the color of his hair. His stomach stood out proudly, and his face held a few small moles on it.

"Mr. Harris, let's get down to it. How can I help?"

"Well, Mr. Lee, my wife has filed for a divorce, and I want to contest it," Michael said flatly, handing him the divorce petition.

Mr. Lee looked over all the papers, then back at Michael. "Did you cheat?"

Michael nodded. "Yes, I did, but so did she."

"Do you have proof of her infidelity?" Aaron Lee questioned.

"Well, no, I don't, but I do have pictures of her cuddling up with another man," he admitted.

"Really? Well, I'm not sure if that's going to persuade the judge to side with you. Let me ask you a question. If she cheated, why do you want to save this marriage?" Mr. Lee asked.

"Because I love her," Michael stated.

"Have you two acquired any property together?"

"Yes, we have a house, a truck, a few different accounts held by both of us, but I don't care about any of that. I just want my wife back," Michael explained.

"I understand that, but we have to think on both sides of the coin. If the judge doesn't grant your request, there are assets you two will have to split."

"I just want my wife back," Michael exclaimed. "I don't want this divorce, especially when I'm not the only one to blame here."

"Please elaborate," Aaron replied.

Michael leaned back in his chair and began sharing his story to Mr. Lee. "In 2010, I was incarcerated for possession of cocaine and intent to deliver. I was looking at twenty years in prison, but I pled down to a lesser charge and got three instead. I did a year and a half and got out on parole. I have three months left. Anyway, while I was incarcerated, my wife in the beginning visited me every weekend, but as time went on, it went from every weekend to every other weekend. I would call home at times and wouldn't get an answer. I didn't think much of it at first because my wife was and still is very ambitious. That is, until my sister Tammy began writing me, telling me that my wife was messing around on me. At first I didn't believe her, but then she sent me pictures of my wife with some man I've never seen. I began having suspicions that something was indeed going on. I mean, she was all hugged up with this man. More pictures were sent, and I became resentful and wanted my revenge. When I got out, I spent my first week at home, and my wife acted as if she missed me so much, like that other nigga never existed. I think that I could've handled it if she had told me what she had done, but she chose not to. So I started hanging out with my sister and met her homegirl Nikki. We kind of hit it off, and I ended up sleeping with her. I used protection, but the condom broke, and she ended up pregnant. I couldn't believe my luck. For five years I was able to keep my son a secret, until recently, which is why I'm here," Michael divulged.

"I see. So your hope is that this marriage can be salvaged?" Mr. Lee asked.

Michael shook his head and frowned. "Sir, that's what I've been saying. Listen, since the separation, she has also been seeing another man. I can't say if she has slept with him, but she has been out with him."

"How do you know that?" Mr. Lee asked as he was writing notes on his pad.

"Because I've seen them together. Me and this guy actually had words," Michael told him.

"No disrespect, and this is off the record, but are you sure that you want to stay married to this woman? It seems like the both of you have issues with infidelity," Mr. Lee said as he leaned back in his chair, staring at Michael.

"I'm positive. I love her, and no other woman has ever had a place in my heart. We recently spent time together, and I know the feeling is mutual. We just need help finding our way back to each other. Mr. Lee, listen,

I've thought about this, and yes, we both have made our mistakes, but we can fix them. I'm sure of it," Michael explained.

"I understand that you are no longer living in the home?" Mr. Lee inquired.

"No, she put me out," Michael laughed.

"Well, you know, technically, being that you two are married and your name is on the deed . . . well, let's back up. Did she legally put you out of the home?" Mr. Lee questioned.

"No, sir, she just told me to get out, and I left," Michael replied.

"Okay, so technically that's still your home. I'm not sure if the situation was violent—"

"Oh, no, sir, it wasn't," Michael replied, cutting Mr. Lee off mid-sentence. "But I just don't want to make the situation worse by moving back in."

"Well, I have enough information here to get started. Depending on who the judge is, we may be able to get you what you want. In most cases, the judge will order mediation, especially when there are assets involved. So we will work on this. Is there anything else you like me to do?" Mr. Lee asked.

"No, sir, I just want to save my marriage," Michael replied. "Well, yes, there is something else. Do you handle child custody cases, or can you refer me to a good attorney?"

"I don't handle those types of cases, but let me check around to see who is the best attorney for that." Mr. Lee picked up his phone and waited, then said, "Felicia, can you pull up a list of family law attorneys please? Print them out and bring them in for me."

After the attorney got off the phone, he looked at Michael. "Now we wait for her to bring in those documents. I need you to sign a few documents right here, and if you will agree to my fee to represent you in this case, we will be all set."

Michael looked over the documents. "Thirty-five hundred up front, huh? Hold that thought." Michael took out his cell phone to call his mother. "Hey, you still got that money I gave you to put up a while back?"

"I do. What's going on?" she asked.

"I need some of it for the attorney I'm hiring," he told her.

"Okay. Do you need me to go get it and bring it to you now?"

"No, ma'am. I'm going to write him a check, and I will replace the funds later. Just want to make sure I had it available."

"Now, Michael, you know I'd never take your money," Sharon fussed.

"I know, but I also gave it to you with the expectation that if you needed something, you would use it. That's what I told you to do anyway. But I will call you later when I leave. I love you."

"I love you too, son," Sharon replied and hung up.

Michael looked at Mr. Lee. "Okay, it's a go." After he signed all the documents, he wrote out the check and thanked Mr. Lee. He got his documents and left.

Michael sat in his car for a few moments looking over the family law attorneys, and he sighed, "I'm going to take this one step at a time." He pulled off after deciding to wait on filing for custody of Tavon, at least until after the court situation with Paula was over.

He had a gut feeling that Paula was probably going to feel some kind of way about him contesting the divorce, but when he said, "I do," it was for life with him. He didn't want to be one of those guys who jumped from marriage to marriage. Paula would see things his way sooner or later.

***

A week later, Michael received the text that he knew was coming.

Paula: I mean, really, Michael?

Michael: Really, Michael, what?

Paula: You hired an attorney to fight the divorce?

Michael: You got the paperwork, right? So why you asking me this shit? If you aren't texting me to agree on your own accord to counseling, then we have nothing to talk about.

Paula: That's some petty-ass bullshit.

Michael: Yeah, and it's some childish bullshit for you to continue to listen to rumors.

Paula: Nigga, you're the one who did this.

Michael: Yeah, yeah, yeah. I already heard all that. Come at me with something more recent. Come at me with something valid.

Paula: Just sign the damn papers.

Michael: Yeah, wait on it, my dear wife, lol.

Paula: You're a stupid ass.

Michael: I love you too, baby.

After Michael sent that last text, he started laughing. "She's not going to keep playing games with me."

Chapter 17

Two Weeks Later, Saturday, 7:00 p.m.

Michael had been cooped up in the house for a couple of days, outside of going to work and visiting his mother and Miguel, and Sean felt that it was time for him to get out and mingle.

"Man, we are tired of seeing you mope around here like a lovesick puppy. It's killing our vibe. Let's go chill at the car wash, y'all. It's time we got out a bit," Sean suggested.

"I agree. This is a bachelor's pad, and you tripping. We know you love Paula, but damn, I can bet you she ain't just sitting around pouting over you. Getting out of here sounds good to me," Miguel agreed, looking at Michael.

Michael shrugged. "Hell, you guys are right, and I guess anything is better than sitting around here. But let's do something other than the car wash. We too damn old for that shit."

"Where to then?" Miguel asked.

"Let's go to Blake's Pool Hall," Sean suggested.

"Cool with me. Let me go get changed." Michael got up and walked into the back room. It had been two weeks since he had seen or heard from Paula. He hadn't called her, nor had he texted her. He figured he'd let things play out how they should. He had ignored Aaron Lee's advice about moving back into the house with Paula. He figured that if he did that, she'd definitely retreat and move further away from him. He would just wait and bide his time.

After he was dressed, he walked out and started doing a quick dance shuffle. "Y'all niggas ready to go fuck up a couple of hundred on this pool table?"

"Who? I got about a hundred to fuck up, not hundreds. I'm not planning on losing any money anyway." Sean laughed.

"We'll see what you talking about when we get there, bruh," Miguel spoke up.

"Oh, so now y'all teaming up on me?"

"Hell naw. Both of y'all money coming to me." Miguel laughed.

The three guys headed out the door and to the car. When they got in Sean's Hummer, he pulled out his half-smoked blunt. "Y'all don't mind, do you?"

"Man, you know I'm not supposed to be around that shit," Michael argued.

"Oh, fuck, my bad." He laughed, "I forgot you on parole."

"How the fuck you forget that shit at this time but you remember anytime you feel like I'ma do something that will get you hemmed up, bruh?" Michael fussed.

"Man, you know he a scary-ass nigga." Miguel laughed.

"That's foul, man," Sean replied as he got out of the Hummer to smoke his blunt. After he smoked it, they were on their way.

They pulled up to the pool hall, and it was packed.

"Oh, shit, I forgot this was two-dollar draft night," Michael said.

"Man, you aren't going to get drunk, are you?" Miguel said.

Michael laughed, "Nah, man, I have no desire to get drunk tonight. Hell, the way I'm feeling, I might just fuck something."

"Aw shit, nigga. You not gonna even talk to a woman, much less fuck one. You so stuck on your wife, your player card has been revoked." Miguel laughed.

"And you know once you get that card revoked, it's hard to get it back." Sean laughed as he pointed at Michael.

"Man, fuck that shit y'all talking about. I still got it, and I can prove it," Michael replied.

"Oh, yeah? Put some money on it," Sean said.

"Damn, is everything about money to you?" Michael asked.

"Well, hell, I want in on that bet too," Miguel chimed in.

"So, listen, what you want to bet? Don't be scared, Michael. I got fifty on it myself," Sean said as he pulled his money out.

"Here's my fifty too. So what you going to do, player?" Miguel laughed.

"Man, fuck y'all. Here go my fifty right here," Michael replied.

"Nah, buddy, that's a hundred out if you lose," Miguel corrected him.

"I know that, nigga. Let's just go in. I need to see whose daughter I'm going to fuck tonight," Michael laughed.

The guys walked into the pool hall, and as soon as they hit the threshold, sitting at the bar were Paula, Tasha, and Angela.

Sean started laughing. "Michael, just give me my money now."

Miguel started laughing as well but quickly stopped, knowing that Michael could possibly turn the whole place out. "Michael, man, do you want to go somewhere else?"

"No, I'm good. I'm not going to leave because shawty here," he replied, walking to the far side of the bar.

"Man, I hope he ain't going to show out," Sean whispered.

"If he say he good, he good. Stop being so paranoid," Miguel replied.

The guys sat down and ordered a pitcher of beer. The music boomed, and the chatter of voices filled the room. Michael tried to keep his eyes from venturing over to where Paula was sitting, but from time to time, they drifted off to where she was sitting.

There was a group of females seated next to them, and Sean and Miguel were engaging them in conversation.

Miguel looked at Michael, leaned over, and said, "Michael, this lady here . . ." he started, then looked at the woman. "What's your name again, cutie pie?"

"Pam," she replied.

"Pam here is interested in talking to you. What you got to say about that?" Miguel asked as he sipped his third cup of beer.

Michael once again glanced over to where Paula was, and realizing that she wasn't going to acknowledge his presence, he smiled at Pam. "Hey, cutie, I'm Michael. Why don't you ladies move your party over here? Let's all get acquainted."

"I'm down for that," Pam replied.

The ladies moved their chairs to the table where Michael and the other guys were sitting. As they talked and laughed, Michael almost forgot that his wife was there, until she and her whole group walked over. Michael knew that Paula was being an asshole, and it tickled him that she had even walked over.

"Good evening, Michael. What are you doing here?" she asked.

"Same thing you are. I'm just trying to enjoy myself a bit." He placed his arm around Pam's shoulder. "Oh, how rude of me. This is Pam. Pam, this is Paula."

Paula smiled mischievously and reached out to shake Pam's hand. "Hello, I'm Michael's wife."

Sean choked on his drink, and Miguel patted him on the back. "Um, ladies, let's go over to the bar for a moment," Miguel said, praying that all the ladies would follow suit. Everyone walked away, except for Angela, who was trying to linger.

Tasha walked over and pulled Angela by the arm and said, "Come on, girl, give them their space."

Michael said, staring at Paula with a hint of dangerous amusement flickering in his eyes, "What do you think you are doing, Paula? I'm not bothering you, so why are you over here?"

"Oh, I just felt like fucking up your little party." Paula laughed.

She tried to walk away, but Michael reached out and grabbed her arm. "Well, damn, since you almost succeeded in doing that, then you come on over here and sit down, because truth being told, you're not going anywhere just yet."

Michael was far from playing with Paula, and from the way he was staring, Paula knew he was serious. *Dare I try him?*

As if reading her mind, Michael smiled. "Go ahead and try me please. This is the night. I have nothing else to lose."

"I'm not even trying to do this. Enjoy your night," she said, realizing that her stunt may have been a mistake.

"We both gonna have a great night," Michael growled as he tightened his grip on Paula's arm. "Let's go outside and talk," he suggested, staring at her with the lust in his eyes that Paula knew all too well.

She cleared her throat and glanced nervously around the room and looked back at Michael. "Fine."

Michael turned his cup of beer up, swallowing the last bit, but he didn't release Paula's arm. When he stood, he slid his chair back, and it tumbled over, but he didn't care. He walked out, pulling Paula behind him.

Tasha, Angela, Sean, and Miguel followed them. "Ay, Michael, you need to slow your roll, man," Sean cried, not feeling the attention that Michael was getting.

"I'm telling y'all to go back inside. This has nothing to do with y'all. None of y'all," he growled, looking at Paula's crew as well.

"I'm not going anywhere. You tripping, bruh," Sean retorted.

"Paula, tell these fools that you agreed to come out here with me. See, that's what's wrong now. Everybody got their nose in our shit. Listen, just go back in the pool hall and let us talk."

Tasha looked at Paula. "You good, cuz?"

"Yeah, I'm okay. Y'all can go back in. If I need you guys, I will call you. We are just gonna sit out here and talk," Paula said, giving everyone the assurance that she was outside with Michael because she wanted to be.

After everyone walked back into the pool hall, Michael took Paula around to the side of the building where it was dark and quiet. He then pushed her up against the cold brick exterior and began kissing her. She wrapped her arms around his neck and kissed him back. Michael lifted her dress and snatched her panties off, tossing them to the ground. He pulled his pants and drawers down enough to only expose his ass and free his dick and lifted her up against the wall and slammed his dick inside her warm, wet woman cave. She moaned as Michael tortured her pussy. He was hitting the sides of her walls and biting her on her neck. She had a handful of his hair and was accepting the punishment that Michael was laying down on her. He then let her down and turned her around, pushing her downward. She grabbed her ankles as Michael slid inside from the back, pushing inside her, pounding her insides stroke by stroke.

"That nigga can't fuck you like I can. Have you fucked him? Huh? Answer me," he growled as he slapped her ass.

"Oh, my fucking gosh. Michael, damn, fuck me."

"I asked you a question. You fuck that nigga?" Michael asked again.

He started getting angrier and angrier, knowing that by her not answering, she had given her pussy to another nigga. Michael stopped in mid-stroke. His dick went soft, and as he pulled completely out of her, he pushed her, causing her to hit the ground.

"I should beat your damn ass. You fucked that nigga, didn't you?"

Paula didn't know what to say or what to do. Michael had never reacted to her in such a manner. "Michael, how the hell is it okay for you to create a whole other family while we were married, but I'm wrong for doing me?" Paula stood up and fixed her dress. Her panties were a lost cause. She took her phone out of her bra to text Tasha to let her know she was ready to go, but Michael knocked it out of her hand.

"You think you got all the answers, but you are so off the mark you couldn't even imagine. But you fucked old dude, so I guess you are happy. Was it good? Huh? Was it worth it?" he asked as he walked up on Paula.

She backed up until her back was against the wall once more. She was getting nervous staring into Michael's black eyes. "Michael, move," she whispered, trying to walk around him only to be blocked by him.

"Make me. Move me, Paula," Michael said.

"Please move," Paula whispered again.

Michael wasn't listening, as if he were no longer there.

Paula started trembling from fear. "Michael?"

Michael suddenly began to laugh and stepped aside. "Get the hell out my face."

Paula took off, not waiting to see if he was behind her. Michael fixed his clothes and waited a few moments before walking back around to the front of the pool hall, and just as he'd hoped, Paula was leaving. He walked back into the pool hall and told Miguel and Sean that he was ready to go. Pam was talking to another guy, but Michael didn't give a fuck.

As they were leaving the pool hall, Michael lay back in the back seat and didn't say another word. When they got to Miguel's crib, Michael grabbed a bottle of gin and began drowning his sorrows. He finally felt what Paula must have felt, and it didn't feel good at all.

Chapter 18

The next morning, Michael decided to take his attorney's advice. He was moving back into his and Paula's home whether she liked it or not. If she wanted him out, she was going to have to get the courts involved.

Michael walked into the house reeking of liquor. "I see y'all bitches up in here like everything is cool. Well, until the divorce is granted and final, I still live here. Tasha, you sitting here like you all righteous and shit. Well, you see now that my life is going downhill. Now that my wife hates me, I feel like all secrets must be told. Or have you already told, little cuz?"

"Tell me what? What is he talking about, Tasha?" Paula asked, looking back and forth between the two of them.

"I don't know what he is talking about, Paula," Tasha replied.

"Tell your cousin that it was you who wrote me and told me about her having an affair not even thirty days into my incarceration," Michael laughed.

"Cheated? I never cheated on you period. Tasha, what the fuck is he talking about?" Paula questioned.

Tasha couldn't speak, but Michael could and did. "What you mean you never cheated? I saw pictures of you all cuddled up with a nigga sitting on a couch at Tasha's house."

"You saw what? I have never . . ." Paula's words halted as she remembered meeting Tasha's man friend once, and she insisted they take a picture. Her "two most important people," she had said. "Tasha, why would you lie on me like that? You know that I never cheated on my husband."

Michael sat down on the couch, stone-faced, trying to piece together what was taking place. Paula couldn't be innocent, because if she was, that meant that he was the cause of the breakdown of his marriage.

Tasha began to cry. "You two weren't right for each other. When Angela came to me with the idea to split you two up, I said yes, but I only did it to help you."

"Help me? You destroyed my marriage. Why? You hated the thought of us being together that much?" Paula fumed.

Michael laughed, "Naw, she wanted to fuck me too."

Tasha looked at Paula, then Michael. "Shut your mouth."

"Nooo, if I'm losing my wife, I might as well reveal more truths."

"You're drunk. Paula, don't listen to him," Tasha whispered.

Paula growled through gritted teeth while keeping her eyes locked on Michael, "What truths?"

Tasha began stumbling over her words. "Girl, that nigga drunk. Don't listen to him."

"Drunk I am, but I'm not going to lie on my dick. I fucked you, and you got pregnant and had your reliable, kindhearted, dumbass, foolish-ass cousin accompany you to abort a baby I paid for, bitch. But I'm a dirty nigga." He laughed nastily as he walked into the back bedroom.

Tasha sat in silence as her mouth opened, forming the words that wouldn't come out.

"Tasha, is that true? You fucked the one nigga you knew I loved and the very nigga you warned me about?" Paula questioned.

"You don't understand," Tasha began.

"No, suddenly I understand perfectly fine. Get the fuck out of my house. I can't believe this. Oh, my God," Paula cried, holding her stomach. She felt like she was about to throw up.

"Paula, wait. I can't let things happen like this. Tammy came to me and asked me to help her get you out of Michael's life. I was in love with him and was furious that he went after you and married you. I thought I was a better fit for him, but then you—"

"Shut the fuck up, Tasha. I don't want to hear this bullshit." Paula couldn't believe that Tasha was standing in front of her, confessing that she had been in love with her husband and had been in cahoots with Tammy. "Of all people I thought I could trust. Nooo, not you, Tash. Dammit."

Paula grabbed her keys and walked out with Tasha racing behind her. "We didn't put a gun to his head, Paula. He strayed on his own."

"Yeah, you didn't put a gun to his head, but you handed him a loaded muthafuckin' gun shooting blanks. Tasha, you told my husband that I was unfaithful to him. And it was a lie. Even went so far as to show him innocent pictures that were taken at your crib with your nigga."

"Paula, stop and talk to me please," Tasha cried, throwing her hands up in despair.

Paula placed her keys into the keyhole to unlock her car door and turned to face Tasha. "You know, all those days I confided in you, you were deliberately pushing me away from Michael all because you wanted to fuck my husband. You've always wanted what I had. Even when my mother died, you just had to get attention. You were a leech then and now. Well, I guess we got more in common than DNA. You're pathetic, Tasha. You couldn't get your own man, so you decided to share mine. What's sad, though, is that even after you fucked him, he still chose me."

Paula unlocked her door, slammed it, and spun off, throwing gravel in Tasha's direction. She couldn't think straight and had nowhere to go to vent. She had left Michael's and Tasha's trifling asses at her house, and they were probably fucking on her suede couch. Paula screamed loudly and pressed the pedal to the metal and sped off down 85 South: destination, South Carolina, her only safe haven.

Michael and Tasha

When Paula pulled off, a drunken Michael ran out of the house, stumbling down the steps. "You let her leave?"

"How the fuck was I supposed to stop her?" Tasha answered angrily.

"You happy now? Y'all got what the hell you wanted, damn meddling assholes. My marriage is apparently fucking over, and my life is over. I just lost everything I ever loved," Michael cried.

"You're blaming me? You bitch-ass nigga, you're the one who walked in here and started confessing your sins to her. It's your own damn fault," Tasha yelled.

Michael walked back to the porch and sat down on the top step. He dropped his head and his shoulders shook.

"Is this nigga crying?" Tasha whispered to herself, looking around to make sure no one was watching. She walked over and sat down next to Michael. "You want me to suck your dick?"

Michael looked up and frowned. "Bitch, I wouldn't let you eat my asshole clean after I took a shit much less suck my dick. I hate you muthafuckas. All of you. You know, I caught the last part of what she said to you, and she had a few things right. I would have never chosen you over Paula. To be honest, you were a lousy fuck, and your pussy was raunchy. Get the hell off of my porch."

"Michael, I didn't force you to do shit with yo' dick. You did it all freely. Remember that," Tasha replied angrily as she stood up and walked down the steps to her car. She got in and pulled off.

"It ain't over by a long shot," Michael swore.

Seems like no one can be trusted these days. Betrayal from my husband and my cousin. Fuck them all. I will never forget this shit.
—Paula Smith Harris

Man, I think I really fucking lost my wife for sure. My drunk ass just handed her a smoking gun to hand over to the damn judge. I'm still gonna fight for my marriage no matter how fucked up I am.
—Michael Harris

I can't believe Michael just spilled the tea about me and him. Paula is sure to never forgive me, but I honestly love my cousin, and no matter what, I will earn her trust back . . . but damn, the dick was good.
—Tasha Smith

Chapter 19

It's a Wrap

Three hours after hitting the highway, Paula pulled into the parking lot of Tripp's studio. He had given her a key to his house, but she didn't want to go there without informing him that she was in town.

Paula walked into Tripp's office and sat at his desk and waited for him to come in. She loved the way his office was laid out and the decor of it as well. The carpet was a beautiful shade of burgundy. He had a three-piece black and burgundy sectional with matching plush armchairs, and a crystal bar with matching end tables throughout the office. There were expensive paintings and beautiful mirrors that cascaded the walls. The adjoining room was his executive meeting room, and there was a long cherry-oak table that was designed to seat fourteen people with a throne leather armchair at the head of the table. Paula knew it was Tripp's chair, and she smiled as she walked over to it and sat down in it. She looked up at the crystal chandelier that hung from the ceiling. She definitely felt at home.

She walked around the office, wondering where Tripp could possibly be. He wasn't anywhere in sight, and she was ready to get something to eat. She decided to seek him out, but as she sauntered down the hallway, she heard loud voices coming from a small room toward the back room. She tiptoed toward the door, which was cracked open, and she covered her mouth to stifle her gasp.

Tripp was standing over a man's body, wiping what appeared to be blood from his knuckles. The man wasn't moving, and Paula didn't know if he was dead or alive, and she wasn't going to stay around to find out. She walked slowly backward in hopes that she wasn't seen, and as soon as she felt she was far enough away safely, she ran down the hall, grabbed her purse, and rushed out of the building.

She sat in her car for a few minutes, allowing her nerves to calm down. She couldn't get out of her mind the sight of Tripp standing there with blood dripping from his hands and whoever the man was lying on the floor. She wondered what he had done. She decided that she wasn't going back to North Carolina, and she wasn't going to spend any money for a hotel. She decided to go to Tripp's apartment and call him but changed her mind quickly. She grabbed her cell phone and dialed Tripp's number.

"Hey, babe, what's going on?" he asked in a calm voice, which kind of disturbed Paula.

"I'm in town and I'm at your office, but I don't see your car," she lied. "Are you here?"

"Yeah, but I'm kind of busy. Go on to the apartment, and I will be there in about an hour," he told her.

"Okay," she replied quietly.

Paula laid her head on the steering wheel, trying to decipher where she had fucked up to have so much drama piling up in her life all at once. She wanted to crank her car and drive a little bit farther, but she didn't have a clue where she wanted to go, and she didn't have the energy to drive back to North Carolina. She scrolled through her phone and ran across the number of her cousin

Carla, who stayed right on the edge of South Carolina and Tennessee. She hadn't seen her in ages. She dialed Carla's number, and when she finally picked up, Paula immediately began to talk. "Cuz, it's Paula."

"Paula who?"

"Don't play, girl."

"Who playing? Shit, we ain't heard from you in so long." Carla laughed. "What's going on?"

Paula explained her situation to Carla, who was amped for action. "Bitch, come get me. I'm going to come and chill with you for a couple of days, but you know what it is, right?"

Paula knew that Carla was a no-nonsense type of chick and didn't mind getting her hands dirty if need be.

Paula pulled out of Tripp's studio's parking lot and drove another forty-five minutes to Carla's house. When she arrived, Carla was sitting on the porch looking rough. Her hair was in braids that looked like they were two weeks overdue for a touch-up. She had on a T-shirt that looked like it was two sizes too big and jogging shorts with flip-flops.

"Hey, cuz," Carla yelled as Paula got out of her truck.

"What's up, Big C?" Paula said as she walked up and hugged Carla. "Where is Auntie Lisha?"

"She in the house cooking. Go on in the house and speak to her, and then we can sit down, and you can tell me what the hell is going on," Carla said as she pulled on the Black & Mild she was holding.

"All right. I'll be right back," Paula said as she walked into the house. When the creaky screen door slammed behind her, Paula almost jumped out of her skin.

"Wow, everything is almost the same as it was when I was a little girl," Paula whispered as she gazed upon the old furniture that was still seemingly in good condition. The house smelled of fresh collard greens and fried chicken cooking. The old clock that hung on the wall was still fifteen minutes faster than any other clock in the house. The hardwood floors creaked more than they ever did from what Paula remembered, and the walls were somewhat dingy from age.

When Paula walked into the kitchen, her aunt Lisha was standing in front of the table, shucking corn. "Hey, Auntie," Paula cried as she walked over to give her a hug.

Her aunt looked up and gasped, "Oh, my God." She dropped the corn and embraced the young girl she hadn't seen in ages. When she released her, she took a good look at her. "Paula, you are looking just like your daddy."

Paula smiled and closed her eyes as she hugged her aunt for a second time. She had to admit she missed her family.

"What brings you to Tennessee?" her aunt asked.

"I just felt like I needed to get away from North Carolina for a while. I hope you don't mind if I crash here for a few days," Paula said, picking the crust off a piece of chicken that her aunt had just taken out of the fryer.

"Now you know I don't mind," she replied, popping Paula's hand.

Paula laughed and rubbed her hand.

"You know I ain't never liked y'all putting y'all nasty hands in my food. That's your piece." Lisha laughed.

"Do you need any help with anything?" Paula asked.

"No, I got this. Did you bring that handsome husband of yours?"

Paula's eyes shifted to the left, then back up at her aunt. "No, ma'am. I think that may be over."

"Sounds like you aren't sure. Make sure that whatever you do, it's what you really want." Lisha flipped the chicken that was left in the fryer.

"So much has happened, and I'm not sure it can be fixed." Paula sighed, picking the chicken skin again and, for a second time, having her hand popped by her aunt. Paula flinched and laughed, "It's habit."

"I know it is, but listen, baby girl, nothing is unforgivable. If it's in your heart to do so, do it. The last thing you want is to live the rest of your life with regret."

"You're right," Paula replied. Paula kissed her aunt on the cheek and walked back outside with Carla.

She told Carla about her marriage and the betrayal of her husband and her cousin. Carla shook her head and slid her flip-flops off her feet. "I used to tell you that damn Tasha wasn't right. She wanted your life. Hell, all the money you were left from your mom and Uncle Jack, you could've left North Carolina."

"And you know what? I've still got the majority of that money in my savings account. I didn't have any need for it because I obtained a good job, and the money I made from that has been plentiful," Paula shared with her cousin.

"I can believe that. You have always been responsible," Carla replied.

"Just not with my life," Paula cried.

"What you mean?"

"I mean I left my husband only to jump into bed with the next man. I knew it was a mistake, but I was fucking hurt. I had just found out that my husband had a kid with another woman and that he had been cheating for damn near five years. I fucked this nigga I met in South Carolina at the Crown Vic event."

"Oh, shit. My homegirl is in that club chapter. I was supposed to have gone, but Momma needed me here." Carla said, "So who was this dude?"

"Tripp Moore," Paula answered.

Carla stared at Paula in shock. "The owner of the Crown Vic MC's club?"

"I guess," Paula said, though she hadn't known that before.

"Paula, please tell me that you aren't literally involved with him."

"Well, I was, but I can't see him anymore. Not after what I just saw," Paula said.

"I hope you're finished. He is a very bad guy. I mean, I've heard stories about him from my homegirl. They say that he is a kindhearted man with a demon spirit. If you fuck him over, everybody will pay."

Carla told Paula what she knew about Tripp Moore. He was a living icon in the streets of South Carolina. He was known for smuggling dope, guns, and prostitutes abroad. He didn't move anything less than a kilo. He wasn't a street hustler making his money from corner to corner. He was the real deal, with people making the deliveries for him. But Tripp was different from your average criminal. He took his hard-earned illegal cash and invested it into various businesses. Once he'd started making the big dollars, he left the drug game alone, although here and there he would set up plays for his main partner to grab dope and cash.

Even though Tripp was out of the game, his name still held weight in the streets, and niggas knew that if Tripp's money or businesses were ever in jeopardy and he had to get involved to get his shit fixed, there was trouble coming. He was well respected in the business world and the streets. He was a prominent street king.

"All right, y'all, dinner is ready," Lisha yelled from inside the house.

"Come on, girl. You know she don't like for us to hold dinner up." Carla laughed.

"Nothing has changed." Paula laughed, but deep inside she felt worse than she had initially felt. What if Tripp decided to come after her? Could he find out that she was there in his office when he did whatever he did to the man whose body he was standing over? "What a way to go, Paula," she whispered, scolding herself.

She sat down at the table with her family, and they ate dinner. Afterward, while Paula and Carla cleaned up the kitchen, Lisha gathered a few old pictures. After they were done, they all sat in the front room, looking through the photo albums. Paula saw one picture that she had to have. It was one of her mother, pregnant with her, sitting on her father's lap.

"I've got to have this picture. Auntie, do you think I can take a few of these tomorrow and get them copied?"

"That will be fine with me," Lisha replied.

Paula and Carla continued to look through the pictures, and Paula started laughing. "Oh, my God. Look at us."

Carla looked and pushed Paula, laughing, "Child, we look rough."

It was a picture of them standing under an apple tree. Paula had on a red and blue striped shirt with a pair of dirty jeans and no shoes, and Carla had on a pair of tan shorts with a gray tank top.

"Girl, what were we thinking?" Paula laughed.

Suddenly the front door swung open. "Missy, come and give me a hug. Lisha told me you were here, and dang it, she wasn't lying."

"Uncle Stan. Oh, my God." Paula laughed as she stood up and walked over to him and gave him a hug.

"You ain't missed no meals, have you? Just all grown up," he said. "Where the food at, Lisha? I smell it."

"You ain't ate yet, fool?" Lisha asked, walking into the kitchen to fix him a plate.

"Naw. Oh, John and David are outside. They will be in here in a few," Stan replied.

Carla and Paula walked outside, leaving the photo album on the couch.

The night turned out to be one of the best nights Paula had experienced in a long time. They drank a few drinks and danced.

"Watch my feet. Y'all can't move like this, huh?" her uncle Stan asked as he shuffled his feet to Lebrado's "Fire."

"Shit, I think I got you, Unc," Paula laughed as she jumped down and started shuffling her feet.

"Awww, shit now. It's a close call, Unc." Carla laughed.

"Chile, she ain't got nothing on this. Watch me move," he announced as he dropped down to the ground in a James Brown–style split.

Paula laughed, "Okay, okay, you got me. But what can you do with this?" Paula spun and dropped down slow and got back up and spun around once more.

"Oh, hell, I can't do nothing with it. My goddamn back done went out on me. Somebody help me up," Stan groaned.

"See, that's what your old ass gets for trying to act young. Get up on this porch and sit down somewhere." Lisha laughed as she pulled on Stan's arm to help him get up.

When Paula finally lay down for the night and went to sleep, all the thoughts that plagued her mind had disappeared.

Chapter 20

Tasha hadn't heard from Paula in almost one week. She had called and texted her repeatedly but got no response at all. She had called Michael's phone a few times, but he was ignoring her also. When she called Tripp, she was expecting to be ignored by him as well but was surprised to find that she was wrong.

"Hey, Tripp, this is Tasha. Is Paula down there with you by any chance?"

"No. She was supposed to have met me at my house last week, and she wasn't there when I got there. What's going on? Is she okay?"

"I hope so. Listen, we had a slight disagreement, and she ran off. I haven't heard from her since."

"Where the hell is she?"

"I wish I knew. If you hear from her, can you please ask her to call me? Or can you just text me and let me know she is there?" Tasha asked.

"Yeah, and you do the same. Tasha, if I find out that you or anyone has hurt her, you will answer to me."

Tasha cringed at the sound of his voice. She felt the sting of his words even though he was calm when he said them.

When she hung up, she called Angela. Angela didn't answer the phone, and Tasha decided to take a drive over there, hoping that Paula was there. She was sadly disappointed when she arrived. Angela informed her that she hadn't talked to or seen Paula either.

"Where the hell can she be?" Tasha sighed.

Tripp hung up from talking with Tasha and started pacing. "Where the hell could she be?" He grabbed his phone and dialed her number and was immediately greeted by her voicemail. He slung his phone against the wall. He walked out of his office and down the hall, where Shock was making a few beats.

"Ay, man, I need you to get on the phone with your people and see if they can put some work in for me. This girl either somewhere hurt or she playing games, which is gonna get her hurt."

"I'm on it, Tripp."

"Cool."

Paula spent ten days with her Tennessee family, and when she left, Carla was in the passenger's seat beside her. Paula was glad that she had decided to go with her. She needed someone by her side who wasn't trying to gain anything from her or after her husband.

"Damn, cuz, I'm so glad you decided to ride with me. Man, I really enjoyed my stay," Paula admitted as they rode down 85 North.

"Hell, I need to get away just as much as you needed me to come with you. Shit, I had lost my identity. I know you can girlie me up." Carla laughed.

"You're perfect just as you are," Paula replied.

Carla gave Paula that "I know you're lying" stare and playfully rolled her eyes. "Bitch, I know you lying. Hell, my feet can cut through steel." Carla laughed.

Paula laughed and shook her head. "Yeah, I must say those feet are tough."

"But on the real, I want one of those bitches to act up while I'm there. I'm given 'em that ol' Tenn-to-the-C ass whooping for real," Carla said as she leaned back in her seat.

Carla was asleep within ten minutes, and Paula smiled as Carla began snoring. She turned the radio up and headed home. Paula sighed as she passed the WELCOME TO NORTH CAROLINA sign. She instantly felt ill. She hated the thought of returning to Burlington, but she had to face all those who had caused her so much grief.

Paula had made the decision to stay at the Hyatt Suites before she left Tennessee and had already made her reservations and paid for a week in advance. She didn't know if Michael was still at the house, and even if he wasn't, she didn't want Tasha or Tripp to pull up on her. She was going to grab a tray from Cook Out for herself and Carla and then go to the room and relax.

Three hours after passing the welcome sign, Paula was pulling up to the hotel. She had gotten a two-bedroom suite and was ready to get a bath, eat, and go to sleep. She figured she would go to Angela's the following day.

Because they went to sleep early, Paula and Carla were up early. Paula accessed her DVR through the app to watch the recorded *Love & Hip Hop Atlanta* episodes that she had missed.

"I wished my hair fell across my shoulders like that," Carla said as she watched Rasheeda swinging hers.

"Girl, that's probably all weave, and if it's not, them hoes got the money it takes to make their shit swing," Paula commented.

As they continued to watch the show, Carla laughed, "Those some dumb-ass hoes. They make themselves look desperate for a man."

Paula laughed. "So, Carla, you want me to wash your hair and flat iron it? I can get it just like those women on TV. I got some great products."

"Um, cuz, you got dreads. What you need with flat irons?" Carla asked.

"I do hair here and there. Come on. Let's do this," Paula replied as she jumped up to go get hair supplies.

"Kinda like the old days when we used to play dress-up," Carla reminded her.

"Hell yes. I miss those days."

An hour later Paula had Carla's hair laid. She kept flipping it and moving her head to the left and right. "Girl, you did that," Carla admitted.

"I know I did. Now come on. I've got a cute-ass denim outfit you can put on. We're about to get dressed and ride out," Paula said.

After they got dressed and ate breakfast, they headed out to go visit Angela. When they pulled up in Angela's yard, Paula sat in the car for a minute. She wasn't sure if she wanted to see Angela, but she had been calling her for days, and she wanted to at least ease her mind and let her know that she was okay. She hoped she wouldn't bring up Tasha, because she didn't want to discuss her and definitely didn't want to see her.

When she got out of the car and walked up to Angela's porch, the door flew open. "Bitch, where the hell have you been? I've been worried sick," Angela cried.

"I went to spend some time with my dad's family for a while. Angela, I'd like you to meet my cousin Carla. Carla, this is my best friend, Angela."

As they walked into the house, Angela looked at Carla's butt and nodded. "Yep, I see the family resemblance."

Paula hit Angela on the arm and started laughing. "You so damn crazy."

They all sat down and started laughing and talking. Paula was happy that Tasha's name wasn't brought up.

"Ay, let's hit the club tonight," Paula suggested.

"I'm all for it," Angela agreed.

"I am too," Carla chimed in.

"Hell, I've got to go to work in the morning, but I can stand one night of fun. But listen, I don't want to go to any club here. Let's hit up Raleigh."

"Shit, that sounds good to me. Let me go get my clothes together, and I'ma ride with y'all back to your house," Angela said as she stood up.

"I'm not at the house. I'm staying at a hotel right now," Paula told her.

"You're staying where?" Angela asked.

"At the Hyatt. Before I went to Tennessee, Michael had his attorney draw up paperwork saying that until the divorce and a judgment, he is entitled to live there. And I honestly don't want to be around him. So he can have it," Paula explained.

"But your mother left you that house. How the fuck is Michael forcing himself in there?"

"It's marital property even though it's rightfully mine. When we got married, it became ours," Paula replied.

"That's fucked up, but you know damn well you don't have to stay in a hotel. You always got a place to lay your head here," Angela told her.

"I know, but I just didn't want to really be anywhere that Michael or anyone else could find me. I'm good, girl. Go on and get your stuff so we can go," Paula said with a smile.

Angela packed a small bag, and they headed back to the hotel. When they walked in, Paula walked to the cabinet and yelled lightly, "Dammit, I ain't got not one bit of liquor."

"We got to go get some, bitch. I need some blunts anyway," Angela said.

"Shit, you smoke?" Carla asked.

"My weed is my medicine. I can't see without it," Angela laughed.

"Bitch, where you at? I can't see either," Carla said with her eyes closed, feeling around as if she couldn't see.

"Both of y'all need rehab." Paula laughed.

"Paula, you know what, maybe if you hit a blunt every now and then, you'd forget your troubles. Weed is a very good stress reliever," Angela told her.

"I guess. But I'm good. I don't need to smoke that shit. Are y'all riding to the store with me?"

"I'm going to chill here," Carla replied.

"I'ma ride because I got to get a few things myself," Angela replied.

Paula walked to the door and turned and looked at Carla. "You sure you don't want to ride?"

"I'm good here," Carla said.

"Okay, I will be back shortly then."

Paula and Angela headed out to the ABC store to pick up a bottle of Patrón tequila while Carla stayed back to get dressed.

"So you are really going through with the divorce?" Angela asked as they drove down Maple Avenue.

"Girl, yes. I'm so over all the damn drama and bullshit that I've had to deal with since being married to Michael. It's time for me to move on," Paula exclaimed.

"You're going to kick it with Tripp instead?" Angela continued to pry.

"Naw. I'ma tell you why later. But I don't have time in my life for the bullshit with him either," Paula replied.

"Damn, you two seemed so perfect together though. I mean, I know I acted like a bitch around him, but I mean, he seemed cool."

"Yeah, you just don't know the half. The last few weeks have been hell with me and men. I'd rather be alone than deal with them. But listen, let's change the subject, because this one is making me sick."

"Okay. I feel you," Angela said.

They pulled up to the liquor store and got out. As they were walking down the aisle, they ran smack dab into the path of Nikki and Tammy.

"Umph, girl, look at this shit." Nikki laughed.

"I know this bitch ain't referring to me. She'd better just move on. I swear she can get it today." Paula laughed.

"Bougie-ass heffa couldn't even hold on to her damn husband. I got him, boo." Nikki laughed.

Paula attempted to rush her, but Angela restrained her. "Not here, baby girl."

Paula turned and grabbed the two bottles that she was going to buy, and after paying for them, she got into her car and waited for Nikki and Tammy to come out. Angela looked at her, wondering what she was about to do. Paula didn't say a word, but her knee was jumping like crazy.

"Paula, what are you up to?"

"I'ma whoop this ho's ass. I've been itching to do it, and today is the day," Paula replied, not looking at Angela.

Angela's eyes grew wide as she watched Paula, who was barely blinking. Her chest was rising and falling hard. "Um, Paula, maybe you should calm down a bit."

"Here they come," Paula exclaimed as she turned her car on.

Nikki and Tammy walked out laughing until they saw Paula still sitting there. Paula smiled and waved. Nikki paused a bit, but after Tammy pushed her a few times, she got in her car. When she was pulling out, Paula pulled up quickly on her bumper. Angela put her seat belt on and prayed that Paula didn't kill them all. Nikki pulled out of the lot fast with her tires screeching loudly, and Paula followed suit. Every road that Nikki turned down, Paula turned down too, getting as close to her bumper as she could get.

"Yeah, I'm still here, bitch. Pull the fuck over," Paula yelled out the window.

Finally, Nikki pulled over on a dirt road with a dead end. When they hopped out, she started yelling, "You trying to kill all of us over a nigga? Bitch, you crazier than I thought," Nikki yelled.

"Paula, just take your ass on home now," Tammy yelled, jumping out of the car as well.

"She too damn worried about me to go home, but I'm ready for your ass, Paula," Nikki yelled.

Paula laughed, disgusted. "Bitch, you so irrelevant to my life. You got the whole nigga and a seed. Grow yo' family tree, bitch. I don't want his ass period, but I promise you that the next time you think about approaching me, you're gonna think twice, because I'm about to roll yo' bougie ass."

And with that, Paula dived at Nikki, knocking her back on the ground. As she drove her fist repeatedly into Nikki's face, Tammy rushed forward and grabbed Paula by her dreads and began pulling her off of Nikki, which then caused Angela to join in.

Angela pulled Tammy away from Paula and slung her to the ground and stood over her with her finger in Tammy's face. "Don't put your fucking hands on her, bitch. This is between her and Nikki. I promise I will let her knock your motherfucking ass out if you even attempt to jump in again," Angela growled.

Tammy slid back away from Angela but didn't attempt to intervene in the fight again. Paula regained her composure and dived at Nikki once again. She punched her a few more times and stood up.

"Go find my husband and tell him to man up on yo' ghetto ass, move out of my house and into yours, give me the divorce I've been begging him to give me, and leave me alone, because I don't want his ass no more."

Nikki didn't say a word as she wiped her face with her shirt, wincing as pain swept through her.

Paula and Angela jumped in the car and drove off. As they pulled up to the hotel, Angela's phone began to ring, and she told Paula that she would be in right behind her. Paula hoped it wasn't Tasha, and if it was, she hoped Angela wouldn't tell her where she was. She didn't want to see her ass period.

Paula walked into the room, laughing and talking junk.

"What the hell is wrong with your clothes and hair?" Carla asked angrily once Paula walked in and sat down.

"Bitch, those hoes just tried to jump me. Michael's baby momma and his fucking sister."

"Those bitches did what? Oh, hell naw. Now we need to take a ride. Angela should've spanked both their asses for trying that shit."

Carla stomped to the closet and pulled out an aluminum bat and a small torch she'd brought with her. "Carla, what the fuck you gonna do with that?" Paula questioned.

"I'ma fuck me a ho up. I hit 'em and you fry 'em."

"Oh, hell naw, girl. You done lost yo' mind." Paula laughed.

"Well, fuck it. You hit 'em and I fry 'em. Either way, they gon' regret fucking with you."

"Noooo, baby girl, it's handled. I beat the brakes off that trick," Paula told her.

"That's all well and good, but I didn't do anything, and our motto since childhood when you stayed around us is, 'You fuck with one, you fuck with all.' I ain't had my turn." Carla smiled and dropped the bat. "I got something even better."

When Carla ran to her bedroom, Paula sat down on the couch, shaking her head, eyes glued to Carla's bedroom door. When she came out, she had some black tape and brass knuckles. "I'ma knock a bitch out old-school style."

"Carla, chill. It's all good."

"Bitch, you sure? Because damn, I'm ready," Carla replied, dancing around.

"Yeah, I'm sure, Rocky," Paula laughed.

Angela walked in a few minutes later with the bag holding the alcohol and two blunts. She and Carla were going to blaze up before they headed out.

"Bitch, why the fuck didn't y'all come and scoop me up so I could get my hands dirty today?" Carla asked as Angela set the drinks on the table.

"Hell, Paula didn't need any help. Now when the other bitch tried to—" Angela started but was interrupted by Carla.

"Other bitch? So it was two on one?" Carla asked, jumping up and down and amping herself up all over again.

"Yeah, but I handled her. Girl, look at you looking all sexy. You look good mad."

"Oh, my God. I know you ain't cracking on my cousin." Paula laughed.

"You rather I crack on you? You jealous?" Angela teased.

"Go on, do you, but I don't think Carla is going for that shit." Paula laughed as she walked over to the cabinet and pulled out the plastic wineglasses she had gotten at Walmart the day before.

Carla and Angela laughed and talked while Paula poured the drinks. She was just glad that Carla's mind was off Nikki and Tammy even though hers wasn't. She was low-key angry because Michael had to have told that bitch that she had left town. How else would she have known?

"Ay, come on now, y'all. Let's start drinking so we can get the hell out of here," Paula said as she handed out the glasses of liquor. After a few shots and Carla and Angela smoked their blunt, they headed out.

They arrived at the club, and the three ladies had a wonderful time. Paula danced with Angela and Carla and noticed that a few guys were checking her out, but the daring glances she threw them when they would have approached her kept them at bay. She wasn't there to find, chat with, mingle with, nor build with a nigga. She was there to have fun with her girls before her court hearing.

Chapter 21

The Next Morning

Paula got up and got dressed for court. She didn't want to disturb Carla, especially after the night they had just had. She was amazed at how well Carla and Angela got along. She actually retired before they did. She thought Angela would've spent the night, as late as it had gotten, but when she didn't see her on the couch, she figured Angela had gone on home.

While Paula was brushing her teeth, she heard a low murmuring coming from the other bedroom. She frowned and turned the water off and squinted, as if doing that would help her hear more clearly. She heard laughing and two familiar voices. She rinsed her mouth and dried her hands and walked out of the bathroom and knocked on the bedroom door. She burst out laughing when Angela opened the door.

"What the fuck is this?" Paula laughed.

Carla spoke up first. "Shit, cuz, we just chilled and fell asleep. Nothing more or less."

"Well, not yet." Angela laughed, smacking Carla across the ass.

Paula walked away stunned but amused. "Are you ready to go, Angela? I mean, you are still going with me, right?" Paula asked.

"You know I am. I wouldn't be anywhere else. I just got to go home and take a shower and get dressed," Angela replied.

"All right, well, take my truck and go on and do what you got to do, and then come pick me up," Paula told her.

"All right. Carla, are you going?" Angela asked as she sat down to put her shoes on.

"No, I'm gonna chill here. I will go if Paula wants me to though," Carla answered.

"Naw, you good. I don't think this is going to take too long. At least I hope not. All she needs to say is, 'Divorce granted,' and I'm out of there. Plus, I'ma go to work afterward."

"Okay, well, I'm gonna just chill. I might go to the pool," Carla said.

"Hell, I don't have to work, so I might come back and go to the pool with you," Angela said as she grabbed her coat. "Be back in a few."

When Angela walked out, Paula looked at Carla. "Y'all muthafuckas ain't slick, cuz, but Angela is a cool chick."

"I don't know what you mean," Carla denied as she walked back to her room.

"Yeah, right, you don't know. Just don't do shit in my room or on this hotel couch, bitch." Paula laughed.

An hour later, Angela was back, and she and Paula headed to the courthouse. Neither one of them spoke, but Angela couldn't help but wonder where Tasha was and why she wasn't accompanying them to Paula's hearing.

When they pulled up, Paula sat in the car, vigorously rubbing her hands together.

"You good, fam?" Angela asked.

Paula didn't say a word, but when she looked over at Angela, Angela felt her pain. She reached over and hugged her friend. When she released her, Paula was wiping at her eyes and smiling. "I'm good, you ready?"

Angela smiled. "Are you ready? That's the question."

"I am," Paula replied as she got out of the car.

The Hearing

Michael Harris sat in the courtroom across from his wife, Paula Smith Harris, waiting for the judge to decide if he was going to be granted mediation and marriage counseling. He was going to fight for his marriage, and he didn't care what anybody thought about it. He had replayed his and her relationship over and over again, and he could admit that, yes, he had his faults, but so did Paula.

"All rise for the Honorable Judge Karen Duluth," the bailiff ordered.

The judge walked in and took her seat, and once the courtroom attendants sat back down, Michael glanced over at his wife. She was just as beautiful as the day he first met her. He remembered that she had on the light blue dress that fit her perfectly. Her dreads were short and curly, and her eyes glimmered like diamonds. She had caught his eye as soon as she walked in the building. He escorted her and her cousin to their table and took the chance of asking her to dance. He held his breath waiting for her answer, and the moment she said yes, he let go of his breath and his heart. He fell instantly in love.

Now, thirteen years later, he might just lose his heart. He loved his wife, and yes, he had fucked up, but he didn't feel that he should lose everything he had with Paula.

The judge began to speak. "In reading both parties' affidavits, I'm riddled with more questions and concerns. It seems that neither party has stayed firm on the 'better or worse' clause of their marriage."

Michael glanced over at Paula and saw the anger in her demeanor. She looked over at him with a questioning stare, then back at the judge. She looked like she wanted to say something, but her attorney, who Michael thought was too sexy to be an attorney, whispered something to her, and she sat down, shaking her head. Paula looked over her shoulder and shook her head. Michael followed her gaze and grew hotter than the sun in August. There, sitting in the second row, was her friend Angela and some nigga Michael had never seen before. Did she really have the audacity to bring a new nigga with her to court? The guy must have felt Michael staring at him, because he looked over and kind of nodded.

Oh, this nigga want beef? Well, he can get it and then some. As Michael continued to glare, his anger was replaced with embarrassment as a young lady walked over to the man and slid in next to him. The man leaned over and whispered in the woman's ear, and she looked over at Michael and shook her head. Michael turned around quickly and stared at the judge.

"I'm going to reschedule this hearing for one month, and within that month's time, I want you two to go see a marriage counselor, one visit. If nothing is reconcilable, then when court reconvenes, the divorce will be granted. Mrs. Harris, I do understand that there was infidelity and a possible child created outside of the marriage, but I can't ignore Mr. Harris's request for counseling. Mr. Harris, I am ordering a DNA test with regard to the child in question, and based on all the findings at the end of the one month, I will make my decision. I also understand that there were several properties obtained during the marriage, which will also be divided if the divorce is granted or wanted equally."

"But I obtained those properties by myself," Paula yelled.

"Ma'am, I understand that, but we won't tolerate such an outburst in this courtroom. Your property became partly his once you two said, 'I do.'"

Paula sat back down, furious that her assets were mentioned in the divorce. If Michael thought that he was getting anything her money paid for to take care of another bitch and her bastard child, he had another think coming. She would burn that house down and sell her vehicles for dirt cheap and purchase a new house later. *Fuck he think?*

Michael sighed as he watched how angry Paula got. He shook his head at the thought of her hating him for what he had done to her, but it wasn't entirely his fault. She cheated first.

"This court will reconvene in thirty days. I hope you both take this time to evaluate every aspect of divorce and whether it's what you really want. Mrs. Harris, I am granting this time to Mr. Harris, but to you as well. In looking at your response, it isn't clear if this is what you want either. That is my ruling."

As the judge slammed her gavel down, Paula stared at Michael, then rolled her eyes. Michael smiled, thinking, *so she doesn't want the divorce either, huh? Interesting.*

Michael left the courtroom. He stood on the steps, talking to his lawyer and waiting for Paula to walk out. He wanted to talk to her, but when she emerged, she had Angela's mouth in her ear. He decided that he would give her time to cool off, but they were going to talk. When he left, he drove straight to his mother's house. He had been staying there again since the day Paula had disappeared.

He hated the way Paula looked at him. He could feel so many emotions from her eyes, pain and confusion, but mostly he felt hatred streaming from her. He had to win her back, but how?

***

"Boy, that was brutal." Angela sighed as she and Paula left the courtroom.

"Yeah, but I'm just glad this shit is almost over. The judge said one session with a therapist and it's over. Three more damn weeks and I'm free," Paula replied.

Angela couldn't tell what her best friend was feeling at that moment, but she had to speak about Tasha's absence. "I know this is a lot for you, and I'ma ride with you until this is over, but you need all the support you can get. Why isn't Tasha here? I've noticed that since you've been back, you haven't mentioned her or been around her. I haven't seen her myself, but I know something is going on, so tell me what's up."

Paula sighed and shook her head. "I'll tell you when we get in the car."

Once they were in the car, Paula told Angela what had transpired between her, Tasha, and Michael, and told her that as a result of that, she left. She also admitted that the night they were at the club, she felt that Tasha or Angela had told Michael that she was there with Tripp.

"And speaking of Tripp," Paula said, "girl, I went down to his studio before I left for Tennessee. He had murdered someone. I'm sure of it."

"Girl, what the fuck happened?" Angela asked.

"I walked into the building and began looking around, and I looked into a room, and he was standing over some guy lying on the floor. The man on the floor was bleeding awfully bad, and Tripp was wiping blood from his hands. Angela, I know that man is dead."

"He didn't see you, did he?" Angela asked.

"Hell no. I dipped out that bitch so damn fast. When I drove away, I didn't look back." Paula admitted, "He keeps calling and texting, but I don't want to ever talk to him again. Carla had heard of him, and she told me some things about him. I just hope he goes away for good."

"Damn, I'm sorry. You've been through the ringer lately, but God isn't going to see you hurting for long. Give your troubles over to Him, and watch Him work it out. I promise you, He will," Angela told her.

"Look at you getting all religious on me," Paula laughed.

"Yeah, but it's a fact. I may not always act like I'm God-fearing, but He hears all my troubles, and I give Him all the glory. Think about it," Angela replied as she leaned forward and turned the radio on and started bopping to "Bullet Proof" by Yo Gotti.

Paula shook her head once more and started laughing.

Michael sat on his mother's porch, smoking a cigarette and watching cars ride past, wondering what the hell he was going to do about his marriage. He knew he probably looked desperate, but he didn't care. He wanted his wife back, and he was willing to do whatever it took to win her back. Nikki and Tasha were mistakes he'd made. He didn't even remember fucking Tasha's trifling ass, but being drunk, he was capable of anything. Waking up to her lying naked next to him, he knew what it was. But from what he remembered, she hadn't been drinking much at all, so whatever happened she was partly responsible for. He ran his hands through his dreads, agitated. "Michael, you're just so damn stupid," he scolded himself.

Michael put his cigarette out and walked back into the house. He lay across his bed, and at about four thirty, he decided to call his boys. He needed to get out of the house before he went crazier than he already was.

"What are y'all doing today? I need to get a drink. Are y'all down to maybe go to the pool room tonight?" Michael asked once Miguel picked up.

"I'm always down, but I don't know about Sean. You know how his ass can be."

"All right, I'ma be on the way in a few minutes. I swear, I need tonight to be better than today."

"Oh, that's right. Today was your court date. What happened?" Miguel asked.

"Man, it's on hold. They are letting us talk to a marriage counselor. They wanted to be fair to me, but Paula was so damn mad. I don't think there is no hope, but I'm not gonna give up just yet. I need to get drunk."

"But tomorrow is a workday, and I don't think we should pull an all-nighter," Miguel said.

"I don't really care at this point. I just need to get out for a while." Michael put his Nikes on and grabbed a light jacket. "All right, I'ma see y'all in a few minutes."

"Ay, you know things gon' work out no matter what happens between you and Paula. Let me get with Sean and see if he wants to go. Talk to you when you get here," Miguel said before hanging up.

Michael pulled up to his house about twenty minutes after he got off the phone with Miguel. He didn't get out of the car, but he called him to let him know he was outside. Sean and Miguel rode together, and Michael drove behind them. When they arrived at the pool room, they found a parking space close to the entrance of the facility. There were very few people there, which was even better in Michael's opinion.

When they walked in, they sat down at the bar and ordered their drinks.

"Ay, let's go sit at that table right there," Miguel said as he headed in the direction, not waiting for anyone to reply. They sat down, and Michael immediately started talking about his marriage woes. Miguel listened, but Sean was barely paying attention. As Michael continued complaining about his marriage problems, Sean began sucking his teeth and rolling his eyes upward.

"Am I bothering you?" Michael asked crossly.

"Matter of fact," Sean began but was stopped quickly by Miguel.

"Sean, you need to just chill."

"No, fuck that. He's sitting here acting like a real bitch. So what his wife left him? I'm sick of coming out with him just to hear about Paula's recent antics. Fuck."

"First of all, who the hell are you calling a bitch?" Michael growled.

"Nigga, I didn't call you a bitch. What I said was that you're crying like one. Paula got you acting like a fool. Ask yourself this question: why, after finding out about your one indiscretion, was she so willing to walk away that damn easy? Man, that bitch was ready to go. And now she is pulling at your heartstrings like you a fucking puppet. Every single day it's Paula this and Paula that. Man the fuck up, and accept the shit for what it is—a goddamn wrap."

"Sean, chill the fuck out," Miguel growled.

"Chill out? Man, you know for yourself that he is making a total fool out of himself chasing after a bitch who don't want his ass," Sean argued.

Before he could utter another word, Michael landed a two-punch combo to his face, causing him to fly backward. Michael turned up the remainder of his drink and walked out. Miguel shook his head and walked out behind him.

"Bruh, you know how Sean is. Don't leave like that. Y'all boys," Miguel told him.

"Fuck that nigga. I'm done. You can chill with him, but I'm not trying to be around dude like that. That's your boy, and I met him on the strength of you, so fuck him."

Michael walked off and got in his car. Miguel waited for him to pull off, and he headed back inside.

Sean was sitting at the table, massaging his cheek. "Ay, you need to do something about that nigga."

"You need to learn to curb your mouth. Michael wasn't hurting you by talking about his problems. You act like you want him or something. Every time he around, you acting funny and shit," Miguel fumed.

Sean didn't say anything, which caused Miguel to look at him hard. "Nigga, you better say something."

"It's not Michael I'm interested in. It's you. Shit, since everybody spilling their guts, there goes mine. You always jumping to that nigga's defense, you are always there for dude, and you don't see me. You don't see me wanting you," Sean replied.

"Nigga, I know you playing, and if you aren't, you better act like you are. Laugh or something, bitch nigga," Miguel growled as he loomed over Sean.

Sean didn't say a word, and he didn't look at Miguel either.

"Let me get the fuck out of here. I like pussy, nigga, not dick, and I damn sho' don't want no dookie dick. You got me all the way fucked up. Goddammit."

"Let me finish my drink, and I will be ready to go," Sean said.

"Ready for what? Nigga, I'ma catch a cab, and let me tell you what it is from this point on—not muthafucking shit. You got to get out my damn house asap. Dammit, you a punk? Man, damn." Miguel walked out of the pool room and called Michael.

"Yeah?" Michael answered.

"Nigga, turn around and come get me. You not gonna believe what the fuck just happened. I need to sleep on your momma's couch tonight," Miguel said.

"Damn, I'm turning around," Michael replied.

"Don't hang up though, nigga. I can't believe this shit," Miguel fumed.

"Bruh, what the fuck happened?" Michael asked.

"This nigga just said he a whole damn gay man. Talking about he wants me and is basically jealous of our friendship."

"What?" Michael yelled. Michael laughed hard, which angered Miguel, so he hung up. When Michael pulled up, Miguel could see that he was still laughing but was trying to hold a straight face.

When he got in the car, Michael pulled off and glanced over at Miguel. "So um, you just left your boyfriend at the pool room, huh?" Michael laughed even more after Miguel gave him the middle finger.

"Man, that shit ain't funny. This dude literally said he wanted me, and I told him that he better laugh or something, and when he didn't, I wanted to punch him in his shit like you did, but I didn't want to go to jail."

Michael sat quietly listening, and once Miguel finished, Michael looked at Miguel with tears of laughter glittering in his eyes. "So umm, is he a top or bottom type of guy?"

"You know what? Fuck you, man," Miguel replied, laughing.

They drove laughing and talking, and when they pulled up to Michael's mother's house, Michael looked at Miguel. "You know ain't shit gon' happen right? You get the couch, my nigga."

Miguel cringed. "I wish I hadn't told yo' ass now. Are you gon' let this shit die down ever?" he asked, laughing.

"I'm done. For real I am." Michael laughed some more.

When they walked into the house, Michael grabbed Miguel a sheet, pillow, and blanket, and went to bed himself. Although his day had started off wrong, he had to admit that he felt better.

The following morning, Michael overheard Miguel telling Sean that he had until the end of the month to be out of his house. Michael walked in, humming. "So you just aren't ready to play the family man, huh?"

Miguel shot him an angry but amused stare. "You know what? Fuck you."

"Hey now, watch that language in my house," Sharon warned them as she walked into the kitchen.

"Yes, ma'am." Miguel laughed.

Michael laughed and headed out for work. He felt energized and ready to take on the world.

Chapter 22

Paula returned to work tired but ready. She knew that as of late her work performance was minimum compared to her usual performance, but she was going to make up for it all. She wasn't going to let her personal issues interfere with her job anymore. She had worked too hard in obtaining her reputation at her job and didn't want anyone to look at her as if she were like any other worker there. Chandra had been very understanding of her problems, and she had to respect her for that. Paula had money saved from when her mother and father died, and even with that, she felt the need to work.

When she walked into the office, she was greeted by a new face. There was a light-skinned woman sitting behind a desk in the office beside hers. She frowned and began praying that she hadn't been fired. She had called in daily, as well as worked on several client files, billing issues, and anything else that Chandra had sent to her email. She was confused at what was transpiring.

She walked into her office and flipped the light on. All her belongings were still in place, which kind of eased her mind until Chandra walked in. "Hey, sweetie. Listen, can you come into my office? I need to talk to you."

"Yes, I will be in shortly," Paula replied.

When Chandra walked away, Paula felt her heart sink to her stomach. She stood up and sat back down, feeling her knees weaken. Finally she walked to Chandra's office and knocked on the door.

"Come on in, Paula," she answered.

Paula walked in and stood at the door for a few seconds until Chandra looked up and smiled. "Girl, come in. We've just got to talk about a few things."

"Am I fired?" Paula blurted out.

"Just come in and close the door." Chandra laughed.

Paula closed the door and sat down, bracing herself for the inevitable.

The day arrived when Paula and Michael had to meet with the marriage counselor. They hadn't seen nor spoken to one another since the day of the divorce hearing. As they sat in the waiting area, they didn't speak at all, but they did sneak glances at one another here and there.

Damn, I can smell his cologne all the way over here. He looks so damn good, but his ass is as sorry as they come, Paula thought as she quickly looked back down at her phone, seeing him look up at her. She pretended to be playing *Candy Crush* on her phone.

Yeah, she checking me out, and she looks tasty sitting over there in those tight jeans. Damn, her ass looked delicious when we were walking in here. Shit, is that Gossip she is wearing? That's what it smells like. She did that shit on purpose. She knows I love it when she wears that. Michael shifted in his seat, trying to readjust his "man."

After a few minutes, the receptionist's phone rang, and then she looked up. "Mr. and Mrs. Harris, you can go in now."

Michael stood, and like any gentleman would, he waited for Paula to stand and followed her into the room.

When they entered the room, they were greeted by a middle-aged white woman with shoulder-length curly gray hair. "Please come and have a seat." She led them to a two-seater couch, which meant that Michael and Paula had to sit next to each other.

"How are you two doing today? My name is Amanda Tate, and you are Mr. and Mrs. Harris, correct?" She sat down across from them.

"Yes," Paula and Michael both answered.

"I've been going through your file, and from what I've read, I'm gathering that one of you wants a divorce and the other doesn't. Is that true?" Amanda inquired.

"Ma'am, I really don't see any need for us to be here. This marriage is over as far as I'm concerned," Paula explained in a rushed voice.

"And I," Michael started, glaring at Paula, "feel that things are repairable if we both give it a try and keep other people out of our business."

"Keep other people out of our business? I know damn well you didn't say that." Paula laughed angrily.

"Paula, you just need to give me a chance to fix my mistakes," Michael sighed.

"I've done that, and now I'm just ready for this to be over," Paula replied, glaring back at Michael.

Michael sat upward and turned toward Paula in amazement. "When did you attempt to talk things out? That is a lie, and you know it."

"Oh, so now I'm a liar? Listen here, you asshole," Paula started but was interrupted by Amanda.

"Wait a minute, you two. Let's just slow things down a little bit, shall we?" Amanda advised.

"Look, I love—" Michael started, but again Amanda intervened.

"Mr. Harris, why don't we start with you telling me how you and Mrs. Harris met?"

Michael began telling her the story while Paula sat back at first. She smiled, remembering their first time talking. Then she started getting frustrated, tapping her fingers and rolling her eyes. After Michael finished, Amanda looked at Paula. "Did you disagree with any part that he just told me?"

"No."

"Well, I watched you as he talked, and at first you were smiling, but then your whole demeanor changed. Why is that?" Amanda inquired.

"I just grew bored listening to him, that's all. Our marriage didn't mean that much to him, because if it did, he wouldn't have done the things he did to destroy it," Paula shared.

"Okay, Paula, but you haven't been the model wife either. We aren't even divorced yet, and you picked up with another man. I mean, you just sat here and lied to this lady, saying that you have tried to reconcile, and you know it was a lie," Michael growled.

"So you're gonna sit there and say that I didn't take the time to get to know your son? I didn't take the time to talk with you and go out on a date with you? Really, Michael?"

"During all our years together, you weren't one hundred percent righteous. You put your job ahead of us a lot of the time, and I swallowed that, and yes, you did come around and try to work things out for a couple of days, but just as soon as we started getting along, you fell back yet again. I mean, I thought we were headed somewhere," Michael replied.

"Hell, if we were headed somewhere, that's all over with now, and you know why. Look, lady, please just sign the document saying that this is irreconcilable so I can go," Paula groaned.

"You seem angry, Mrs. Harris," the therapist commented.

"Hell yes, I'm angry. I don't give a damn what he says I didn't do as a wife. I know what the fuck I did do, and that was honor my vows. I loved this man, and I trusted him with the one thing he should have cherished more than some ghetto-ass pussy, and that was my heart. All those nights he couldn't get that dick—which seemed to stop growing after he hit the age of sixteen—up to fuck me, I never once cheated," Paula yelled. "Look, all I want is out of this bullshit-ass marriage."

"Girl, stop playing. We had sex, made love, however you want to put it, all the time, and I guarantee you there isn't anything sixteen years old about my dick. He had your ass running."

"Okay, okay, that's a little too much. You two really have a lot to work out, but I'm not sure if a reconciliation is what's best for you," Amanda told them.

"How can you say that? She isn't even giving this counseling a try. Please, Paula, I made a damn mistake."

"You made a mistake? We know that's a lie. You made one mistake that lasted almost five years and one kid. And another mistake that not only killed any chance of us reconciling, but it ruined my relationship with a person I truly care about. Naw, nigga, go be the family man you were playing the day I attempted to put yo' low-life ass out."

"Mrs. Harris, the order says—"

"Ms. Tate, I know exactly what the order states, and I'm here. It doesn't state that I have to change my mind or go one day further afterward. Listen, I just want out of this marriage. I did what I was told, and now I'm done."

Paula stood up to leave, and Michael dropped to his knees. "Paula, please wait," he cried. "I know I messed up, baby, but I swear I never meant for you to be hurt. When things first started with Nikki and me, I was young, fresh out of prison, and my head was filled with so many different stories of your infidelity that I lost it. Then when she got pregnant, she threatened to tell you about us and Tavon if I tried to leave her alone. I'm sorry. Paula, on God, I will do anything to save our marriage."

Paula had never seen Michael cry. He appeared to be sincere, but how could she forgive him. How could she trust him? She dropped her head and shook it as tears dropped. "Michael, you broke us. You allowed others to get in your head, and you fucked two other women and had a child by one of them. How can I forgive that? Every time I look at you, I see deceit. How can we move forward?"

Paula shook her head and walked out of the office. Michael sat in the office a bit longer and then stood to leave.

After Michael left the therapist's office, he drove around for a little while and then decided to go home. Miguel called to see how the session went, and after Michael told him the details, Miguel sighed, "Man, it may be over for real. You have to just accept it and move on."

"Yeah, I guess. Look, I will talk to you later. I need to lie down for a while," Michael told him.

"All right. I'm here if you need to talk," Miguel told him.

"Thanks, man," Michael said.

Michael refused to give up on his marriage, and he was going to win her back or lose it all trying. He sat around and moped for a few hours until he finally figured out what he was going to do. He called Paula and asked her if she would meet him at the park. He promised her that if she agreed to meet him and listen to him and still felt that a divorce was what she wanted, he wouldn't stand in her way and would give her the freedom that she desired.

"Michael, I will go out with you to talk, and that's it. I don't know what I want to do, but I give you my word that I'll try to resolve shit, even if it's only to discuss division of property."

"I'm trying to show you that I can change and I can be the man you need me to be. I'm not sure what you want from me. Tell me what you need from me, and I will do it."

"First of all, you can get that damn DNA test done. You've been holding off, and I need to know for sure if you popped that seed in that trash Nikki's ass or not."

Michael sighed and closed his eyes and said quietly into the receiver, "I'm going to prove to you that I'm trying to change. I'm going to be honest with you, as I should have been from the very beginning. I don't need a DNA test where Tavon is concerned. He is my son, and I won't deny that. He looks just like me, but that was a mistake I made when I first got out of prison, and I swear to you that I haven't slept with Nikki since back then."

Just then, Paula's phone beeped. She glanced at it and saw Tasha's name pop up. "I have an incoming call. I will call you right back."

"But wait. We got to finish this conversation," Michael replied agitatedly. But before he could utter another word, Paula had hung up.

"What do you want, Tasha?" she asked softly.

"Paula, you are my cousin, and I miss you. Can we please go somewhere and talk?" Tasha pleaded.

"Tasha, where was that cousin bond when you had my husband's dick in your pussy? You weren't worried about me then. I have to go. I'm meeting Michael."

"So you are going to reconcile with him and to hell with me, huh?" Tasha asked angrily.

"Whether I reconcile with Michael or not has nothing to do with you. I don't owe either of you shit." Paula hung up and stared at her phone before slinging it onto the couch. She was torn between following her heart or leaving both of them to rot in their own trifling world.

Michael stared at his phone after Paula hung up in his face. Who had called her? Who was she talking to? It drove him crazy just thinking about it.

He walked over to the bar and poured a shot of vodka and downed it in one gulp. He shook his head and poured one more. He knew what he had to do if Paula refused to take him back. He turned another drink up and headed to his room to get some rest. He and Paula were meeting the following day, and it was going to be either a rewarding and blissful meeting or a bittersweet one.

The following day, Michael got up and got dressed. He put on his black and gray balling pants and a gray T-shirt. His face looked ragged and worn. He shaved and put Visine in his eyes to hide the redness from the lack of sleep. When he walked out, his mother was in the kitchen, cooking breakfast.

"You going to eat something?"

"No, ma'am. I'm not hungry," he sighed.

Sharon sat down next to him and rubbed his hands. "Everything is going to be all right. You just got to believe it. I wish you wouldn't let this situation bring you down so much."

"Mom, it's going to be okay. I promise you that, after today, if Paula decides that a divorce is what she wants still, she will get it. I love you. I have to go." Michael stood up and kissed her on the head and walked out.

Sharon stood up and walked to the door and watched Michael pull off. She rubbed the top of her head and suddenly had a sinking, sickening feeling that this day would end very badly. She raced to her room and grabbed her Bible and began praying hard for God to help her son.

Paula awoke and stretched. "Let me get up and get dressed," she sighed. She walked to the bathroom and smiled as she greeted Carla. "You cooked breakfast?"

"Who? Not I. I ate some cereal. I can pour you a bowl if you like," Carla replied.

Paula laughed, "I will grab something later. Girl, how about Tasha called me yesterday asking if we could talk. I'm not ready to see her ass. And I got a call from Michael asking me to meet with him today, and I'm going to, and he promised that if I still wanted the divorce, he wouldn't fight it. I'm so ready for this. There ain't nothing he can say to me to change my mind."

Carla laughed, "Tasha is your fam. You're going to have to talk to her sooner or later."

"I prefer later."

"You want me to go with you?" Carla asked.

"Naw, this is something I gotta do all by my lonesome. Let me go on and get dressed so I can get outta here. I'ma have to grab me a biscuit while I'm out since yo' ass didn't cook." Paula laughed.

After Paula dressed down in her jeans and a sweatshirt and Tims, she stood in the mirror and checked her face. She wasn't going to wear any makeup, nor was she gonna have her hair up. Her dreads fell down across her shoulders, and she smiled. Then a feeling of sadness washed over her. It was almost over, and she didn't know how to feel about it. Her phone began to ring, and she walked out of the bathroom to grab it.

"Oh, shit, he needs to stop calling me," she groaned as she saw Tripp's name across her screen.

"Why don't you block his number, cuz?"

"Honestly, the thought never crossed my mind. Let me do that now." Paula laughed.

Carla stood back and watched her cousin, and she didn't know what it was, but something didn't seem right. "Are you sure you don't want me to ride with you?"

"I'm sure. I will be back shortly," she replied as she grabbed her keys and walked out of the suite.

Carla shook her head. She didn't know what it was, but her stomach began to knot up. "God, take care of my cousin."

Paula stopped by Biscuitville and got a sausage, egg, and cheese biscuit and an orange juice. After she ate, she headed to the park where she was to meet Michael. When she got there, he was already sitting on the bleachers.

"Hello," she said as she walked up.

"How are you?" he replied.

"I'm good. What did you want to say to me?"

"Paula, let's start fresh. No lies, no deceit. Just me and you and a new life. We don't have to get remarried again right away. We can just start slow and take our time to rekindle what we had. You know we were great together."

Paula looked at Michael and frowned. She loved him, no doubt, but then all she could see was his face in between her cousin's legs.

"Michael, I just can't. I probably could have forgiven you in time for Nikki and your son, but I cannot get the image of you and Tasha out of my head. That was just foul and nasty. I can't fuck you after you've been with her."

"But you already have, and that was so long ago." Michael's voice trailed off as he realized that he had spoken a bit too much.

Paula stood up to leave. "Really? How could you say that shit? You know goddamn well that if I had known that you slept with my cousin, I would have never fucked you again."

"I didn't mean it like that. Oh, my God, this isn't going like I expected," Michael cried as he pushed his dreads back. Michael stood up and turned to say something to Paula, but she stopped him.

"I'm sorry. I cannot do this," she whispered.

Paula turned and started toward her car, but before she could make it, she heard Michael's voice scream, "Paula."

Paula turned, and as she did, she heard screaming and witnessed several people scattering from the park. Paula's eyes widened as she saw Michael standing before her with a small-caliber gun.

"Michael," she yelled.

"I love you, and I'm sorry for hurting you. I hope this will make up for that pain. I can't live without you," he cried.

Pow.

Michael shot himself in the head, and as his body fell to the ground, Paula ran forward, screaming, "Nooooo."

Chapter 23

Three Months Later

Michael was sitting in his room at his mother's house, gazing out the window. His mind was on Paula, wondering if he would see her before she left.

Shooting himself was the defining event in his life. The bullet didn't penetrate beyond his skull, but it did cause significant swelling. The doctors decided to medically induce a coma, which he was in for eight days. When he awoke, he was staring at the face of an angel: his wife. From what he was told, she was there daily. Michael reached out to her, and when she took his hand and his vision focused enough to where he could see her, he quickly turned his head, trying to focus on any other object in the room. A lump formed in his throat as his wife's gaze told him in unspoken words that it was over.

"Hey," Paula had whispered.

Michael had smiled and whispered, "Hello." Paula had tried to pull away, but Michael held her hand tight. "I'm sorry."

Paula shook her head and leaned over. "No need to be sorry. I forgive you, Michael."

Michael smiled and fell back to sleep. When he woke up, he was surrounded by his family and friends, but Paula wasn't there.

He regretted his actions and was put in the psych ward for three months before he was released from the hospital. Once he arrived home, Tammy was there with a letter from Paula, and she was accompanied by his mother and Miguel.

"We didn't want to give you this letter until we were sure you could handle it. Here you go," Tammy said as she handed Michael the letter.

Michael sat down slowly on the couch, and with shaky hands, he opened the letter.

Dear Michael,

We have been through a lot these last few months, and I know it wasn't all your fault. You were led to believe so many untruths that one can't blame you for feeling betrayed, but you should have come to me out of the gate. Instead, those secrets and lies have snowballed into what we are now: divorced. I love you, though, and that will never change. I have accepted a job in Seattle, Washington, and will be moving soon, but I couldn't leave without telling you how I felt.

I haven't been an angel through this ordeal, and I deeply apologize for my actions. While you were in a coma, Nikki came by with an attorney, informing me that if you passed, she felt she was entitled to your insurance money, your 401(k) from work, and your social security for Tavon. We had a DNA test, and due to the severity of the situation, the court put a rush on the results. What you do with these papers is totally up to you, but I will say that I hope you won't turn your back on the child who loves you and who you love and have been there for since day one.

Michael frowned and pulled the papers out. "I'm not the father." Michael dropped the letter and broke down. He suddenly realized that his family and friends were there for him to help him deal with the knowledge that Tavon wasn't his.

They quickly surrounded him and consoled him until he went into his room and lay across his bed. His mother kept his room door ajar for fear of what he would do to himself. She knew that only one person could help him, and that was Paula. After ten minutes of listening to his family whisper about him, Michael stood up and closed his door.

Miguel said that he was going to the store, and he asked if anyone needed anything. Sharon asked him to bring her a pack of Salem Lights.

"Mom, you don't smoke anymore," Tammy cried in shock.

"I do today. Miguel, just bring me what I asked for please," Sharon replied, rolling her eyes at Tammy.

When Miguel left, Tammy sat in the living room, staring at Michael's shut door. Everything that her brother was enduring was her fault. She stood up and tiptoed to his door. She placed her ear to it and could hear him sobbing. She pushed the door open and slowly walked in. She paused as Michael's eyes clashed with hers.

"Is this what you wanted?" he asked softly. "Did you know that Tavon wasn't mine?"

Tammy shut the door and took a deep breath. She had made up her mind that whatever happened beyond that point, she was going to accept it, but she couldn't keep bullshitting. Michael could've died, and all because she was jealous.

"Michael, you know that, ever since we were kids, you were the favorite and I was the black sheep, but you always made me feel special. You were my big brother."

She laughed and looked at Michael. "I couldn't stand that she was in your life. She took you away from me, and there I was, taking a back seat yet again to someone else. Even with Mom, Paula was a favorite, and I felt like I was alone. When you got locked up, I started taking up the slack in the streets where you had left off. Boy, when Momma found out, she read me like I wasn't shit. But she never said one word to you, and I know she knew what you were doing."

Michael shook his head. "I got cursed out daily. Mom told me that she was disappointed in me and that Paula deserved more than a drug pusher. She even told me that I wasn't a good role model for you. She loved us both equally but differently. Everything you just said to me, Tammy, you could have told me a long time ago."

"When? Michael, you were always busy. I didn't have anyone to really talk to. The day I ran into Tasha, we were at this club, and she started telling me how Paula couldn't wait for you to leave because she had a new guy within days of your incarceration. At first I wasn't going to say anything, but a few days after she told me that, she started sending me pictures of Paula with a guy. I printed them off my phone to send them to you, but I changed my mind. Tasha called me a few weeks later and asked me if I had sent you the pictures, and I told her no. That's when she asked me for your address so she could send them. She said she was tired of her goody-two-shoes cousin getting one over on people. I gave her the address, thinking that it was better her than me."

"You didn't wonder if Tasha was telling the truth? Do you know that Tasha was lying about that and it's that lie that started all of this?" Michael told her through clenched teeth.

"I honestly didn't care if it was a lie. She had taken you from me, and once you got locked up, she had Mom.

They went everywhere. I felt like I was being replaced," Tammy admitted, looking down at her hands, then back up at Michael. "To be honest though, deep down I knew she wasn't cheating, even after seeing those pictures. Tasha had her own agenda and so did I, but I swear I didn't know you were going to get out and link up with Nikki. When you did, I was overjoyed. I figured that Paula would find out and it would be over with. Hell, Nikki wasn't wifey material, so I wasn't worried about her taking my place. But then she got pregnant, and you and Paula were still kicking it, and then years later, yet again, Tasha jumped in my ear, telling me that Paula was talking about having a baby with you. I just couldn't have that, so that's when I pumped Nikki up to go along with me to break you two up. All it took was a hit of coke here and there and the game was on. Tasha helped also by texting Paula and pretending to be sharing shit from Facebook with her when, in actuality, the pictures were staged by all of us."

Michael looked at her. "Did you or did you not know that Tavon wasn't mine?"

"With all truth laid out on the table, I didn't know," Tammy replied.

"I think that you need to talk to Mom and then seek help. Something is seriously wrong with you. I never would have thought that you could betray me like you have. All this bullshit because you wanted to be the center of attention. I swear, I want to hate you, but I can't. It's gonna take a while and counseling, but hopefully we will one day be okay," Michael replied, looking out his bedroom window.

Tammy stood up and walked over to Michael to hug him.

"We aren't there yet," he said, refusing the hug.

Tammy patted him on the shoulder. "For what it's worth, I'm deeply sorry for everything I've done, and I will do everything you have asked."

"Good."

Tammy stood, staring at Michael for a brief moment before he looked up and shook his head. "One hug."

Tammy walked back over and hugged Michael and walked out of his room. She decided to talk to her mother as well, and when it was over, Sharon admitted to Tammy that she was disappointed, but she owned up to showing favoritism at times. She told Tammy that she needed to make things right however she could with Michael, and Tammy agreed and knew exactly how to do it.

She hugged her mother and told her that she would return the following day to check on her brother. She grabbed her car keys and walked out the door.

The next morning, Michael was awakened by his mother. "You have a phone call, son."

"Who is it?"

"It's the police. It's about Tavon."

Michael sat up immediately. "What's wrong with Tavon?"

"Here, you better talk to them yourself," she replied, walking forward to give him the phone. Michael knew it wasn't good by the look on his mother's face.

Nikki

"I'm so foolish. I've allowed these men and drugs to ruin my life. It's over for me," she cried as she laid her head down on the table in the interrogation room.

"Ma'am, we have a few questions we need to ask you," said the detective who was sitting across from her.

Nikki raised her head slightly and sneered with tears streaming down her cheeks, "Fuck you. I want an attorney. I know my rights."

"Take her to her cell." The detective opened the door to leave. He turned back around and shook his head. "You're pathetic."

Nikki stood as the woman officer walked forward, and she felt herself shaking slightly. She had never been inside a jail cell before, and she was terrified of the unknown.

"Open cell block C," the guard yelled out, and the doors opened.

Upon entry, Nikki was handed a mattress and a plastic container, which contained one pillow, a rag, and a towel. She was then given a mini toothbrush and toothpaste. As they thrust her inside the block, Nikki jumped as she heard the clanking of the steel doors closing behind her.

Nikki walked to the empty bed and set her thin mattress and container down on the cold steel bed frame. She looked around and felt the piercing stares from a few of her bunkmates.

"If I have to kill a ho up in here, I will." She grumbled to herself, "This can't be my life."

Nikki fixed her bed up and lay down on the thin mattress and pretended to sleep. She decided that she would deal with her situation the following day.

As morning approached, Nikki was up before anyone else, trying to get a quick shower and lie back down before they brought in breakfast. After her quick shower, she walked back to her bunk and sat down. She bowed her head and said a brief prayer. She wondered what was going to happen at her first appearance. Would her parents be there?

She sighed and lay back down and fell back to sleep. A little after eight, she awoke for breakfast. When she grabbed her tray, she frowned at its contents. The cup of milk was hot, the eggs were runny, and the one slice of bacon was hard and black on the edges. She grabbed the only appealing item on the tray, which was an orange. After she picked the orange up, she pushed the tray away and walked back to her bunk. A tall and big white woman grabbed the tray that she left behind and smashed the food quickly. Nikki sighed as she sat down on her bunk and searched the room and caught sight of two black females watching her hard. She quickly looked away and peeled her orange and began to eat it. As she slid the last piece in her mouth, she noticed that one of the ladies was walking in her direction. She braced herself for whatever was about to jump off.

"Ay, yo' name Nikki?" the lady asked.

"Yeah, and?" Nikki replied, trying to sound hard.

"Listen, I suggest you avert your frustrations. You're wanted on the phone," the woman replied blankly.

Nikki frowned, wondering who could be asking for her and how anyone outside of her parents would know that she was locked up.

She stood up and followed the woman to the phone, where her friend was waiting for them with the phone outstretched. She took the phone and placed it to her ear with the two women standing close to her, one in front and the other behind her.

"Hello?" she said into the receiver.

"Bitch, pay close attention to what I'm about to say. Listen to me real good," the voice on the other end of the phone replied.

Nikki listened to the person talking, and as she did, she felt her body begin to get weak. She nodded her head as the tears began to fall. After she gave the phone to the lady who had handed it to her, she slowly walked back to her bunk, and she could hear the ladies laughing and overheard one talking. "Yeah, we got you. Anything else you need?"

Carla and Paula were sitting in Golden Corral, discussing her move. Paula decided it was time to share her news with Carla about the changes that were taking place in her life. She had been asked if she would be willing to relocate and head up a new company that they were starting in Seattle. Chandra had explained to her that even with everything Paula had been going through, she always made sure that her work was on point and completed. She worked through the worst of times and always displayed the ability to be a boss.

At first Paula didn't know what to do, but after a long night of thinking, she agreed. She was going to be president of Bennent Care Solutions, and they were doubling her current salary. They also were giving her moving expenses, as well as a bonus.

She had signed her house over to Michael, and other than her mother's personal items that she had held on to, she was going to let Michael keep the furnishings. She also left him $25,000 of the money that her mother had left her. She wanted Tavon to be taken care of. She was supposed to have left right away, but when everything happened with Tavon, she felt she was needed there.

"Are you going with me to Seattle?" Paula asked Carla as she bit into her chicken.

Carla looked up. "Are you serious?"

"Hell yeah. We just started reconnecting, and I don't want to be in Seattle by myself. Will you go with me?" Paula asked again.

"You damn right I will. Girl, that just made my day."
Carla jumped up and hugged Paula.

"I might need you to go before me so you can get things
in order for me. I've got the furniture being delivered,
and I have to pick up the keys and all, but I have a few
last-minute things to handle here. Do you think you can
do that for me?"

"I got you," Carla replied.

"Cool. I will get your plane ticket tomorrow."

"Plane. Bitch, I ain't ever flown before," Carla exclaimed.

"Girl, you will be okay. I can guarantee you that."

"Shit, I will do it because I ain't no punk, but what if
that muthafucka go down?" Carla laughed.

"Girl, don't think so negative." Paula laughed.

"All right, but that's a real question."

Paula shook her head. "Is your food good?"

"I understand you trying to change the subject and shit.
It's cool." Carla laughed.

They finished up their meal and left, and once they
were back at the hotel, Paula took out her laptop and
checked the flights to Seattle. She and Carla sat down
and put her itinerary together. She was going to leave a
week from that day, and Paula was going to get her some
money to tide her over until she followed.

That evening, Carla called Angela over while Paula
went out to a briefing that Chandra had called at the last
minute.

"What's up, chick?" Angela said when she walked in.

"Oh, nothing, just sitting here chilling. I didn't want
to sit here by myself tonight. Paula was called in to a
meeting, so I figured I'd call you to keep me company."

"Is that right? I'm glad you called." Angela sat down on
the couch.

"I wanted to tell you that I've enjoyed meeting you and
hanging out with you. You made coming here worth-
while," Carla said.

"Shit, you saying that like you going somewhere," Angela laughed.

"I am. Paula asked me to go with her to Seattle, and I agreed to go."

"What? Paula ain't even said shit to me about leaving." Angela was upset and didn't try to hide it.

"Well, don't let on that I told you. I assumed she told you, but she's probably gonna do it in her own time."

Angela sat quietly for a minute and let out a long sigh. "I need a blunt on that one and a damn drink," Angela said as she pulled out her bag and rolled a blunt. She took a few pulls and passed it to Carla, who took a few pulls and handed it back to Angela. Angela got up and walked to the kitchenette and poured a drink. As she stood there sipping on gin, Carla walked up behind her and wrapped her arms around her waist. Angela turned around, and they kissed one another for the first time. After all the joking and playing around that they had been doing, Carla was ready to see what Angela could do.

Angela and Carla walked into the bedroom and kissed, fingered, tasted, and climaxed as only the two women could. When it was over, they lay in bed and talked about how they were going to keep in touch and visit one another when Carla left for Seattle. Carla didn't know if she believed Angela, but she was hopeful, because she really had grown very fond of her.

When Paula returned, she could hear the moaning and kissing sounds that were coming from Carla's room. She instantly knew who was in there, and without thinking, she laughed and said, "Get it, girl."

She clamped her hand over her mouth, and ten minutes later, both Carla and Angela were coming out of the room.

"Something you need to tell me?" Angela asked as she stood with her hands on her hips.

"Um, is there something you need to tell me?" Paula asked, smirking.

"Bitch, you knew I was going to make Carla mine, so don't play. Why didn't you tell me?" Angela replied.

Carla mushed Angela's shoulder. "I told you not to say anything."

"I couldn't wait," Angela replied.

Paula shook her head and sat down at the table. "Well, I was offered a job to head up a new company in Seattle, and I accepted. I leave in a couple of weeks."

"I can't believe this. You are leaving me?" Angela asked.

"Girl, it's time for a new start in life for me, and this is a great opportunity. I wanted to tell you, but I didn't know how. Thanks to bigmouth over there, I was forced to. You can come visit whenever you want to. You know that."

"Yeah, but it won't be the same." She pouted for a few seconds and then smiled. "But I'm happy for you."

"Thank you. Now don't let me keep you two. Go back to doing what you were doing. I'll just go in my room and pretend that I'm not listening," Paula laughed.

"You so silly." Carla laughed, but she and Angela went back in the room, and just as Paula had expected, they started up again, and she listened.

Wednesday, November 12

Michael sat in the waiting area of the Department of Social Services, waiting to speak to the social worker who was on Tavon's case. His mother was with him, and she was very concerned about her son's well-being. He had endured so much in the past year, and losing Tavon, she feared, would be his tipping point. She had never seen Michael look so torn and worn out.

"Mr. Harris?" a tall, young white woman asked as she approached him.

"Yes, that's me," he replied, standing up to greet the woman.

"I'm Elizabeth Warren, and I'm overseeing Tavon's case. Please follow me to my office so we can talk."

Michael and his mother walked into the office and sat down. "Why did we have to meet you here instead of the courthouse?"

"Well, I want to explain to you what's going on before the hearing this afternoon. I know you have questions, and I want to answer them as best I can. Yesterday, the police were called to Miss Nikki DeLeon's home, and upon their arrival, Tavon was found in the back room, dirty, hungry, and in the middle of a bad situation. There was a huge quantity of marijuana present, as well as heroin. Miss DeLeon was passed out on the couch when the police arrived, and the door was wide open. She has been charged with possession of a controlled substance and child endangerment, as the drugs were out in the open in Miss DeLeon's bedroom. There is a placement hearing this afternoon."

"Why is the hearing necessary? I will care for my son, and he can stay with me as of tonight. A hearing isn't necessary," Michael explained.

"I understand what you are saying, sir, but we have to make sure that Tavon is placed in a safe environment. Upon looking over your information, we have learned that you have a criminal history involving drugs," the caseworker explained.

"Look," Michael started a bit harshly, which caused his mother to tap his knee, alerting him to calm down. "Ma'am," Michael started again, "I'm Tavon's father, and I've been in his life since day one. Yes, I have a history, but if you check, you will learn that I've held down a job since being released and I haven't gotten in any new trouble."

Mrs. Warren thumbed through her folder and looked up at Michael. "Well, I see here that there was a DNA test taken, and Tavon isn't your child. Again, we have to weigh all the factors in this case. Our job is to protect the child."

Michael stood up. "If you weren't going to give me my son, then why did you call me here?"

"Mr. Harris, we aren't saying that Tavon won't be able to live with you, but we have to follow up on every factor of this case."

Michael sighed and wiped at his face. "I hear you. Come on, Mom. Let's get ready to go to court."

Michael and his mother walked out of the building, and when he got into his car, he just sat there.

"Son, it's gonna all work out. You gotta have faith."

"How much faith can I have right now? I lost my wife and now possibly my son. What more does God want from me? I swear, I will make whatever change I need in order to get my son. Why is this happening to me?" Michael cried.

Sharon didn't know what to say, but she smiled anyway. "Son, just have faith." Sharon's phone began to ring, and she answered, still patting Michael on the shoulder.

"Hey, Tammy. Yes, there's a lot going on. Oh, you heard what's going on? Okay, let me tell him." Sharon looked at Michael. "Tammy wants you to pick her up so she can ride to court with us."

Michael didn't say a word. He started the car and pulled off.

"I guess we're on the way," Sharon said into the phone before hanging up.

Michael picked Tammy up, and they rode in silence to the courthouse. When Michael pulled up to the courthouse and parked, he sighed, "I'm getting real tired of seeing this damn place."

Sharon looked over at him and leaned over a bit. "Son, this time around you aren't alone."

"I appreciate you guys for being here."

Tammy didn't say a word, but she nodded as she prayed that things would work out for her brother.

They got out of the car and walked into the courthouse. They asked a person in passing where courtroom D was, and after the person explained how to get there, they headed on up. Michael and his family sat in the third row and waited. There were several other families present, and Michael wondered why they were there.

After about an hour of them listening to the two other cases, the door in the back of the courtroom opened and Nikki was being led inside. She had on a gray jumpsuit and was handcuffed.

After they sat her down at the front table and took the handcuffs off, she immediately turned and looked over at them. Michael felt sick and turned his head, but Sharon caught the exchange between Nikki and Tammy and looked at Tammy questioningly. Tammy looked over at her mother, and with an unhidden glare, Sharon knew what Tammy had done. She shook her head and looked away, and Tammy felt like she had failed yet again. She dropped her head. When the judge walked in, she addressed the court and asked that Michael join them up front. Michael stood and made his way forward and sat down. Nikki asked to address the court and was granted her request.

"Your Honor, I am requesting that my son, Tavon Harris, be placed in the custody of Michael Harris. He is and has been a positive role model and father to our son. I won't contest the process at all."

Sharon glanced sharply at Tammy, and Tammy looked at her, afraid that her mother would be scolding her silently. Sharon nodded and clamped her hand inside Tammy's and smiled. Tammy knew that her secret was safe with her mother. Anything she had done, she did for the sake of her brother. She just hoped it didn't backfire on them all by losing Tavon for good. She felt that her brother deserved a win for once.

The night before, Tammy had called the police anonymously and reported that there were drugs in the home. She knew where they were located, and she knew that, as usual, Tavon would be in his room. What she didn't know was that her homegirls would be in the same cell block as Nikki. It all played in her favor. When Ashley called her, she told her to put Nikki on the phone, and when she did, she threatened to have the ladies fuck her up every day that she was in there if she didn't say exactly what she had just said to the judge. Nikki knew that she couldn't fight those drug charges and had pled guilty just an hour earlier in a separate courtroom.

"Miss DeLeon, I respect your request, and I will look into placement for Tavon, but I can assure you it won't be today. I understand that there are a few things in Mr. Harris's background that need to be addressed, and we cannot place the child until we are sure that he will be in a safe environment. Now, Mr. Harris, I applaud you for being here, and I won't hold your criminal history against you, but I do have an issue with your recent issues. I have learned that you recently attempted suicide. Is that correct?"

Michael stood up and cleared his throat. "Yes, ma'am, I did. I'm not gonna lie and say I didn't, but I have learned and been in therapy and will continue to do what I have to do to ensure that I am mentally stable not only for my son but for myself. I made a bad judgment error, and I regret it very much so, but, Your Honor, I love my son, and I want him with me."

"I have documents here given to me by the social worker that state you are not actually the child's father."

"A DNA test was done while I was in a coma, and yes, it does prove that I am not technically his father, but I am all he knows, and he is all I know. I need him in my life. I can promise you that my love hasn't change for him at all since finding out I was not his father. I have a supportive family, and they are here with me now. I swear to you that I will do everything in my power to ensure that Tavon is safe and healthy. I've been there since the day he was born, and I'm going to continue to be there. No disrespect to you, this court, or even the social workers present, but I will fight this until the day my son is placed back in my care."

The judge sat back and looked at Michael and then read over the paperwork. "Mr. Harris, I feel how ad-amant you are about the child in question, and I'm going to set another hearing for a week from today, next Wednesday. I want to talk to you and your therapist to-gether and then one on one. I am also going to talk with the child in question to see how he feels about staying with you. We are not here to tear families apart, but we must ensure that the environment is safe and stable. I hope you understand that."

"Yes, ma'am, I do. May I ask the social workers if my son is okay? Have they seen him? Does he need anything?" Michael inquired.

The social worker stood up and smiled. "Your Honor, I'm Elizabeth Warren, and I will answer that question." She looked at Michael and replied, "He is shaken up a bit, but he is adjusting as well as expected. He has everything he needs at this moment."

"May I see him?" Michael asked.

"I apologize, but that's not going to be possible at this juncture. It may affect the child negatively in adjusting to his temporary environment," Elizabeth replied.

Michael looked down and felt like his whole world was shattering around him, but instead of exploding, he calmly nodded his head. "Yes, ma'am, I understand."

The judge dismissed them and called up the next case. Michael and his family walked out of the courtroom, and Mrs. Warren, along with two other people, approached him. "Mr. Harris, please understand that we are only doing what we have to do. We aren't going to oppose you getting your son. Please make sure that you follow what the judge has ordered, and everything will work out for you."

Tammy and her mother patted Michael on the back, and he sighed and smiled briefly. He hoped that the social worker was being honest. He immediately called his therapist to schedule an appointment. He needed to vent, and that was the only place where it would be looked upon as healthy.

Chapter 24

Paula and Angela went to the airport to see Carla off. Paula hugged her tightly and thanked her for going ahead of her to set things up. Angela hugged her also and gave her a long kiss. "I will see you soon, okay?"

"Okay. I will miss you," Carla said.

"You know I'ma miss you and that big ol' booty."

Carla laughed and sighed as she heard her flight being called. "Okay, here goes nothing. Pray for me, bitches."

They all laughed and watched Carla board the flight.

"Where to now, *chica?*" Angela asked.

"I need to go to the house and get a few belongings. I'm waiting to hear from the trucking company that is shipping my vehicles to Seattle. I also need to go into the office for a little while."

"Okay, let's go," Angela replied as they walked out of the airport.

Carla sat on the plane, wishing that Angela could've gone with her. She had fallen for her, and she felt a pain with each mile the plane took away from her. She wasn't going to be with her, and she was going to do everything in her power to influence her to come with them sooner rather than later.

She closed her eyes as the skies led her to Seattle. She prayed that this was the right decision for her.

Monday Afternoon, South Carolina

Tripp

Tripp was growing very frustrated with Paula. He had been calling and texting her for over three weeks and still had gotten no response from her. It wasn't that he was in love with her. He had access to plenty of women. He was angry because she was being disrespectful toward him and ignoring him, which was something he couldn't and wouldn't tolerate. She could easily pick up the phone and tell him that she was going to work on her marriage, that she was seeing someone else, or that she simply wasn't interested in him. Ignoring him just wasn't gonna work.

He had called Tasha a few times, and at first, she was very responsive, but the last few times he called her, she too was ignoring his calls. Tripp was ready to explode.

"Ay, Shock, what's up?" Tripp asked as he walked into the studio.

"Shit, trying to get this beat together for Trey," Shock replied as he leaned back in his chair to talk to Tripp.

"That's what's up. Have you heard from your ol' jump off from North Carolina?" Tripp asked as he sat down on top of the table next to the music mixer.

"Nah, I haven't. Why you ask?" Shock questioned.

"I need you to call her in a few to see if she answers the phone for you. If she does, I want you to see if she has heard from Paula, and then I'm gonna call her to see if she is just missing my calls or ignoring me."

"Still haven't heard from her, huh?" Shock asked.

Tripp looked at Shock sideways and shook his head. "Do you think I'd be asking you to call that tramp if I had? Come on, be smarter than that. I swear, if it weren't for your musical talents, you'd be useless. I don't know what the fuck y'all would do if I weren't around. Just do what the fuck I asked you to do," Tripp fussed.

Shock felt like his head was tightening. He hated when Tripp talked to him like he did, but he knew that if he attempted to do anything, Tripp's goons would be on his ass. He shook it off and pulled out his cell phone and dialed Tasha's number. She picked up on the third ring.

"Hey, boss," Tasha answered.

"What's up, baby? How are you doing?" Shock asked.

Tripp motioned for him to put the speaker on so he could hear the conversation as well. Shock did, and Tripp leaned closer to hear Tasha.

"I been good. Just trying to maintain a bit," she replied.

"That's what's up. So how Paula doing?" Shock asked.

"I guess she's okay. She hasn't spoken to me since she's been back. I tried calling her, but she won't answer."

"Damn, shawty, I hope shit gets better between you two. I'ma try to come up and see you soon if that's cool," Shock told her.

Tripp started nodding his head as Shock talked to Tasha. After a few more minutes, Tripp motioned for Shock to wrap the conversation up.

"All right, Tasha. I'ma holla at you soon," Shock said.

"Okay, baby," Tasha replied and hung up.

Tripp smiled. "You know what? You do got some kind of sense about yourself. We are going to North Carolina tomorrow."

"Tripp, I've never seen you so gone over a woman like this before," Shock told him.

"Naw, it's not about me being gone. At this point I'm out for blood, my nigga. She has shown me she ain't shit, and now this is about me getting my face back. Bitch got me calling her, texting her, and acting all loony over her fat ass. I will never go so far out for a bitch again. I promise you that. Be ready to pull out early."

"But, Tripp, man, I got work to do, and I'm booked until Friday," Shock explained.

"Whose shit is this? Huh? I can shut this whole mothafucking building down for good. The fuck you mean? Nigga, I pay you to work for me. Now we leave tomorrow morning," Tripp growled before slamming out of the studio.

Shock sat back in his chair, staring at the door. He was going to have to find his own way. He had enough money to start his own business, but he knew if he left Tripp's establishment, Tripp would make his life hell. He picked up the phone and called his receptionist and informed her that an emergency had arisen and he needed to clear his calendar for a few days. She told him that she would make the proper phone calls. He thanked her, sighed, and finished mixing the music he was working on, and once he was finished, he left and went home to pack.

Tuesday Night

"I can't believe you are really leaving," Tasha whispered as she watched Paula pack up.

Paula was packing up the last of her clothes that would be going with her on the plane. "Tasha, there's really nothing left for me here," Paula replied, and she pulled the last of her jeans out of the closet.

"I'm just going to miss you so much," Tasha said as tears slowly rolled down her cheeks.

"I'ma miss you too, but we will still talk," Paula replied.

"It won't be the same." Tasha sniffled.

Paula looked at Tasha and sat down next to her. "Tasha, let's be honest. It would never have been the same between you and me. You violated our relationship, but you are still my cousin, and I will still love you no matter what." Paula paused, then continued, "I just can't fuck with you like that anymore."

"I am so sorry I violated your marriage. I'm sorry I hurt you and caused so much turmoil in your life. I love you, cousin, and will always." Tasha stood up and started crying. Paula hugged her, and as hard as she tried not to, she cried too. "Paula, I have to tell you something, but I don't want you to hate me any more than you already do. Michael and I never slept together."

Paula's head snapped back, and she stepped away from Tasha. "What?"

"That night that we were at Trinity's and you and Tripp left, Angela ended up leaving with some chick, and I stayed behind. Michael sat at the table he was at and drank himself under it. I had never seen him drink like that, and the pain that was etched on his face killed me. I couldn't leave him like that. I ended up having to call a taxi and escort him home. Michael made it as far as the couch and collapsed. Nothing happened, but I made it look like it did. The baby I aborted was Shock's baby, but when I told him I was pregnant, he refused to even talk to me afterward. I was confused and wasn't in my right mind. I kind of felt responsible for Michael even being there that night."

"Why, Tasha?" Paula asked with her voice and hands trembling.

"Because I texted him and told him that we were there."
"Really?"

"You had left your cell phone, and I texted him, pretending to be you, and invited him to join us," Tasha admitted.

Paula drew her hand back and slapped Tasha across the face hard. Tasha grabbed her face, and tears began to trail down her cheeks. "I deserved that, and I'm truly sorry. I don't know what came over me. I was lost in a world of corruption. Please, Paula, don't leave with hatred in your heart toward me."

Paula sat down on her couch, shaking from Tasha's truth.

"I guess you were right, Paula. I have been envious of you."

"Tasha, if you are looking for sympathy, you are crying up the wrong river, but even in saying that, I can't leave hating you. I wish you the very best in all that you do."

Paula stood up and told Tasha to leave, but before Tasha walked out, she asked Paula to call her before she left the following day.

"I don't know if I can do that. I don't even know if there is a relationship here to salvage. Like I said earlier, I will always love you. No matter what you have done, you are my family, but I'm done with you."

"Really, Paula? After everything we've been through, you gonna just leave it like that?" Tasha asked.

"Tasha, you just said that you understood. Are you smoking crack or something? I don't understand your logic in asking me that shit," Paula snapped.

"Blood is thicker than water, and no dick or none thereof should interfere. I knew you were going to act like this."

"You're three screws loose from crazy and one word off from an ass whooping. Just get the fuck out," Paula demanded.

"Fuck you, Paula, and I mean that."

"Seems we share a mutual thought," Paula retorted.

Tasha slammed out the door without saying another word.

Paula leaned against her front door for a minute once Tasha was gone, then headed back into her bedroom to finish packing. After she packed up the clothes from the closet, she decided to call it a night. She had two days to get the rest of her belongings together, and she was tired.

Wednesday Morning

Tasha jumped out of her bed as loud banging startled her. "Who is it?" she yelled. The banging started again, and she tossed her robe on and swung the door open. "What?"

"Hello, Tasha," Tripp drawled as he sauntered into her house without waiting to be invited in. Shock followed and stared at Tasha apologetically.

"What the hell is this?" Tasha asked.

"Where is Paula?" Tripp asked coldly.

"Why do you want to know?" Tasha asked, folding her arms across her chest.

"Bitch, don't play with me," Tripp growled.

"I'm not playing. I don't know where Paula is at," Tasha responded nonchalantly.

"Let's see if this jogs your memory," Tripp replied as he grabbed her roughly and placed his Glock at her head. "Now do you know where the hell she at?"

"Tripp, you acting a fool. Let her go," Shock yelled.

"Nigga, shut the fuck up. You in love with this ho? I don't think so, not after all the shit you been saying about her. Especially about the li'l bastard you were happy she got rid of," Tripp sneered with a dark look in his eyes.

"Man, I didn't come all the way here to get locked up for murdering somebody. You looking like a damn psycho chasing behind a woman who don't want you," Shock retorted.

"Fuck you, nigga. You gon' do whatever the fuck I say, or you can die too. Now once again, ho, where the hell is your cousin at?" Tripp questioned.

"She probably at work," Tasha stuttered.

"Let's go," Tripp ordered, looking at Shock.

Shock followed him, and once they were gone, Tasha picked up her phone and made a quick call. She was shaken, but she didn't know what to do, and she needed advice.

Tripp drove around after leaving Tasha's house and then Paula's job. He rode past her house several times but didn't see her truck or car in the driveway. "Where the fuck is this bitch at?"

"Man, just chill, get something to eat, and start back looking once you get your bearings," Shock suggested.

"Yeah, I can do that," he agreed and drove to Kentucky Fried Chicken. They ordered their food and sat in the car and ate. After they finished, they sat in the parking lot for a few more minutes before resuming their search for Tripp's missing lady.

Chapter 25

Wednesday Afternoon

Michael again found himself seated in the courtroom in a battle of his heart, but this time it wasn't his wife he was fighting for—it was a child he would always consider his son. The judge was in her chambers talking to Tavon, trying to make a decision whether he should stay with Michael or remain in foster care. When she returned, she gave Michael the best news he could ever get. Tavon would be placed in his care throughout the adoption process. Nikki had waived her rights to be heard, as she was dealing with the fifteen-year sentence she had recently received as the result of a plea agreement.

When Michael walked out of the courtroom with Tavon by his side, he paused and felt Tavon snatched away from him as he yelled out in glee and took off running. Once Tavon reached Paula, he hugged her around her waist.

Michael finally allowed his legs to move, and he walked slowly over to Paula. "I'm glad you are here, but why are you here?"

Paula looked up and smiled. "I wanted to see you gain custody of your son."

"But how did you know we were here?" Michael questioned.

Paula looked in the direction of Tammy, who smiled at Michael and turned quickly to talk to her mother and Miguel.

"Well, I'm glad you're here," Michael said.

They walked out of the same courthouse where they had fought for and against their marriage. The odd thing was that they were there for the main reason that destroyed them: Tavon.

Michael asked Paula if she would join them for a celebration, and she accepted his invitation. Angela also accompanied them, along with the rest of the family, to their house, and they immediately sparked up the grill. It was a homecoming party for Tavon that would always be remembered.

Tammy sat in the living room, watching television, while Michael and Miguel went outside to man the grill. Sharon was in the kitchen putting together the sides after asking the ladies to leave her to it.

"Hey, wait a minute. Do y'all hear that?" Tammy asked, frowning as she turned the television down.

"Not me. What's wrong with you? What are you hearing?" Paula asked. She didn't have to wait long for an answer, because she heard exactly what Tammy was hearing. There were raised voices coming from the front yard.

The ladies rushed outside, and Tammy instantly shielded Tavon and then ushered him back into the house. Standing in the street yelling and arguing with Michael and Miguel was Tripp.

"Nigga, I know who the fuck you are. I started doing my homework on yo' ass when I first learned who you were. Just like you're a street nigga, I'm one too. You are so out of your element. This ain't South Carolina, and you don't hold weight here, but I do, and I will bust yo' ass. If Paula wants to leave with you, that's on her, but don't come here threatening shit," Michael sneered.

Tripp turned and looked at Shock, who was still seated in the vehicle. "Nigga, yo' bitch ass just gonna sit in there and do nothing?"

"This is your fight. I ain't got shit to do with this. You should learn to curb yo' tongue when talking to me too, bitch," Shock growled.

"I'll tell yo' ass what, I'ma kill yo' ass after I take care of this bastard." Tripp laughed nastily.

"Oh, yeah?" Shock retorted as he got out of the car.

Michael and Miguel watched the two frienemies going at it.

Just then, Paula ran to Michael's side. "Tripp, why are you here? What do you want?"

"I decided to come pay you a visit since you seem to be hiding from me. I texted your phone, I've called you several times, and nothing. So this is what you doing? You going back to your husband?" Tripp seethed.

"Whatever I'm doing is none of your concern. If I haven't called you back or returned any of your messages, that should've given you all the answers you want." Paula yelled, "Leave now."

Miguel stood, staring at Tripp with a dark, masked expression on his face. He wasn't going to move. He was waiting for Tripp to make any wrong move, and he was going to flip.

Michael walked Paula back to the porch and turned around and advanced slowly on Tripp. "You heard what my wife said, homie. Leave."

Tripp laughed, "I got you." He turned as if he were leaving and swung back around quickly with his pistol in his hand. "Nigga, I bet you won't have her."

As he took aim, Paula screamed and rushed forward, throwing her body in front of Michael's like a shield.

Pow. Pow. Pow. Pow.

When the dust cleared and the screaming increased around them, Paula stood against Michael and shook her head, then whispered, "This is all my fault. I couldn't let you take the heat for me."

Michael had Paula wrapped up in his arms with tears sliding down his face.

"Call the police," Sharon yelled as she raced out of the house, holding her own gun.

"Ma. What the hell?" Tammy cried.

"I've always told y'all, I'ma protect what's mine."

When Paula and Michael turned, they saw Tripp lying next to his Crown Vic with blood oozing under him.

Sharon, who was an old G, peeped what was about to go down. She'd grabbed her .45 out of her purse and opened fire on Tripp before he could successfully aim his gun and kill her son. Tripp was only able to let off one shot in the air as she filled his body with three bullets.

The police and crime scene units arrived on scene immediately afterward, and after hours of talking with neighbors, they'd heard each person's account of what happened, including Shock's statement that Tripp's main reason for being there was to kill Michael. Finding Tripp's loaded and recently fired gun in his hand, they decided that no charges would be filed against Sharon.

The police took Shock and Sharon in to get their written statements and had Tripp's vehicle towed in as evidence. Once the police left, no one was in the mood to eat. Paula felt responsible for everything that had happened and apologized for everything repeatedly.

"Paula, listen, I appreciate your apology, but right now my focus is on my mother and Tavon. I appreciate you being there for us today and even coming to hang out with us for the time that you did, but I'ma have to ask you to leave. I went through so much to prove to you that I wasn't this monster I was painted to be, but you wanted to believe everyone else, knowing me better than any one of those bitches. Granted, I fucked up with Nikki, and if I could take it back, I would, but that's something I can't take back. Although it ruined our lives"—he paused and looked at Tavon—"I can't say that it was all for nothing."

Paula smiled. "You don't have to say another word. Goodbye, Michael."

Paula and Michael embraced, and when they let one another go, they both felt that it was the end.

Paula looked at the door and saw Tavon. "Tell him I said goodbye, okay?"

"You tell him yourself," Michael replied.

"I'd rather not," she said sadly.

"Don't look so down with your good-pussy-having ass." Michael laughed, trying to mask his pain.

Paula laughed, "Leave it to you to say some crazy shit, but ay, you spoke the truth, and only a nigga with good dick can appreciate good pussy."

Michael laughed and watched Paula and Angela get in the car and drive off. He felt like his heart was breaking all over again, but he had to suck it up and focus on the little man who needed his attention.

Tavon ran out. "Where is Paula?"

"She had to leave, but she told me to hug you real tight and to tell you goodbye," Michael explained as he hugged Tavon tightly.

"Is she coming back?"

"I don't think so, son." Michael was devastated by the disappointment on Tavon's face. "Come on, let's go in the house and get you ready for bed."

Michael took one last glance in the direction that Paula and Angela had driven off in. He sighed and swallowed the lump that was rising in his throat.

Paula watched Michael in the side mirror and smiled as she realized that he was growing up, so to speak. He had put Tavon first even with the information that he wasn't his. She could've easily been hurt, but after spending time with him and growing a fondness for him, she couldn't even be mad. Tavon needed Michael in his life, and Michael needed him. She looked over at Angela. "I'ma miss you."

"Bitch, you already know I'ma miss yo' ass. But as soon as you get settled, I'm coming to visit, so make sure you have my bed ready." Angela laughed, trying to keep the mood cheerful.

"You promise?" Paula asked.

"Pinky promise."

Paula linked her pinky with Angela's and smiled. "Keep an eye on Michael and Tavon for me."

Angela looked at Paula and laughed, "Bitch, I'm too much of a man for you to have me all emotional and shit."

Paula started laughing, and as they pulled up to Paula's hotel, Angela cut the headlights off and they both got out. Angela paused at the front of the car. "I'ma go ahead and bounce, okay?"

"You aren't coming in?" Paula asked.

"Naw. I don't think my heart can take seeing you prepare to leave. Listen, I love you, and I will call you tomorrow night," Angela said, stepping to Paula quickly and hugging her tightly. They hugged for what seemed like forever, and when they separated, Angela dipped her head and wiped at her eyes. "See you later, sis."

"See you later," Paula repeated. She stood and watched Angela pull off. Angela blew the horn as she drove off.

"Damn, I'ma miss that bitch." Paula sighed as she walked into the building.

Several hours later, Shock walked out of the interrogation room, called Tasha, and asked her to pick him up from the police station.

"What the hell happened?" she asked.

"I'll explain when you get here," he replied.

"Fuck that. Is my cousin okay?" She grabbed her keys and walked out the door.

"She is fine. Just come and get me." He hung up.

Shock sat back, trying to figure out what he could tell the guys back in South Carolina about why he had returned and Tripp hadn't, why he was alive and Tripp wasn't. He had to figure something out and quick. He wasn't going to run from the situation, but he had to make it work all around for him. He wasn't expecting Tripp to get shot by the old woman. He had planned on killing Tripp himself. Shock smiled at the irony of the situation. From the moment he met Tripp, Tripp had always gone for bad, and now his bad ass was in the morgue, lying on a table and being dissected.

Suddenly an idea popped in his head. He was going to tell them the truth—well, semi-truth—and take over Tripp's empire.

A few minutes later, Tasha was calling him to let him know that she was in the parking lot. He got up and walked out with a smile on his face.

"What's going on? Why am I picking you up here, and where the hell is Tripp?" Tasha asked once he got in the car.

"Tripp is dead. That's what. I need you to drive me to South Carolina, and once we are there, I need you to back me on everything I say. Your cousin's life and Michael's are in jeopardy, and I don't want to add more drama to their lives. You understand what I'm saying, right?"

Tasha sighed, "Anything to right my wrong. Yeah, I understand."

Tasha's heart was beating fast, and her nerves were on 10,000. She was terrified of what was about to occur, but she felt the need to do what was right.

She told Shock that she needed to stop by her house and get a few items. Once they were at her home, Tasha got out, and Shock sat in the car and waited for her. Ten minutes later, she was back out, and she and Shock drove off into the unknown.

Thursday Morning

Paula walked into the hotel, went to her room, and lay down on her bed. Sleep was the furthest thing from her mind. The day's events were replaying in her head. She couldn't believe that Tripp was dead. She tossed and turned the whole night. At nine thirty, she had her bags in the lobby and was waiting for her Uber to arrive. She looked at her phone and saw that she didn't have any messages from Michael at all. Angela had texted her, telling her to have a safe trip and that she loved her.

When the Uber arrived, Paula, with the driver's help, loaded the car up with her belongings, and they headed to the airport. When she arrived, she checked her luggage and waited to board the plane. Her phone beeped.

Maybe Tavon and I can visit once you're stable in your new city. I love you, and I wish you well. Good luck and have a safe flight. Please let me know that you arrive in Seattle safely.

Paula smiled and texted back: You know you can visit, and I will contact you once we land. Thank you, Michael, and I wish you the best as well. Take care of Tavon and yourself.

Paula felt bad at how she and Tasha left things. Maybe she was overreacting, especially since she and Michael were over. She didn't know where her head was at with Tasha, but she wouldn't feel right leaving without at least saying goodbye.

She dialed Tasha's number but didn't get an answer. She sent her a quick text: Love you no matter what.

She put her phone away. She grabbed a *Forbes* magazine and sighed, "My face is going to be on here one day."

As they called for her flight, she took a look around and sighed, "Welp, so long, North Carolina."

She boarded the plane and found her seat and got settled in. She checked her phone once more before the plane took off and still hadn't heard back from Tasha. She turned the phone off, and for some reason, she was feeling like she was leaving something behind.

An announcement sounded out throughout the plane. "We would like to thank you for choosing Delta Airlines. Please buckle up and turn all cell phones and electronic devices off. I'm Douglas Ray, and I will be your captain on this flight. The flight attendants will be around shortly to offer refreshments. Enjoy your flight."

"Here goes," Paula whispered to herself. As the plane ascended into the air, Paula lay her head back against the seat with her eyes closed, holding her breath as her stomach began doing flip-flops. She prayed that they would make it safely to Seattle. She always got nervous when she had to fly.

Once they were in the air safely, she began to wonder why Tasha hadn't contacted her. She hadn't heard a peep from her. She shrugged it off and figured that she would reach out sooner or later.

Eight hours later, Paula had arrived in Seattle. She was in awe of how fresh the air smelled compared to the air in North Carolina. She took in the beautiful landscape that surrounded the airport.

"Hey, girl. You made it," Carla shrieked as she saw Paula walking through the airport.

"Yes, I did. Is the city as beautiful as I imagined?" Paula asked.

"Better, bitch. Was Angela okay when you left?" Carla asked.

"She was good. You know she was sad, but I told her that I'd fly her out in a heartbeat if she felt like she wanted to come," Paula explained.

"I hate to spring this on you, but I really need to go back to North Carolina. I miss her," Carla admitted.

Paula smiled. "When?"

"Next week?" Carla asked with a raised eyebrow.

"That's fine. Next week it is. Now let's embrace the city of Seattle."

The two ladies walked out of the airport, and Paula excitedly wondered what wonderful adventures her life was about to embark on. "Here's to a new lifestyle," she screamed before getting into the taxi that was taking her to her new home.

Chapter 26

Friday morning, Shock and Tasha were sitting in Tripp's office, talking to three of Tripp's main hitters.

"What the fuck happened up there?" Jack growled, holding his pistol in his hand.

"And we ain't trying to hear no bullshit. We got a copy of the police report. My question to you is, how the fuck did you figure you could come back here knowing your bitch ass is a snitch and backslider?" Dorian asked as he punched Shock in the face.

Shock's head rocked back and forth, and blood trickled down his mouth and chin. He looked at the men with a bewildered look. His plan wasn't going how he expected.

"What are you looking at us like that for? You thought we weren't going to find out about you bailing on a homie just when he needed you the most? Tell me what you thought you would gain from that," said Ice, the third man who was standing off to the side.

"Man, I don't know what y'all talking about," Shock replied.

"Oh, yeah? Is that your final answer?" Ice asked as he cracked his knuckles.

"I swear I don't," Shock replied.

Ice looked over at Tasha, who was now standing up and moving away from Shock.

Shock frowned and shook his head. "You fucking bitch." He knew at that point that Tasha had told them everything.

"No, nigga, don't look at me like that. I wasn't the one who told them. I just verified everything," Tasha replied.

"You really are a piece of shit. You just killed your whole fucking family, bitch."

"I don't give a fuck, and you can call me what you want to call me, but Paula turned her back on me over a mothafucking nigga. I'm her blood, and she treated me like I was nothing, so fuck her and that nigga," Tasha sneered.

Shock shook his head and started laughing. "You know what? You are sad. You wanted so much to be like your cousin that you gonna let these bastards kill her? What is it? Do you think you can have her life if she is out the picture? Let me save you the trouble of thinking that. Paula is more woman than you will ever be. You will never have her life. You are nothing like her."

Tasha walked over to Shock and slapped him as hard as she could. She walked away from him, but deep down in her gut, she knew he was telling the truth.

"You're one to talk about loyalty and wanting to take someone's place, Shock. Especially since you told me that you had planned to kill Tripp yourself. You know the report says that the bullets that were pulled from Tripp's body didn't match Sharon's gun at all. They matched the gun that you had. You know, the one we went and picked up from where you tossed it before the police arrived?" Tasha laughed, sharing every detail that Shock had shared with her.

Shock looked at Tasha for a moment. "Why are you doing this?"

"Nigga, you made me kill my baby. You used me, and you knew you only brought me here to place blame on me for Tripp's death. That's why when I went to my house to pick up my clothes, I called Kisha and gave her a quick rundown on what had happened, and she told me to leave everything up to her." Tasha laughed again. "You know, it's funny that when I needed someone, she was the only person there for me. Not my cousin, not my best friend, not even you, but she was. We became good friends, and we stayed in touch. Nigga, fuck you, and I pray you go straight to hell for the pain you caused me."

Just then, the door opened, and Kisha walked in, and Shock looked up and shook his head once more.

"You must be shocked to see me, Shock," she laughed. "I'm sorry, Tasha, but just like they say, 'The sins of the father . . .' Somebody, namely you, has gotta pay for the sins of the cousin. We aren't going to go all around the world searching for anybody. You will do."

Pow.

Before Tasha could say a word, Kisha shot her once in the forehead. Tasha's body dropped, and Shock began to panic.

"Don't worry, nigga. I'm not going to shoot you," Kisha promised.

Ice moved away from the door and walked forward and pulled out the drawer to Tripp's desk. "This should do." He pulled out a straight razor and walked back over to where Shock was sitting. He grabbed Shock's head and tilted it back. Silence fell upon the room as Ice slowly and menacingly sliced Shock's throat, allowing the blood to flow freely.

After Shock was dead, Ice ordered the others to clean up the mess as he silently prayed, *this kill was for you, Tripp. Rest in peace, my brother.*

Ice sat down at Tripp's desk and lit a cigar as he wiped the wetness from his eyes. Tripp was gone and never coming back. He knew that Tripp should've left shit alone with that bitch Paula, but it was too late to think about that now. "Ay, we gon' have to kill that bitch and that nigga. We sparing no muthafucka."

"What do you have in mind?" Kisha asked.

"We about to take an extended trip, baby girl."

Kisha nodded and walked out.

Chapter 27

Six Months Later

Paula settled into her new environment very quickly. She had made a few friends within a month's time. Chance, her next-door neighbor, and his wife, Shawna, were the first to embrace her. They showed her around Seattle and introduced her to some of the most influential business associates in the local area. They all had children, and she utilized her knowledge and coercion tactics to reel in a few new clients.

"Hi, Paula. What have you got planned for the weekend?" Shawna asked as the two were exiting the lovely high-rise building where she rented an apartment.

Paula fell in love with the apartment immediately, as the rooms were spacious and the wonderful view that overlooked the city was its high point. Tower 12 was very expensive, and she wasn't sure that she wanted to stay there any longer than her company was paying for. The rent was $3,000 a month, and even though she could afford it, she wasn't crazy. She wasn't about to pay that amount of money for an apartment. If she was going to pay that much a month, it would be for a home that she was purchasing. Paula decided that she would save her money, and after her year's lease was over, she'd put a down payment on her very own home.

"I'm not sure yet. What are you guys doing?" Paula asked as she went through her mail.

"We're having a party Saturday for Chance's birthday. We'd love for you to attend."

"Sounds like a plan to me. Should I bring anything?" Paula asked as she reached her car.

"Nope, just come on by. We've got everything covered."

"Count me in," Paula said as she waved her hand and got into her car.

It was the day that she was pitching a major move for their company. They were embarking on creating another franchise of daycares. The company's other centers throughout the country were a success. Now she wanted to discuss going global. She hoped that they'd embrace her idea, as she had put in a lot of time and research for a global reach.

Paula drove down the interstate and merged onto the road to get to her office. She loved the scenery. Each morning she passed the Space Needle as she headed in and always was amazed that she was seeing it in person.

When she finally arrived, she grabbed her briefcase and pocketbook, got out of her car, and walked into the building.

"Hello, Ms. Harris. You have had eight calls from Mr. Harris, and he says it's urgent that you call him back," Tracy, her secretary, informed her.

"Okay, thanks. I wonder why he hasn't called my cell."

Paula walked into her office and set everything down and pulled her phone from her purse. She searched her call log and saw that he had indeed called her over twenty-seven times.

"What the hell is going on?" she pondered.

Before she could call him back, Evelyn walked in and sat down. "Boss lady, I need some advice about the new location in Ohio. I have to staff it just right. In my hands, I have two of the most qualified ladies for the management position. Tap one."

Paula laughed, "Hell naw. I'm not gon' touch shit. Just pick one. You will make the right decision. I have to make a call right quick, okay?"

"I can take a hint. Bye." Evelyn laughed as she walked out.

Paula walked behind her and closed the door. She walked back over to her desk, but before she could call Michael, he was calling her.

"Yes, Michael?"

"Paula, someone took Tavon," Michael cried.

"Who took him?" Paula asked as her heartbeat quickened.

"Some of your pussy-ass nigga's people. They said if I ever want to see him alive again, you and I have to follow their instructions and ride down to South Carolina."

Paula could hear the pain and fear in his voice. "Okay, we got to think this out," Paula began.

"Think what out?" Michael fumed.

"No, I mean, we have to call the police," Paula rambled.

"The bastards said that if we contact the police, my son would surely die. I know I've betrayed your trust, but don't make my son pay for my sins," Michael begged.

Paula sat at her desk with tears falling from her eyes, leaving several splattered drips on her laptop. "I'm on my way. I will catch the next flight out, and, Michael?"

"What?" he whispered.

"Tavon is going to be okay. We will fix this."

Michael hung up without a response. Paula wasn't going to take a chance that they'd get out alive, so she called her family in South Carolina for assistance.

Michael was pacing back and forth, praying Tavon was being treated okay. He wanted to go get him alone, but the letter said that if he arrived without Paula, Tavon would die. He was so mad and convinced that he and Paula were going to die. He was okay with that, as long as Tavon could live. If he couldn't, at least they'd die together. He hadn't told Tavon's mother because she was facing her own fate in jail. He had to deal with it himself.

His phone beeped, and he looked down and noticed it was his mother. What was he going to tell her? She was most likely calling to talk to Tavon. He ignored her call and put her on snooze. He couldn't deal with any extra stress.

As he sat back, he rubbed his hands through his hair. He was dog tired and hadn't had any peace since he'd gotten home and found his son gone. How the hell could someone scoop him up at a bus stop? He was beside himself, and it hurt because there was nothing he could do. Someone else was holding him by the nut sack, and he had to suffer that pain.

His phone beeped again, and he quickly picked it up, hoping that it was Kisha with Tavon on the phone. He couldn't believe that he was so gullible to fall for such a deviant slut.

He opened up the text, and it was Paula.

We aren't going to ride the storm alone. I got a plan.

He texted back: Paula, don't do nothing stupid. Any wrong move, Tavon is dead.

A few moments passed, and Paula's response canceled his disapproval.

Paula: Tavon could already be dead. I'm sorry to say that, but it's a fact. And if he isn't, how do you know they won't kill him anyway once we get there?

Michael hated Paula for bringing those thugs into their lives. But most of all he hated himself for allowing that bitch to come into his life and trick him.

Michael reluctantly texted back: What do you have planned?

Paula: I'll tell you once I'm there. My flight leaves at eight tonight, and I will be there by two in the morning. I will catch a taxi to your house when I get there. Have you heard anything from them? I'm at a loss. How did they know about Tavon?

Michael frowned. Just get here.

Paula didn't respond, but Michael knew she was going to ask again once she arrived.

Ice and Kisha

"Hey, little fella, we aren't going to hurt you. We just need to talk to your dad. Everything is going to be all right," Kisha whispered, trying to calm Tavon.

"Get that little nigga a bottle of water. He gonna dehydrate with all that damn crying he doing. Man, shut the fuck up," Ice growled as he advanced in the room where Tavon was located.

"Do not yell at him, and don't come in here like you going to do something to him," Kisha hissed. Kisha wasn't okay with kidnapping Tavon. She just thought they were going to make the little boy an orphan.

"You know, I don't know what the fuck you got on your mind, but that little muthafucka gon' die along with his daddy. I didn't do all this just to let someone point the finger at me for murder. If you good with that, then you can get the fuck on," Ice snarled.

Kisha turned and looked at the frightened child and then back at Ice. She didn't want to admit it, but he was right. If she left, she knew that he would kill the young boy, and she couldn't have a child's blood on her hands. She'd kill Ice first and raise Tavon as her own child after they killed Michael and Paula.

"Miss Kisha, are you mad at me about something?" Tavon sniffed.

"No, but just be quiet, okay? Are you hungry?"

He nodded.

"I'ma go get him something to eat. I'll be back though."

Ice looked at her and smiled. "I knew you'd see it my way. I'll go get the li'l menace something to eat, and you stay here with him. Keep him quiet."

Once he was out of the room and walking down the hall, Kisha walked over quickly to Tavon. "I won't let him hurt you, but you got to be quiet, okay? Trust me, you will not get hurt."

Tavon looked up with tears in his eyes. "Is he going to kill my daddy?"

Kisha looked at him sadly and nodded. " I'm sorry," she whispered and walked away.

Carla and Angela

Angela and Carla were at home and eating dinner when Carla's phone began to ring. "It's Paula." She smiled and screamed in delight, "Hey, cuz."

As Angela motioned for Carla to tell Paula hello for her, she frowned as Carla's smile disappeared and her mouth dropped open.

"Oh, my God. Paula, are you serious? No. Yes, I'll call them right now and let them know to be expecting your call. Yes, I love you too." Carla hung up.

Angela glared at her, waiting for her to tell her what was going on.

"Babe, you're not gon' believe this. Tavon has been kidnapped, and Paula and Michael are being summoned to South Carolina. I need to call Darius and Snook. We gotta take a trip, bitch."

Angela stood up and began to walk away.

"Babe, where are you going? We haven't eaten yet," Carla cried out.

"Fuck, you said we gotta take a trip, so let's go," Angela replied.

Carla could see the concern and anger on her lady's face, and she felt the same, but they had to eat and figure things out. "Angela, she is still in Seattle. Let's eat, and then we can go check on Michael. But I got to make this call. Come on now, sit down."

Angela sat back down, but seafood was the last thing on her mind. She closed her eyes and prayed for her friend and the survival of Tavon. She also prayed for Michael while Carla made her calls. Shit was about to get real.

Michael sat at the kitchen table, staring at a bottle of gin and a bottle of Percocet.

"I can end it all right now," he said. "This is the second time that my son has been taken from me." Soon a terrible wave of anger began to replace the feeling of pain and fear. "Fuck it," he yelled.

He began to punch at the walls, leaving cracks in the wake of his wrath. He knocked over the table and began destroying the house. Before long he found himself hunched over, yelling Tavon's name out repeatedly.

Just as a second wave of anger began to seize him, he heard a bang at the door. He rushed over and opened it, hoping beyond hope that Kisha and her niggas had changed their minds and were bringing Tavon back home. Instead, it was Angela and Carla.

He turned disappointedly and walked away.

As the two ladies walked in, they took in the destruction that Michael had caused, stepping cautiously through the broken glass from the table he had tossed around. Angela's eyes caught a glimpse of the pill bottle on the floor next to shards of broken glass from the gin bottle. She glared at Michael and rushed over.

"Did you—" she began.

"I didn't. I wanted to, but I didn't."

Angela hugged him. They had never been close friends, but her heart couldn't bear to see him so broken. He looked helpless, hopeless, and terrified. His eyes were shadowed and red.

Michael broke down as he felt her arms engulf him. He needed to feel that at that moment. Suddenly he pulled away.

"I don't deserve your compassion when I don't know if my son is receiving compassion. I just don't know what I'd do if he died because of Paula and me. He doesn't deserve this."

Michael cried while Angela and Carla sat next to him, consoling him. Angela waited about ten minutes before cleaning up the mess that Michael had made.

"Angela, you don't have to do that. I can get all of this up. But thank you," he sighed as he stood.

"It's no problem, really. I need to do something to keep my mind from focusing on what's going on. I know that me and you have had a rough relationship, but I'm so sorry that you're going through this, and I need you to know that we're here for you," Angela assured him.

Michael truly believed her, and as they all began to clean up, Michael began to feel stronger.

Once they were finished, Angela and Carla made sure that it would be okay if they returned, and then they left to go pack a bag. They weren't going to let Paula go to South Carolina alone.

Michael was relieved when Carla and Angela said that they were coming back. He didn't even have to think about it when they approached him with the idea of them staying over. It actually made him realize that he needed his own support team with him, and he knew one person he could call who would go to war with him.

After cleaning up his house, Michael decided that whatever Paula had planned to do, he was about to amplify it ten times over. If they wanted war, they were going to get just that.

Chapter 28

Friday Morning

Paula arrived at Raleigh-Durham International Airport and quickly exited once she retrieved her luggage. She was tired and anxious to see Michael. When she waved down a taxi and was comfortably seated inside, she checked her messages. She smiled as she saw a text message from Darius: a simple green-light meme.

Darius and Snook were Carla's brothers. They were part of the game, located in South Carolina. They were known for their ruthless behavior. After Michael called to inform her of Tavon's abduction, she knew for sure that if they went to South Carolina unprepared and alone, they would surely be killed. One thing she learned from Tripp was that his crew was useless without him. Her cousins were going to face the shit head-on, and she was going to be leading the troops.

Michael just didn't know how much she loved Tavon. She would risk her life to save him, but she refused to go easily.

Paula sent a smiley-face emoji back and closed her eyes to say a prayer. She didn't know if God was going to listen, especially as it appeared that she was about to kill someone or be killed herself. She was terrified at the several possibilities that could occur, death being the worst.

She called Michael to let him know that she'd be there in an hour. When he answered, she heard laughter in the background. Michael was drunk.

"Shello," he sang into the phone.

"Michael. Is everything okay?"

"Hell naw. My son is missing, and I'm drunk as fuck."

"I'll be there in an hour." She heard a familiar laugh in the background. "Is that Angela?"

"It is. We are enjoying what may be our last night alive. Kind of like our own funeral celebration. Hurry on and join us, wifey." Michael hung up before Paula could respond.

She looked at the phone and frowned. "What a jerk."

"I think we going to be in trouble when the missus gets here." Michael laughed.

"Naw, we'll be straight by the time she gets here," Carla interjected.

Miguel, who Michael had called earlier, shook his head. "I told y'all not to drink that whole bottle of VSOP. That shit ain't for everybody."

"Well, she will be here in an hour. She just called," Michael informed them, laughing.

"Oh. Shit," Angela groaned. "Yeah, she gon' be pissed off. Let's try to sober up a little bit."

Everybody got up and began straightening up before Paula got there. Carla walked to the kitchen and made a fresh pot of coffee.

Once Paula arrived at Michael's, she paid the driver, grab the bags, and got out. Carla and Angela were sitting on the steps with only the light from inside the house shining dimly on them. She sighed and walked forward. It was three thirty in the morning, and she was so happy to see some friendly faces.

Paula walked on the porch and was greeted by Angela and Carla with a tight hug. Paula finally felt secure enough to break down. They all sat on the porch consoling Paula.

Michael walked out and stumbled over to where Paula stood and laughed, "Welcome home, dear."

Paula wiped her face and stood up. "I can't believe you are drunk. Do you know what the fuck is about to happen?" she fussed.

"You know what? What the fuck I do know," he slurred, "is that if it weren't for you, my son would still be here right now."

"Okay, now wait a minute," Angela started but was pulled back by Carla.

"Not our business. Let them have their moment," Carla told her.

It hurt Angela to see Paula and Michael in so much pain, but Carla was right. They had to get it out in order for them to work together in getting Tavon back.

"You're really going to say that shit to me? I love that child with everything in me. Even after I knew he was born out of wedlock, I still bonded with him. He is my heart. Why the fuck else would I be here? Huh? Answer that," Paula stormed. Tears flowed from Paula's face, and her body trembled uncontrollably. The wind was blowing lightly, causing the clouds in the sky to move briskly by.

"I just don't know how they found out where y'all lived," Paula pondered.

"Paula, I have to tell you something. I met a chick named Kisha from South Carolina. I didn't think that she could be a friend of Tripp's. I was just so lonely and confused that when she started gracing me with attention, I jumped at it. She told me she was new to the area, and we kind of hooked up here and there. I didn't know that she was using me to get to you. And when they couldn't get to you through me, I assume that they figured the next best way to get to both of us was through Tavon."

Paula dropped her head. "This is all my fault, and I gotta make it right." Suddenly it dawned on her. Tasha was the culprit, and she also assumed that Tasha had to be dead.

"It was Tasha," she whispered.

"Tasha?" Michael asked as he looked at her.

"Yes. She was with them when Tripp got killed. I know for sure that Tasha is dead now. Oh, my God, damn," Paula snapped. "This is crazy. You know, I thought I was doing something when I started going out and found Tripp. I thought it would make me feel vindicated in some way. And all I ended up doing was messing things up worse. Tripp was kind to me until I learned that he was into drugs and murder. I left immediately, and I began to realize that we are all flawed. You are a good man, Michael. I want to say that I forgive you for everything that has happened between me and you. You are a great man and a wonderful husband, and I'll never take that away from you. I was just really hurt," she admitted as she looked into his eyes.

Michael hugged her, and she hugged him back. "Let's talk about how we are going to get our son back," said Paula.

Michael nodded his head. He and the others went inside to make their plans.

Chapter 29

South Carolina, 8:00 a.m.

"Paula, the guy Ice said that once we arrived, you should call him from my phone. He will only talk to you from this point on," said Michael.

Paula walked away from the group with Michael on her ass to make the call.

"Well, is this the one and only Paula? Girl, it's been a minute," Kisha said as she answered the phone.

"Is Tavon okay?" Paula asked. She put the phone on speaker so that Michael could hear what was going on.

"He's fine. Now this is what you're going to do," Kisha started.

"Before we do anything, I need to know for a fact that Tavon is okay," Paula told her.

There was a bit of murmuring in the background, and then they heard young Tavon speak out. "Daddy. Daddy," he cried repeatedly.

"I'm coming, son. Oh, my God. If they've hurt him, I'll kill them with my bare hands," he growled, energized and full of so much anger that he couldn't picture anything other than placing his hands around Kisha's neck and squeezing the life from her body.

While Ice was giving them instructions on where to meet, Miguel, Carla, and Angela were with a huge group of gang members, getting suited up for war. After they got Tavon's location, Paula and Michael walked over and told everyone else what the plan was. It was a good thing that Paula was familiar with the layout of Tripp's studio.

They had agreed to meet Darius and Snook at Carla's mother's home, located deep in the country area.

"We have to be there at ten tonight, so I sent a few of my boys to ride through and see what it looks like over there. They just texted me and said there are about seven men and one bitch lurking around the property. They sent me pictures of the area, and we will look over them and pinpoint our best way in," Darius informed them.

"Yeah, that bitch is Kisha. I still can't believe she did this shit," Paula said.

"Well, we will head out about thirty minutes before you all do, and once we are in place, we will send you a text. We gotta get in quick, and once we have neutralized Ice and Kisha, we will then clean up the bodies, and y'all can head back to NC," Darius continued.

Paula knew that after Ice and Kisha were dead, Darius and his boys were going to do more than get rid of the bodies. They were going to strip that building down and take anything they felt was of value to them. She had also given them Tripp's home address. After tonight, she prayed that she'd be able to hear about her cousins' come-up off of Tripp's money.

"Can we go in and try to rest up for a few hours? I've literally had zero amount of sleep, and I'm sure Michael hasn't had much either," Paula asked.

"Yeah, go in and rest. We will finish up after y'all are refreshed. Don't worry, cuz. We gon' get the li'l man back."

Michael smiled, hearing the reassurance that Darius had just given Paula. It made him feel better about the situation. He also felt a little bit more at ease after hearing his son's voice. He looked at Paula and tapped her on the arm. "Can we talk before we attempt to sleep?"

"Sure, what's up?"

They walked off to the side of the aged, beaten wood house, and once out of eyesight and earshot of the others, Michael hugged Paula with a force that she had never felt.

"Thank you, Paula, not only for being here, because to be honest, you didn't have to come, but also for being the standup woman you've always been to me and now Tavon. You apologized to me earlier, but on my life"—he gritted his teeth as he stared deep into her eyes—"I am so very sorry for betraying you. I wish that I could have a do-over. You know I love having Tavon, but—"

Paula cut him off. "Things happen for a reason. It's all for the best. Tavon needed you, and God saw that. He doesn't make any mistakes, babe. This struggle we're facing right now too will pass. Believe that. We are going to be just fine, together or apart. I will always love you."

They hugged for a few moments before going into the house and lying down. A few hours later, after a bath and eating dinner, they were ready to face their opponents.

Saving Tavon

Paula and Michael stood outside their car outside of Tripp's studio. She shivered at the anticipation of what was to come. She closed her eyes and begged to the heavens that they would make it out alive. She searched the area and breathed in deeply. "You ready?"

Michael swallowed hard and nodded. "Let's go."

As they entered the building, a tall dark-skinned man approached them. "Move," he ordered as he pushed them.

Suddenly the man's grip on Paula's arm slacked, and she turned. He fell to the ground, and Darius stood behind him, smiling. "Told you I got you. Go."

They rushed down the hallway, popping their silencers as they approached them. Suddenly, they heard a voice growl, "Stop right there, or this little bastard gon' get shot right here. I told y'all not to come with the bullshit. Kisha, go get that muthafucka." Ice pointed his gun toward Tavon, who was just a few feet away.

Kisha raced toward Tavon and grabbed him. "Don't worry. I won't let him hurt you."

"Bitch, don't hurt my son," Michael warned.

"I can shoot yo' ass quicker than you could pull that trigga," Darius told him.

"No, please, he has his scope on my son."

The red laser displayed a dot right in the middle of Tavon's forehead.

"Daddy. Daddy," Tavon cried.

Paula stared helplessly at Tavon with a fear that she could really lose him, which sent her mind spiraling. Her fear was soon replaced by anger. *How dare that bitch?* She had helped Ice put her stepson through hell because Tripp couldn't take rejection. The love she had for Tavon had weakened her. As she stared at him, her stomach turned, and her head started hurting. Her eyes collected the tears that had been battling to spring forth since the day Tripp had brought his drama into their lives. She glanced over at Michael, who looked at her and frowned. He knew without her saying a word what her next move was going to be.

As Paula rushed toward Kisha, Michael attempted to stop her. But it was too late. Paula was off.

"Paula, noooooo," he yelled.

Paula moved as swift as a black panther. She was upon Kisha instantly and landed three punches to her face before they fell to the ground. As the pair hit the floor, a muttered popping sound let off.

Michael froze, glaring at the women and praying that his wife was okay.

Once Paula dived on Kisha, Ice was distracted, which allowed Snook to shoot him twice in the chest, leaving two holes, each the size of a golf ball.

Angela ran over and grabbed at her friend. "No," she screamed. She dived on Kisha. She began punching her repeatedly in the face. Every punch got harder as she broke her nose and busted her mouth open. It seemed like Kisha's eyes instantly swelled as Angela got one more hit in before being pulled off her.

"Listen, you two get Paula and take her to the hospital. Brute will carry her down. Michael, you and your homie get little man out of here, and we will stay back and get rid of these bodies. When the police ask you what happened to Paula, tell them that you were all over on Third Street at the park and a white man tried to rob you three. Paula chased him down, causing him to shoot her. I'll call in a report from this burner phone and report a shooting. Okay, let's get going. We ain't got time to waste. And call me when y'all find out if my cousin will live. I'm praying for her," Darius told them.

Michael couldn't get to Tavon fast enough. He checked him over, scooped him up, and ran out of the building. He took his son to the nearest hospital to have him checked out. He was also worried about Paula, but he had to make sure Tavon was straight first.

"Son, we can't speak of this ever. Do you understand me? If you do, they could take you away from me forever."

"No, Daddy. I don't want that. I won't tell anybody," he exclaimed.

The one hope that Michael had at that moment was that Tavon would soon forget about this experience. He was young enough to do just that. He was going to do everything in his power to get him through it.

Back in Tripp's Office

Darius stood over Kisha and smiled. "Before we kill you, bitch, where is all the money kept?"

Carla looked at Angela and shook her head. "You go with Paula. I wanna see this bitch die."

"No. You go with her. It has to look like you were all together in the park when the robbery was attempted. Go make sure Paula is all right. We got this. I'll call you later," Darius told her.

They ran out, even though Carla wanted so badly to see that bitch die.

Once Brute had her in the car, he looked at Angela and grimaced, alerting her that he didn't think Paula was going to make it. Angela rolled her eyes, jumped in the car, and sped off.

MUSC Health University Medical Center

Carla pulled up to the entrance, blowing her horn repeatedly. Once the nurses came out and assessed the situation, they rushed Paula in, who was taken to emergency surgery. Angela was crying terribly, and Carla was doing her best to console her without falling apart herself.

She was beside herself as she watched the doctors work on Paula. One of the nurses walked over and told Angela and Carla that they were going to be moving Paula to surgery located on the second floor and they could go to the waiting room on that floor.

"Why the hell did this happen to her?" Angela asked no one.

Carla stroked her hair. "She will be okay. She just got to be. We got to be strong for her, babe. Come on now. Sit up, and let's go wait for the doctor to come out."

Angela wiped her face and smiled. "I love you, and I'm so glad you are here with me."

"I wouldn't want to be anywhere else," Carla assured her as they walked down the hall and got on the elevator.

Three hours later, the waiting room was filled with people from Carla and Paula's family in South Carolina. Michael and Miguel were also present with Tavon, being carried by his dad.

"How is he?" Carla asked.

"He is healthy. Just shaken up is all." Michael smiled weakly.

Finally, the doctor walked in, and Michael jumped up along with Angela. "How is she?" they asked simultaneously.

"Well, it was kind of touch and go for a moment. She is stabilized and resting. She lost a lot of blood, and the bullet was lodged within her chest. It came very close to hitting her heart. No major organs were injured though. Other than her being in quite of bit of pain, I'd say she is going to be okay."

Michael thanked the doctor repeatedly, and suddenly he slid to the floor on his knees and began to pray. He was happy that things had turned out the way they did, and he knew it was all because of God.

"Can I see her?" Michael asked.

"She will be in recovery for another hour and then moved to a room. We will come and get you then. You look tired. Go and get refreshed, maybe get something to eat, and when you come back, she should be settled in her own room."

Everyone thanked the doctor, and Angela broke down. "He did listen," she cried.

Carla smiled. "Let's go eat. Hey, little man, what you got a taste for?"

Tavon whispered, "Pizza."

Michael tightened his grip slightly on Tavon's hand as a reassurance that he was safe. He knew it was going to take a while before Tavon would trust anyone else. But he was going to do everything he could to make sure that Tavon never experienced such an ordeal again.

They walked down to the cafeteria, and Carla picked up a slice of pizza from the buffet. "I think I'll have pizza too."

Tavon smiled and looked up at Michael, who smiled back. "It's okay." They all sat down after each one of them got a slice of pizza.

Once they finished, they headed back up to where Paula was resting. They had already put her in a room, and the nurses were doing their assessments. Once they were finished, Michael and Tavon walked in first, as they were only allowing two visitors at a time.

Tavon paused at the door as he saw Paula lying in the bed, hooked up to all the machines. "Daddy, is she asleep?"

Michael cleared his throat and nodded. "Yes, son. She is."

"She's so pretty. She's here because of me?" he asked, crying.

"No, son. No. She is here because of some crazy people who were mean," Michael explained.

"I love you, Paula," Tavon said.

Michael looked down at Tavon and back at Paula. He made a promise at that moment that he wasn't going to leave South Carolina without his wife.

After two weeks of Paula resting at her family's home, Michael and his family were heading back to North Carolina.

Epilogue

Paula recovered from her gunshot wounds, and she and Michael rekindled their relationship, but in the end, they decided to part ways for good. They remained friends, and for a while, she threw herself into her work. Finally, after a year, she met her true love, Steven Blake, Chance's cousin. He was a strong, handsome man who treated Paula how she desired. He spoiled her in ways that neither Michael nor Tripp had. He won her heart after breaking through the icy shell that had developed around it. When they got married, it was forever. Paula had two kids with him, and they lived life to the fullest. She often wondered about Tasha and wished that things would've turned out differently for them.

Michael and Tavon lived wonderfully. He made sure that his son didn't want for anything. He was allowed to adopt Tavon, and he felt that it was the best thing to ever happen to him. He visited Paula and Steven about twice a year. He would never have thought that he and Paula could be friends outside of marriage.

He had learned that she wasn't his soul mate, as he finally met a woman who took his mind completely off Paula. He would always love her, but Karen was one hell of a woman, and she accepted him with all his flaws.

Sadly, his mother Sharon died in a church fire a year after his divorce from Paula. The police never found the person who set the fire.

Michael and Tammy's relationship was okay, but he never trusted her 100 percent. He made sure he kept in touch with her once he and Karen moved to Massachusetts.

Angela and Carla continued to see one another, and they eventually went to Seattle and moved in with Paula for a short while until they found their own place. They were happy to see Paula getting back to life after the whole ordeal that happened in South Carolina. Hell, they were just getting back to normal, and they weren't injured. Although they were in a relationship, they both agreed that they didn't want to be exclusive, so they decided on exploring an open relationship, but they had their own rules that they followed. They agreed that they wouldn't bring anyone into the relationship whom the other didn't approve of. It worked for them.

The girls remained close. Carla created her own makeup line. Paula was proud of her cousin's success and supported her in every way. Angela proposed to her years later.

Nikki served ten years of the fifteen-year sentence she had received. She had changed her life for the better. She was involved in the church heavily and gave her life over to God completely. She got a job at a nonprofit rehabilitation center and helped others who were dependent on drugs, sex, or alcohol. She loved herself more than she did before and used her tarnished history to help others. She often thought of Tavon, but she knew that he was good where he was.

Years later, one Sunday evening, while Michael and his wife were visiting Paula and Steven, Michael and Paula walked onto the large balcony, joining everyone outside and watching as their teenage son flirted with one of the neighborhood's babysitters. Michael looked over at Paula. "Do you ever have regrets about us?"

She shook her head. "Not an ounce. I will always cherish what we had, and I wouldn't be who I am today if it weren't for you."

Michael never doubted that. Michael smiled. " I'm so glad we ended things on good terms. I honestly don't know where I'd be if I didn't have you somewhere in my life," Michael admitted.

"All right now, bruh, don't be trying to smooth talk my wife," Steven joked.

"Man, I'd never disrespect you nor Karen like that," Michael replied.

"I know. I was just joking. We're family here," Steven said.

"No doubt." Michael laughed as he sipped his beer.

Carla and Angela were on the grill, cooking some steaks and lobster tails, while Karen was making the salad. Paula had already prepped and cooked her sides and had the entire house smelling good. It was summertime, and they were about to embark on another crusade: taming Tavon's lustful eye. He was a real ladies' man even at his young age.

"Ay, boy, come on back down this way," Michael hollered as Tavon appeared to be walking away with Lisa.

He turned and laughed, "Dad, we're just going for a walk."

"Not tonight, youngblood. Not tonight," Michael opposed.

Everybody started laughing as Tavon turned and headed back in their direction.

Paula looked at Michael and smiled. She may have married the wrong man, but she had the right man as a true friend for life.

The End